Aunt Bea's Legacy

Jeanette Taylor Ford

Cover by Dave Slaney

LONGSHIP
Publishing

In memory of my dear mum, Mona Beatrice, whose love for a certain farmhouse in Hereford (and my own) finally inspired me to write this book.

For Mary, her continued enthusiasm for my books has earned her a cameo role in this one. (Plus she just happens to manage the Hospice charity shop!)

Also, for Margaret, the lovely lady who has owned the same house for many years with her husband and brought up her family there. As 'Aunt Bea' always said, it should be a family home, and indeed it is and hopefully will always be. Thanks to her for giving me permission to use a photo of the house for my cover.

The village and characters in this book are imaginary. However, any similarity to places or people, living or dead is entirely intentional!

Thanks to Dave Slaney for doing his cover magic for me.

Raspberries and Roses

Can one find love
Amid raspberries and roses?
Just give me a chance,
And open your eyes.
The open air,
The beauty of a garden,
But more, the tenderness of a caring soul,
When Fate,
Or a guardian angel
Decides to take a hand,
Anything can happen.
One never knows what's just around the
corner -
Unexpected twists and turns;
That's what life can be,
Amid raspberries and roses.

Aunt Bea's Legacy

Chapter 1
The Letter

"Lucille, you can't be serious! Tell me you're not serious about this – you would have to give up your job, this flat, everything! Even me, because I can't leave here; this is where my work is."

I looked at my fiancé, Jim. He was staring at me, his blue eyes wide, his face reddening with emotion; a vein in his neck beginning to stand out. My thoughts were in turmoil, had been ever since I got the letter from Mr Gamble, a solicitor.

Jim had just read the letter. We were relaxing in my flat after having had dinner out at a restaurant close by. I was upset but not for the reason he thought. I was still upset that my Aunt Beatrice had died, even though it was nearly a month ago now. She had not let on she was ill and I felt guilty that I hadn't been to see her for ages. That's the trouble with life, it gets in the way. It gets in the way of some more important things, like staying in proper touch with the people you love.

"We-ell," my thoughts came out carefully, "I suppose the flat could be rented out while I try this thing, then I would have the option to come back…"

"But the rest! Me – your job – don't you care?"

"Of course I care!" I lost it a bit then and raised my voice. "You're supposed to be helping me here, Jim! Can't you understand how I feel? This Mr – Gamble, doesn't tell me anything. All he's told me is that she has left me her house but to secure it I have to live in it for a year and if not, it will be sold and the money given to various charities. That's really not helpful at all. But I just can't get over that I've lost Aunt Bea, that I'll never see her again."

By this time I was crying. Jim, seeing my distress, put the letter on the occasional table and drew me down beside him on the settee and put his arm around me. I sobbed, leaning against his chest. He stroked my hair and murmured 'there, there, cry it out.' I took him at his word and did.

A while later, when emotions had calmed down, we talked more about this rather strange request.

"I think you should go and see this solicitor chappie and see what he has to say about it. He may know more than he's said in his letter."

I nodded; that seemed a sensible idea..

After Jim had gone, I got ready for bed slowly; all the memories of the times I spent with Aunt Bea came floating through my mind like dandelion seeds wafting on the breeze. As I followed one memory, it led to another. I saw her ready smile, her tinkling laughter and her ever-present bracelets that dangled and jangled on her wrists.

Lying in bed, I thought back to about four weeks ago when dad had called me.

"Hello dad, you don't often call me. To what do I owe this honour?" I joked.

"Oh Lulu, I have some news that's going to upset you," he began. I knew he was upset because he'd just used his baby-name for me, which he tried to remember not to do these days, now that I was twenty-five.

"Oh dad, what's up?" I asked, imagining all sorts of things. "Are you ill? Has Butch died?" (Butch was dad's dog; he was very far from being 'butch', he had to be the gentlest, soppiest dog that ever lived)

"No, Lu, it's not that. It's your Aunt Bea; I'm afraid she is dead."

"Dead? How can she be dead – I was only talking to her on the phone a couple of days ago?"

"I don't really know any details. The police came to tell me that she'd been found on the floor in her house. There was no sign of any break-in or anything so it seems like she died of natural causes but as yet they don't know. They found a card she was going to post addressed to me so they came to find me and ask me if I knew who her next of kin was. Of course I had to tell them that she didn't have any family, except me and you. I told them that I would tell you. I'm sorry I've had to do it over the phone, love."

I sat down slowly, phone in hand, as I listened to my dad. As he finished, I heard the break in his voice and knew he was upset. I imagined him, sitting in his chair by his phone. He still had an old-fashioned phone fixed to the wall so he always had to be near it when he used the phone, which he didn't often. Butch would be sitting, pressed close to him, his big doggy eyes fixed on his master, knowing he was upset. Dad would be comforted; there was no one to comfort me, well not at this moment. Jim would be around later.

"Don't worry about that, dad, I wouldn't expect you to come all this way personally. Oh, I am upset about Aunt Bea! Poor Aunt Bea, dying there alone on her floor..." I stopped as the tears trickled down my cheeks. I reached for a tissue and started to dab my eyes. Once started, I found they wouldn't stop so I pulled a handful from the box. I found myself totally unable to speak for a few moments.

"Do you know when the funeral will be?" I managed at last.

"No. There will have to be a post mortem and so we can't hold the funeral until the body is released. I will let you know."

"Thanks dad. I – I had better go. I'll speak with you soon. Love you," I blurted, afraid I would break down with him still on the phone.

"I love you too, my darling. I'll be in touch when I know anything. Bye for now."

"Bye dad."

When I terminated the call, I let my emotions go and cried. When Jim arrived, my eyes were still reddened and a tear was still inclined to trickle, catching me unawares almost. I couldn't believe the pain I was feeling. This was the first time that death had come so close to me since my mother died when I was eight. It was so long ago that I could only feel faint echoes of how I'd been then. I know that I found life very difficult for a while and was afraid to let my dad out of my sight.

Then Aunt Bea had breezed into our lives and took charge. It was like the sunshine suddenly came out. She cared for me and dad and everything was alright again.

Chapter 2
More Upsetting News

The funeral was held three weeks after Aunt Bea had been discovered. We thought it was never going to happen, the coroner took ages to release the body. Dad, as her closest relative was in charge of the funeral plans.

My fiancé and I travelled over to Herefordshire in his beautiful Mercedes. Although a vintage car, it purred along smoothly. Jim was very proud of the car, which had belonged to his father, who had given it to him a few months before. I knew he had always lusted after it and his dad knew it so he grimly hung onto it, resisting his son's pleadings, until he became ill and could no longer drive. Even so, he still kept it for six months, not wanting to part with it until he finally gave in to Jim's reasonable argument that if he gave it to his son, at least it would still be in the family – and it needed to be kept running to keep it in good shape.

"We might as well be comfortable, having to drive that distance," remarked Jim. I flushed a little, thinking of my beloved ancient jalopy, a Volkswagen Polo. I suppose I could afford a better car really; he kept telling me I should update but I'd had the car a good few years now, ever since I'd passed my test in fact, and I was fond of it – it almost seemed like another person to me, it was my friend.

Anyway, there didn't seem much point in getting another car because I didn't drive much. It was handy to commute into London to my job from Chiswick, where I was living, by tube. I only used the car if I was going out of town to see friends or to go home for a while. Anyway, it's expensive and almost impossible to take a car into the city, never mind park.

I sat back in the Merc as he drove expertly up the M1, and I reflected that it had been ages since I'd gone home. Thinking about Aunt Bea and how guilty I felt as I'd not really seen her since I moved to London, except when she had come to see me, I resolved there and then that I would make sure I saw dad more often.

The last time she came, about a year ago, she met Jim, who I'd been seeing for about six months by then and we'd just got engaged. Hmm, we've been engaged for a year, and as yet, we haven't talked about setting a date...

When we neared Herefordshire, I felt my heart lift and lighten; I was coming home. At that moment, I couldn't help wondering why on earth I had left this beautiful place to live in London. It was the job, of course. I had attended the Catering College in Hereford and got a high qualification. When we were doing a demonstration dinner at the college, I was head-hunted by Joseph Wallis, the chief executive of a large firm in London. He was looking for someone to manage the catering there; apparently, the quality of the food had gone down somewhat and he was looking for someone newly qualified, with up to date knowledge, to bring a diet of healthier foods to his workforce; he was an unusually far-sighted man.

The offer threw me into turmoil; I hadn't planned to go to London but this was an opportunity not to be missed. It was a hard decision; it helped that my dad and Aunt Bea were all for it. They said it was right that I should forge ahead and make a life for myself and London was the place of opportunity. They assured me that they would look after one another and I was not to worry about them but to go and follow my dream. So, I went.

I had been doing this job for four years now and it was great. I had a lovely team of people that worked with me and the people we served were mostly very friendly. I earned a good salary, which is just as well because living in the capital was expensive. When I found my flat in Chiswick, I was very happy because it was a great improvement on my bedsit in Hammersmith. I liked Chiswick, it was a town swallowed up in the expansion of London, a pleasant place to live and so conveniently supplied with a tube station.

When I met Jim at a friend's party, he attracted me with his blond good looks and obviously I must have had the same effect on him, for he never left my side for the rest of the evening and afterwards asked me if he could see me again. Of course, I agreed and we started to see each other regularly and eventually we got engaged. There was no great romantic moment, we just seemed to agree that one day we would marry and he produced a ring, which is a large square diamond. I couldn't wear it at work of course, except for the day I wore it to show my workmates.

I looked at it now; I knew it was valuable but I have never been able to decide if I really liked it. It glinted at me as the sun caught it through the windows of the car and I thought about what it would be like to be married to Jim. He was a high-flyer in his field; to be honest, I didn't really understand what he did, it seemed he had fingers in lots of pies. But there was money in the family too, hence the expensive ring and the posh car. Sometimes I wondered what he saw in me. I was good at my job and lived in a reasonable way on a decent wage, but I was a lot less interested in the 'status quo' than he was and was only interested in money so I could live.

However, there was no doubt that when we married, we would live very comfortably and in fact, he said that I wouldn't have to work at all if I didn't want to. I wasn't sure how I felt about that either; sometimes I thought I would enjoy not working and then I would go into work and enjoy the comradeship and friendship of my fellows there and knew I would miss it. Of course, when we had children I'd have to give it up.

Just as I was following this train of thought, we arrived at my dad's house. After I had left home, he sold our family home in Three Elms Road and bought a two-bedroom bungalow on the Kings Acre Road. Fortunately, it has a good driveway, the road being quite a busy one. We pulled onto the drive and dad was there on the doorstep.

I got out of the car and ran into his arms. He enveloped me in his big bear hug.

"Lulu, oh, it's so good to see you." He let me go and extended his hand towards Jim.

"Jim, welcome. Come in, come in." They shook hands and then he turned and we followed him into the hallway of his little house.

"I have the kettle on, go into the lounge and make yourselves comfortable."

Jim and I did as we were bid. It was a manly room with squashy brown leather chairs and two-seater settee. It wasn't a very big room but it was quite sufficient for a man living alone.

As we sat down, the door moved further open, and there was Butch, wagging his tail in welcome. He came straight to me and I patted his head.

"Hello Butch. Jim, this is my dad's dog, Butch. He's a big softie."

Jim put a tentative hand out towards the dog, Butch nosed him momentarily and then came back to me and sat down beside me, leaning against my leg.

"He seems like a well-trained dog. I'm glad he is not the kind that leaps all over you; I'm not that keen on them, to be honest."

I was astonished. All this time I'd been with Jim, I'd never picked up that he didn't like dogs. I love them, we'd always had dogs when I was growing up – only one at a time but we'd always had one. Butch was a black Labrador; I have always thought that they were my favourite dogs.

Dad came in then, carrying a tray with drinks and a plate of biscuits.

"Just to refresh us."

He set the tray down on a table.

"Actually, I need to tell you something else, Lucy. I didn't want to tell you over the phone because I didn't want to upset you further until you could come here."

Mystified, I looked up questioningly.

"Is it about Aunt Bea?" I asked.

"Yes. The day after she had been found, the police came here to tell me about her. But they also said they were treating her death as suspicious."

"Suspicious? You're not going to tell me someone killed her?

Chapter 3
Puzzling Questions

Jim and I both steadily looked at dad for his answer. I could see he was struggling, after all, Aunt Bea was his sister and she had been like a mother to him after their mother died of breast cancer when dad was only a young teenager.

"The police were suspicious because, when she was found, she had obviously been holding a poker, for it was inches away from her hand where she laid on the floor."

"But she always kept the Aga alight; perhaps she was going to poke it?" I said.

"But she wasn't in the kitchen, she was in the hallway; the dining room and lounge are between the kitchen and the front hall. The police said it looked like she was approaching the front door with the poker."

"How odd; perhaps she thought she had an intruder." I was thoughtful. "Was the front door unlocked?"

"No, and there was no sign of a break-in."

"How did she get discovered? Did you find her?"

"No, she was found by a young man called Mr Baxter. Apparently, he went round to see her every morning and he knew she kept a key under the mat. When there was no sign of her, he was worried, because she was always an early riser, as you know yourself, Lucy. So, he got the back door key out from under the mat and went in to look for her. That's how he found her and immediately called the police once he realised she was dead. She was already cold so she had obviously been lying there for a while."

"Oh, poor Aunt Bea, lying on the floor dying, with no-one to help her!" I could feel my eyes welling up at the thought. Dad put his hand over mine.

"The post-mortem showed that she died of a heart attack and was probably dead before she hit the floor. At least it was mercifully quick. Apparently, she had a heart problem; I knew nothing about it."

"Neither did I, dad. Wasn't that just like Aunt Bea, keeping that to herself?"

Dad nodded. "Yes, it was just her."

Jim spoke for the first time.

"So, it rather looks like she thought she heard something that could be an intruder and had a sudden heart attack and died?"

"It looks that way, yes."

"All very unfortunate," remarked Jim. He put his cup down and yawned. "Sorry, long drive."

"Ah, yes. Now, I only have one spare bedroom...." Dad caught my slight shake of head. "There is a B & B just across the road and they have rooms. Would you like to stay there or..?" he trailed off, looking first at me, then Jim, then me. We had discussed this before we came.

"I will stay here with you, dad, and Jim will go across the road," I said quickly, eager to put dad out of his embarrassment.

"That's right, Mr Dixon. I'd like to go across now and book in, if that's okay with you?"

"Oh yes, do that and Lucy can bring her things in here, then when you're all sorted, we'll go out for some dinner, if that suits you? I'm not much of a one for cooking you know."

"That sounds like a good plan."

Jim and I got up and we went across the road to the B & B. We were shown his room, which looked very comfortable. Jim looked around in satisfaction.

"Looks fine; not quite the standard I'm used to but it will do for a couple of nights."

I loved the small bedroom that was dad's spare room. It was only a single room, so it's just as well that Jim and I weren't expecting to share. I was quite happy to be staying with dad; I hoped to have some private 'daddy-daughter' natter while Jim was enjoying the facilities offered over the road.

We walked down to the Bay Horse to have our dinner. It was close and I knew Jim would want some wine with his meal, dad too, maybe. I think that the Bay Horse would probably not 'be what he was used to' for my fiancé but I also knew the food they served was good. Give Jim his due, although he looked around a bit scathingly, he never said anything, for which I was grateful. One just can't compare a Hereford pub with the posh London restaurants, but give me a Hereford pub any day, I decided. Even though I'm a chef and often have to produce some fine recipes, I do appreciate a well-cooked steak and yummy chips. At least they fill you up and for a decent price, unlike some of those London places that charge you an arm and a leg to give you a meal that makes you want to visit the nearest chip shop on your way home!

It was nine-thirty by the time we set off up the road for dad's house. Jim decided he might as well go back to his B & B now as he was going to be walking past it. I was relieved really as I was quite tired and didn't fancy sitting up too long. He gave me a quick kiss and said goodnight, then shook dad's hand.

"Goodnight, Mr Dixon, I'll come round after breakfast."

"Do call me dad, or father as I'm going to become your father-in-law," said Tom, "Or, if you prefer, call me Tom; 'Mr Dixon' always seems a bit, well, stuffy as we are going to be family."

"Very well – um – Tom. I feel a bit strange calling someone father other than my own – if you don't mind?"

Dad clapped a hand on Jim's shoulder.

"Not at all, my boy, I suggested it after all. Goodnight, then, I hope you sleep well."

We watched Jim let himself into the front door of his boarding house and then we linked arms the way we always did and made our way back to the bungalow.

Once inside, dad let Butch out into the garden and while the dog was out there, made us both a mug of hot chocolate, which had always been our favourite bedtime drink. Butch came back inside and dad shut and locked the back door. We carried our drinks into the lounge and sat down to relax.

"So, when did you last see Aunt Bea?" I asked.

"I'd only seen her the day before. You are aware, I went there often. When the police came to tell me she had died, it was a big shock. Mind you, now I come to think of it, she hasn't been right for some time. She looked all right, but there was – something – something I can't quite put my finger on." Dad frowned into his mug.

"Try, dad, try, please?" I pleaded, leaning towards him and putting my hand on his knee. He covered my hand with his and cleared his throat.

"Well, she seemed not really like herself. You know your Aunt, she was always so cheerful and positive; she smiled and laughed a lot. The last few times I was with her, she didn't come across too bright, you know, she was more – serious, somehow – and a bit, well, jumpy."

"Jumpy? That doesn't sound like Aunt Bea." I frowned.

"No, not at all."

I sipped my chocolate slowly, turning over in my mind what dad had said. I thought about the poker she was holding when she died.

"Do you think someone was terrorising her in some way?" I asked him carefully. Dad looked at me sharply.

"The evidence seems to point that way," dad responded, after he'd obviously thought my question over in his mind.

"But Aunt Bea doesn't have an enemy in the world. Who on earth would want to hurt her – and more to the point – why?"

Chapter 4
The Funeral

The quaint Parish Church in the village of Sutton-on-Wye was absolutely packed for Aunt Bea's funeral. As I walked up the aisle, arm in arm with dad, following the coffin, I was stunned to see so many people. I thought the whole village had turned out to be here; she must have been a well-liked person, I mused.

It seemed the vicar knew her well, for he talked of her in such a way you could tell that he'd had regular dealings with her and had often visited her. She had been a 'pillar of the community' and had done much to help all sorts of people and had led an active church life too. All that I had previously experienced with my aunt was underlined by the knowledge of her from others. It seemed that the village was going to be the poorer without her and that wasn't just an empty saying, such as one often says about a departed one. In this instance it was true.

I was surprised to learn, that apparently Aunt Bea had a thriving business, supplying various outlets with cakes and other confectionary. I had no idea; I was learning more about Aunt Bea than I ever suspected. Certainly those places were now going to have to look elsewhere for their supplies.

After the funeral service in the church, she was laid to rest in the churchyard. I must admit, I don't really like burials and I left the graveside as soon as I could. Jim and I stood on the path until dad was ready to come away. It was a chilly, late March day, even though the sun was doing its best. I stood, shivering a little and stamping my feet, trying to keep warm while we were waiting. Jim was being very good, supportive without being demanding. I thought he was rather quiet for him but perhaps he was just answering the solemnity of the occasion.

As we stood there quietly talking, I noticed a couple of men standing not far away, with a group of villagers but slightly apart. They seemed to be watching me and I wondered why. A few moments later, they started walking towards us and looked very purposeful. One of the men was slightly ahead of the other and as he got within speaking distance of me, he said,

"Excuse me, are you Miss Lucille Dixon?"

"Erm – yes. Who is asking?"

He held out his hand and as I took it to shake, he replied,

"Dan Cooke, Detective Chief Inspector and this is Detective Sergeant Grant."

The other man nodded to me. "Miss Dixon."

D.C.I. Cooke looked questioningly at Jim.

"Oh, er, this is my fiancé, James Netherfield."

"How do you do, sir?"

"Inspector," Jim nodded.

The man turned back to me.

"Excuse this intrusion at this time, Miss, and may I offer you my condolences on your loss?"

"Thank you, my aunt was very dear to me," I wiped a rogue tear from my eye and Jim put his arm protectively round my shoulders.

"May we ask what this is about?" asked Jim gruffly.

"I don't want to bother you at this time but I did want to make your acquaintance, Miss Dixon and to give you my card. I would appreciate it if you would contact me when this upsetting time is concluded; I would like to have a chat with you when you can spare the time in the not-too-distant future. There are a few things I'd like to ask you about. There's no desperate rush, so whenever you're ready."

"Oh! Well, I don't know that there's anything I can help you with, I've been living in London for the past four years."

"I would still like to talk with you, if you would be so kind."

"Yes of course, Chief Inspector." I took the card he held out and he gave me a little nod as did Sergeant Grant and then I watched them walk down the path and out through the gateway.

"Hmm, odd," observed Jim.

"Yes, very," I agreed as I popped the card into my handbag.

"Here comes your dad."

Dad joined us and together we made our way across the road to the village hall where the ladies of the village had got together to put on refreshments.

The next couple of hours were a haze of various people coming up to me and offering their condolences and sharing stories they had of Aunt Bea. It was pleasant really; I know that's a strange thing to say under the circumstances but I enjoyed hearing their memories of my aunt and we even laughed sometimes at some of the stories. It seemed the whole village community was here and wanted to tell me their memories of Aunt Bea. I hadn't a hope of remembering their names or their stories. Eventually, I felt I just needed to get away. People were beginning to leave when Jim came up to me. I realised at that point that he hadn't been in the room for a while.

He drew me to one side.

"Lucy, I'm sorry, but I need to get back to London today. There is a crisis that I need to go back to deal with. Can you be ready to leave in an hour?"

I looked at him, shocked.

"But Jim, what about dad? He should have someone with him, I can't just leave him."

At that point, dad had joined us.

"What's this?"

"Jim says he needs to get back to London this afternoon, he wants to leave in an hour. I can't leave you now, dad! Don't you need me to stay on? I could go back on the train tomorrow."

He patted my arm.

"Don't you worry, Lulu. I will be all right. I have Butch and I have some good friends. I've lived with this alone for the past three weeks so don't worry, I'll be fine. You go with Jim. You don't want to be bothered with waiting around at railway stations and things."

"Are you sure?" I was doubtful.

"Yes, of course I'm sure," he said firmly. "I'm ready to leave here; I had just come to tell you. I have thanked the village ladies for putting on this spread for us but I've had enough now. I just want my quiet home and Butch."

"Okay, dad, if you're really sure. Come on then, let's go." I linked my arm lovingly through his and we waved to the people still in the room. Jim went ahead to open the car.

Minutes later, we were in Jim's car, purring along the twisty road back to dad's bungalow. An hour later, Jim had checked out of his B & B and I hugged dad, promising to call him as soon as I was home in the flat and we were on our way back to London.

I didn't question Jim about having to go back already; he was quiet, his face set like stone. I thought he was probably worried about whatever he was going back to deal with. However, I couldn't help feeling resentful that his work prevented me from staying where I felt I should be – with my father.

Chapter 5
Strategic Plans

The letter came only three days after the funeral. It was a Saturday, so there was nothing I could do about anything until the following week anyway. I had all weekend to think about it. Obviously, Jim didn't want me to go and live back in Herefordshire and I kept swaying back and forth. I loved my job here and my flat – and of course, Jim. Although I was a bit niggled now that I realised we had been engaged a year and as yet he had not suggested naming a day. Maybe some time apart would do us good...?

Telling him about it that night was not a great experience but his suggestion that I should go and see this solicitor was a good idea. I was glad I had an understanding boss; I would make the arrangements as soon as I could. In the meantime, I sent off an email to Mr. Gamble's office to say that I was hoping to come up to Hereford shortly and would like to meet with him and would confirm when I would be coming on Monday after I had been able to speak with my boss.

That done, there was nothing more I could do. When I called dad for my regular weekend call, I told him about the letter and the rather strange conditions of the will. He was as puzzled as I and agreed it was a good idea for me to come and talk with the solicitor.

"I also still have to see that police bloke who wants to see me," I told him, "so I might as well do everything while I'm there."

"Yes, they will expect you to do that. When do you think you will come?"

"I hope about Tuesday, if it can be arranged. I'll let you know as soon as I can."

"Will you come alone or will Jim be coming too?"

"Oh, I will come alone. Jim can't have any more time away from his work so soon after last week."

"Right you are then. In that case, you can stay with me. I was just wondering if I needed to book B & B for him again."

"No need for that. And this time, we'll have the time together that we should have had last week."

"That will be wonderful."

"I will give you a call as soon as I know when I am coming. Must go now, Jim will be round soon and we are going to some friends for the evening."

"Oh well, have a good time. I will wait to hear from you. Goodbye, my dear."

"Goodbye dad. Love you."

"Love you too, my little Lulu."

When I finished the call to dad, I looked at my watch – oh my goodness, I only had half an hour before Jim would arrive! He hated to be late for anything. I flew up the stairs to get myself ready.

****

As it happened, it was Thursday by the time I could get away. I had to be considerate of my workmates and give them time to rearrange the work schedules and get a temporary cook. My second-in-command, Sue Sims, would fulfil my role as supervisor until I got back. At this point, I hadn't warned anyone that this situation might become permanent. I would drive up to Hereford Thursday and would see Mr Gamble on Friday; dad made the appointment for me after I'd called him on Monday to tell him when I'd be coming.

Although my little car is not nearly as comfortable as Jim's purring Merc, I enjoyed the drive. I took it at a leisurely pace, stopping at a service station around halfway, and I had some refreshments and a good break. I walked around a bit to stretch my legs. It was a lovely day for late March, clear and bright, cheerful for a drive in the car.

In spite of the circumstances, as I caught sight of the rolling countryside as I approached Hereford, my heart gave its usual lift. I knew that, wherever I lived, I would always think of Hereford as 'home'; sometimes I felt a deep longing for the place of my nativity; the green hills and valleys, the Malvern Hills, the stunning scenery of the Wye Valley as the river meandered on through the Welsh countryside and the Black Mountains on the west side of the county. Herefordshire is a county without any motorways cutting through it and it gives one the feeling that life is somehow slower and more leisurely there than elsewhere. (I'm sure it probably isn't really for the people who live there.) 'Hiraeth', the Welsh call it – that inbred longing for a place; what a wonderful word.

'Leisurely' was not a word I would now use for Hereford city as I crawled slowly in the line of traffic on my way through to the Whitecross Road. Like everywhere else, the traffic in Hereford had doubled, trebled, in my lifetime and at times the city roads were as clogged as every other city in the United Kingdom. Really, there was no escape, even here.

However, I eventually managed to extricate myself from the majority of traffic at the roundabout as most went off to cross the 'new bridge' or off to the right to head that way. The 'new bridge' was so-called because it was a modern, four-lane bridge crossing the Wye, as opposed to the 'old bridge', built in the days of horses and carts, far too narrow to deal with the demands of modern transportation.

However, today I wasn't crossing the Wye but heading out towards Credenhill. It only took a few minutes then to reach dad's bungalow. He and Butch appeared on the doorstep as I pulled into the driveway. As I climbed out, Butch leaped towards me to give me his usual effusive greeting and I made a fuss of him for a couple of minutes before I stood up to give dad a hug.

"Oh dad, it's so good to be back again. I hated leaving you last week straight after the funeral."

"Don't you worry, I was fine. But I am glad to have you back again. Do you need some help with your things?"

"Well, I guess you could get a bag in for me. I tried not to bring too much but wasn't sure how long I would be here."

We soon got my things in; I didn't have that much, just a suitcase, a coat and my laptop. I locked the car and we dumped my case in my small bedroom.

"Do you want to unpack or have a drink first?"

"How about you go put the kettle on and I'll just unpack my case. It won't take me long and I'll be through in a jiffy."

"It's a plan," dad nodded and headed towards the kitchen. I set to, putting my clothes away in the drawers and hanging a dress, a skirt and a pair of jeans in the small wardrobe and popping two pairs of shoes in the bottom of the same. I was wearing my trainers; they are comfortable for everything, but I also liked to be prepared for more formality, such as when I go and see the solicitor.

While I was there, I hastily sent off a text to Jim to let him know I'd arrived safely. A few moments later, I received one back:

'Glad you have arrived safely. Come back soon.'

I smiled to myself. That was typical of Jim, no 'take care', 'keep me informed', or 'give my best to your father' and no sending his love either. Ah well, I know him well enough to know that the 'come back soon' is as near as I'll get to 'I love you' or 'I miss you'....

About ten minutes later, I was sitting on the sofa in dad's cosy lounge.

"Do you want to nip down The Bay and get something to eat? Or shall we have something here?" Dad asked me.

"Oh, I can't be bothered to go out any more, dad. What have you got in your kitchen? I can probably rustle up something. I'm tired and I'd rather stay home if you don't mind."

"Of course I don't mind, love. While you're here you can do just as you like."

I grinned.

"That's rather a dangerous thing to say, dad!"

"Eh?"

"Fathers shouldn't tell their children they can do what they like – it could cause all sorts of trouble!" I said teasingly.

"Oh, you silly girl! Anyway, as far as I'm concerned you can do what you want. You're a grown woman; I'm not responsible for you anymore."

"I suppose that's true. I never thought of that. Well, that takes the excitement out of any mischief I might have got up to," I laughed. "Now, show me to your kitchen."

*****

Staying with dad was lovely, just like old times when there had just been the two of us with Aunt Bea popping by every day. She had lived with us until I was eighteen; that was when she had finally gone back to live in her beautiful home in Sutton-on-Wye. Dad and I lived alone then while I attended Catering College and it was two years later that I moved to London to work.

Although this was a different house, it was furnished with familiar things; dad had kept everything from the old house that would fit into the bungalow. Obviously, some of the larger pieces of furniture were not here, but all the things that actually make a house a home were around; the nest of tables, the standard lamp with its old-fashioned tasselled lampshade; the rug that dad had hooked himself in front of the fireplace.

Most important was dad himself. Now in his fifties, he was still a handsome man; his hair was now silver but he looked healthy and tanned from the many walks that he took with his faithful hound and the gardening he did. He worked from home, a freelance writer. He had a regular slot in a newspaper and wrote short stories for a woman's magazine – under a woman's name – Elaine Dickman. His stories were very popular. He also had a few books published, crime novels, written under the name of T.D. Thompson. These things kept him comfortably. When I was young, he worked as a reporter and was often away from home when covering events, which was why Aunt Bea was so necessary when my mum died. Give dad his due though, he went away as little as possible, preferring to cover one-day events in the United Kingdom, rather than going abroad for current affairs.

He eventually became sickened about the whole business of reporting; he disliked all the sensationalism and the way they tried to question bereaved people who just wanted to be left alone. So he tried his hand at writing a book in his spare time which was received eagerly by a publisher. The book was well acclaimed and received by the general public and so his new career as an author began. This was good for dad, especially during the years I was at college and Aunt Bea had gone back to her own home.

During this time, Aunt Bea confined herself to much shorter hours at our home, bringing meals that we could just warm up for ourselves and making sure that the house was in reasonable order. Some days she never came at all but she always left us meals. She would prompt dad to eat because he often became completely absorbed in his writing and forgot to eat unless I was at home. Of course, being at a Catering College, I was eager to try out my skills at home so gradually I was doing more and more of the food preparation so now Aunt Bea would confine herself to keeping the house clean. Dad and I were both very grateful for that.

At the weekends, Dad and I would often go over to Sutton-on-Wye to be with her in her own lovely house. I couldn't believe that she had left it to me – on the other hand, I had difficulty in thinking about the possibility of losing it if I didn't comply with her rather strange conditions.

Chapter 6
More Information

Mr Gamble turned out to be, at first glance, a typical solicitor with his white hair carefully done in a side sweep and spectacles perched on his nose. He was tall and thin; he towered above me when he greeted me and shook my hand. However, I soon noticed his eyes, all blue and twinkly and his hand was warm as he drew me into his office.

"Miss Dixon, I am so pleased to meet you at last. I have heard so much about you."

I was startled.

"Have you? Who from?"

"From your aunt of course; I knew her very well, you know."

"Oh! Er, no, I didn't know."

"Do sit down, Miss Dixon. Would you care for a cup of tea? Or Coffee?"

"Oh, um, tea please," I stammered as I sat down on the proffered chair.

Mr Gamble pressed a button on the phone on his desk. "Miss Roberts, would you rustle up some tea for Miss Dixon please? And maybe a couple of biscuits, if you have any? Thank you."

"I have known your aunt for many years. Wonderful lady; I am so sorry that she has gone. May I offer you my condolences, my dear?"

"Thank you. It was a shock."

"A shock to us all, dear girl. I did of course know that Beatrice had a heart problem but I never expected this."

"You knew about her bad heart?" I felt foolish; I felt I must be coming across quite stupid to him but I was taken aback that he had seemed to know Aunt Beatrice rather better than the average solicitor would know a client.

"Oh yes indeed. My home is in the village, you know, and my wife and Beatrice were close friends. When my wife, Alice, died a few years ago, Beatrice and I kept each other company quite a bit. In fact, I had begun to hope..." he petered out and I noticed his rather lovely eyes looked sad. So, Aunt Beatrice had a love interest... I felt sorry for this man; he was obviously as upset about her death as dad and I were.

"Oh, Mr. Gamble, I had no idea! I am so sorry, you have lost her too."

He looked down at his hands, which were clasped together on his large oak desk. I thought, completely irrelevantly what a beautiful desk it was; just as one would expect to find in a 'Matthew & Son'- type solicitor's office. However, instead of piles of musty papers that one would have seen years ago on such a desk, it was laid out with the latest state-of-the-art hi-tech stuff. Somehow, it didn't look quite right. I guessed that Mr. Gamble's desk was something that he didn't want updating when the rest of the modern stuff was brought in. I agreed; I don't think I would have wanted to lose such a wonderful piece of furniture.

The moment was broken by Mr. Gamble's secretary entering with a tray.

"Ah, Miss Roberts, thank you very much."

The woman smiled at me as she set a cup of tea down on the desk in front of me and offered me the sugar bowl. It actually had sugar lumps rather than just granulated and she held a very cute pair of silver sugar tongs ready poised. A moment from my childhood flew back to me and I lusted after a cube, wanting the feel of the solid sugar in my mouth, dissolving gradually as I sucked on it. However, I pushed the lusting aside and shook my head. 'No sugar, thank you.' I smiled back.

I watched as she popped two lumps into Mr Gamble's cup – obviously a man with a sweet tooth – no wonder he liked visiting with Aunt Bea if she dished out cakes to him – not that it was obvious in his thin frame.

Miss Roberts left a plate of chocolate-chip biscuits on the desk and Mr. Gamble encouraged me to take one, which I did and bit into it straight away. It was something to do while I waited for him to begin talking again. Miss Roberts went out and quietly shut the door behind her.

"Yes, life isn't going to be the same now. Beatrice was a good friend and I shall miss going to spend time with her in her wonderful home. You are a very lucky young woman that she has left you her house."

"I am surprised she has left it to me, I thought she would leave it to dad."

"Oh, she was always going to leave it to you. Apparently she and your father talked about it some years ago. He insisted that he didn't need it, he had plenty already. She made her will years ago leaving everything to you. I admit I was surprised when she suddenly changed it and made the condition."

"So, it wasn't always under those conditions?" I sat up, looking at him searchingly. "When did she change it?"

"Around a year ago. A few months later, she gave me a letter that she wanted me to give you on the event of her death. Forgive me for getting you here but I wanted to give it to you personally; I did not want it getting lost in the post."

I nodded. "I can understand that. I don't mind; I was glad of the chance to come back because I had to leave here straight after the funeral because my fiancé needed to leave right away – a crisis at his work, apparently. I was not happy."

"I spoke with your father that evening and he told me you had already gone back. He told me how to contact you in London. Here is the letter. Do you want to read it here, or take it away with you? Or I can go out so you can read it in private."

I took the envelope he held out. It was a plain white envelope with my name written on it, 'Lucille Emily Dixon' in my aunt's flowing handwriting. I looked at it and fingered it.

"If you don't mind, I think I will open it here, if you can give me some time," I replied eventually.

"Not at all, my dear, take as much time as you need."

He stood up, then sat down again and opened a drawer in his desk. He took out a box of tissues, which he placed on the desk near me and then he got up again and left the room, shutting the door gently. I opened the envelope with shaking hands. Inside, there was a single piece of paper which I unfolded and began to read:

My darling Lucy,

If you are reading this, it means that I have passed on. Firstly, I want to tell you once more how much I love you, you were my daughter as much as a child I had borne myself would have been if I had been thus blessed. However, it was not to be but I was blessed to have you instead. You were a great joy in my life; to watch you grow from a lovely child to a beautiful woman and to know that I had a hand in bringing you up gave me so much. You were a wonderful gift to me.

You will know now of the conditions of my will. I had always intended to leave you my home but, after seeing you last year and meeting your fiancé James, I decided to change it slightly. The reason for this will, I hope, become clear in due time. For now, I must just say to you that, if you marry James, or have already married him, you will be well off, settled wherever you choose to live, which will, no doubt, be somewhere near London, and will have no need of River View or the money. Therefore, I wish those less fortunate to be the beneficiaries, although you will still have all my personal effects and money from my business. I hope you will understand my reasoning on this; I think you will because you have a kind heart.

However, if you decide to live in River View for a year and take over my business, I know this will be a big decision for you but it may be what you might need. If you decide to do that, you will find everything that you will ever need at my house and in Sutton-on-Wye.

And now, I must regretfully say farewell to you and to your father – farewell, because I know that we will be together again one day. Death is not the end, just a passing into another phase of one's life, but the love will also live on and is the only thing we can take with us when we leave this world.

Your loving Aunt Bea

I sat with the letter on my lap, a bunch of tissues in my hand as the tears gently trickled down my cheeks. I had already cried so much over losing Aunt Bea but holding a paper with her handwriting in a personal letter to me was moving me again. She had obviously thought about this very carefully and did what she felt was right. And she was right; I did understand. It was just what I would have expected of her; she had a big heart and even after her death she wanted to help people. In spite of my sorrow, I smiled. Oh yes, so like her!

I got up and walked to the door. Upon opening it, I saw Mr Gamble and Miss Roberts talking quietly together. They both looked up and smiled.

"All right, Miss Dixon?" asked Mr. Gamble. "Shall we continue now?"

I nodded and he came towards the door and we both went back into the room and sat down. He reached into another drawer in his desk and brought out a large bunch of keys with a big label on them. I knew they were the keys of River View because I'd seen the big, black, old-fashioned door keys many times before.

"Would you care to borrow the keys of River View? I thought perhaps you would like to look around; it might help you to make your decision."

"Oh yes please! I'd love to look around the house; it would be so good to be there again."

"In any case, under your aunt's will, you will own all that is inside the farmhouse, all your aunt's personal effects and the ownership of her business, the fate of which will be in your hands. You can close it or you can hire someone to run it for you, or whatever you see fit."

I laughed, rather shakily.

"It rather sounds like I have a lot to think about, Mr. Gamble."

"Yes, young lady, you do. I don't envy you your decisions. Still, you have time. Your aunt said you had to decide within two months of her death. We don't want the house to deteriorate too much if it is to be sold. Why don't you stay in the house for a few days? See how you feel when you are there? Get to know the village a bit."

"Yes, I think that's a good suggestion. I will get dad to go there with me now when I get back to his and I can see what I might need in order to spend a few days there. I really do need to make a decision; if I'm going to leave my work I will have to give them notice and arrange to let my flat too – IF I decide to come. I'm afraid it won't go down well with my fiancé; he won't like it at all."

Chapter 7
River View Farmhouse

When I got back, dad and Butch were out so I left a note on the kitchen worktop and headed out towards Sutton-on-Wye. I felt a little guilty that I had not waited for dad but I could feel that big bunch of keys egging me on towards Aunt Bea's house. I knew dad would join me later if he was able.

It took only twenty minutes or so to get there; not quite fifteen minutes along the main road and then about seven minutes to negotiate the more narrow and twisty road that led to the village. Aunt Bea's house was situated just the other side of the main part of the village and down a narrow lane that had obviously been a farm track, now properly tarmac surfaced. River View had once been a farmhouse and had outbuildings. Most of the farmland that had belonged to it had been sold but the house still had a sizeable garden, from what I recalled. When we visited Aunt Bea, we would sit on the patio at the rear of the house on warm days and have our tea.

Beyond the garden was the River Wye; fortunately down quite a steep bank, therefore the house was never in danger of flooding from the river. The nearest neighbour was a nursery and garden centre and on the other side, some distance away, was Sutton Court, which had once been a large estate but was now a nursing home. That was the place furthest from the village and stood secluded in large grounds, surrounded by trees and overlooking the river.

As I stopped my old car outside the front hedge to the house (I couldn't yet say it was my house), I felt my excitement mount as I caught up the large bunch of keys from the seat beside me along with my handbag and got out of the car. I stood for a few moments, looking at this house that my aunt had loved so much. It was a rambling black and white, 'whattle and daub' building such as one often sees in this area.

The front door was in the middle of the house and it had a small, pointed wooden porch around it. Along the side to my right there were two windows and then the sloping side of a lean-to structure at the end of the building. Corresponding windows were above. To my left there were three, no, four windows stretching along the wall, the last window being quite small and again, there were windows above, except there was no window above that small window at the end. I knew that was a barn and it would stretch out at the back at right-angles to the house.

Momentarily, I considered entering the house through the front door but I changed my mind and followed the path round to my right, around the lean-to at the side to the kitchen door, which was the way that Aunt Bea always entered her house and so did everyone else. I found the smaller but still old-fashioned key that I knew would open the door.

Entering into the kitchen, I looked around me. It was dim in here and I realised the curtains were drawn shut; no doubt as a mark of respect to my aunt's passing but also to keep private from any curious stares.

I decided that before I did anything else I would go through the house and open all the curtains and maybe some windows as well. This I did and soon the house was flooded with sunlight filtering in through the small-paned windows. The farmhouse was only one room wide throughout and each room had a window on either side, thereby it was very light and often sunny inside. It was a cheerful house, very much in keeping with Aunt Bea herself.

After letting in some light and opening some windows to let in some air, which frankly was needed because some parts of the house smelt rather musty, I made my way back to the kitchen.

This room was always the hub of the house and, in my memory, always had delicious aromas floating from it. It seemed to me that Aunt Bea usually had something nice in the process of being baked or having just come out of the oven. It was, at first glance, an old-fashioned kitchen with an Aga reigning supreme. However, at second look, there was also a gas cooker on the other side of the room and near it a microwave and the base of a multichef mixer was on the worktop and I knew there were other modern pieces of equipment stashed away that Aunt Bea used regularly. This room had been extended; at one time, so Aunt Bea told me, there had been a small bathroom off the kitchen and another bedroom but these had been knocked out and now the room was a large kitchen/diner.

The old-fashioned wooden cupboards were lined up under a good, solid worktop and also on the walls above. I opened each cupboard and drawer one by one to find all kinds of equipment from mixing bowls to piping bags, baking tins to jam jars – jam jars? There was a whole cupboard full of them! They looked beautiful, obviously new, still in multi-compartmented boxes – hmm...

As I was heading towards the walk-in pantry, I heard a noise. It seemed to come from upstairs; I could have sworn it was footsteps up there.

I stood and listened – nothing. I must have been mistaken. My hand stretched out to open the pantry door – I heard the noise again and I snatched back my hand. Instead, I moved towards the door that led into the next room which Aunt Bea used as a living room. I had to go through that to get to where the stairs were. I went to the bottom of the stairs.

"Hello?" I shouted, feeling slightly silly – after all, I had been up there not long ago. "Is there anybody there?" I stood, concentrating. There was no sound at all. After a few minutes, I shrugged and retraced my steps back to the kitchen. It must be the timbers contracting after I'd opened some windows, I decided.

The pantry was stuffed full of ingredients; flour, sugar, icing sugar, tins of fruit and other things. At least half of the pantry, lined with shelves, was filled with marmalades, lemon curd and pickles, all in the same jars I found in the cupboard, labelled with 'Aunt Bea's Pantry'. How appropriate was that? I smiled; obviously, this was her business: 'Aunt Bea's Pantry' and she sold all these products.

I decided to go out and look at the garden; it was April so I didn't expect it to be exactly blooming. However, as I looked at it, I could see quite a bit of colour. Spring flowers were in abundance, primroses and polyanthus smiled in the sunshine and golden daffodils bobbed their heads in the slight breeze. I was surprised that the grass had recently been cut, it was neat as a new pin; obviously someone was taking care of it. Perhaps Mr. Gamble was paying someone to keep the garden in order until a decision had been made. I made my way around the garden to where I knew was a hidden seat. It was a favourite place of mine.

The seat was so hidden I almost missed it. The climbing plants had been allowed to grow so that the alcove was barely noticeable. I was just about to pull aside some honeysuckle which was in bud but not yet flowering, when I heard a soft footfall behind me, at the same time I heard a voice.

"Excuse me, miss, can I help you?"

I spun around, heart flapping from the shock of someone being there. A man stood looking at me. He was fairly tall, around six feet, I guessed. He wore brown trousers and a red checked casual shirt underneath a zip-up fleecy jacket. He wore thick heavy gloves and in one hand he held secateurs and some green string dangled from a pocket. Hmm, I think I just found my gardener!

As I looked at him, he gazed at me steadily. He wasn't particularly handsome, his dark hair was too long under his cap, his face was unshaven, his cheeks browned from being outdoors. For a moment, I felt myself held in the grip of his gaze, like a frightened rabbit caught in the headlights of a car. I pulled myself together.

"Oh! Erm, hello. I am Lucy and this was my Aunt Bea's house. Are you the gardener?"

"I suppose I am, in a way, although really I'm the next door neighbour. The name's Ken, Ken Baxter."

The name rang a bell – where had I heard it before? Oh yes, my aunt had been found by a Mr Baxter, my dad had told me.

I held out my hand.

"How do you do? I understand you found my poor aunt."

His hand was firm, a little rough (understandable I suppose, given his occupation) but warm and my little hand looked small and very white against his.

"I did, yes."

We stood there, a bit hesitant, each waiting for – something.

"Um, would you care for a cup of tea or something?" I asked. "And then you can tell me about it and about you and Aunt Bea and everything..." my voice faded out as he just stood there, looking at me. I went on quickly.

"Although I am not sure if I can really offer you anything, as I don't know what's in the house and I'm sure there's no milk; I haven't been shopping or anything yet."

He seemed to come to then.

"Thank you for the offer. No, don't worry. Shall we just go and sit on the patio and talk? Maybe, if the water is still turned on, we could have some."

"Oh yes, that's an idea. I like to drink water."

We made our way back to the house. He obviously knew the kitchen well, for he immediately went to the cupboard and found two glasses and then over to the tap, which was actually still on. He ran the water a few minutes, then filled the glasses. I remembered seeing some packets of biscuits in a cupboard and so I fetched a packet out and put them on a plate which Ken took from another place.

We set them on one end of the table and sat down.

"We have a feast," Ken grinned. I smiled back; there was something about him that I was drawn to.

"I remember seeing you at the funeral," he said.

"I don't remember seeing you there," I replied. "Although I met so many people that day my head was spinning."

"I didn't stay for the food afterwards; I only went to the church bit. I was sitting near the back so I'm not surprised you don't remember seeing me. But of course I saw you with your father following the coffin up and down the church. I am sorry for your loss."

"Thank you. I am going to miss her so much; she was like a mother to me. She brought me up, you know, after my mother died."

"Yes, I know. She talked of you often. She was very proud of you because of the success you were making of your life in London."

"Was she? I never realised. I feel so guilty because I didn't make the effort to see her so much after I went to London. Somehow, I just thought – I thought she would always be there, you know?"

He put his hand out tentatively and touched my hand.

"I do know. Don't beat yourself up about it. She understood. And she was very busy with her own business. Do you think you might consider carrying on with it?"

"Oh! Er, I haven't got that far yet; I don't even know half of what she did."

"Well, I can help you there. But don't worry about that for now."

I nodded. To fill the silence that followed that conversation, I reached out and took a biscuit from the plate. Before I put the chocolate digestive to my mouth, however, I said,

"Tell me about how you found her."

"Not much to tell really. I always came first thing in the morning to see Bea. She provides my nursery with jams, jellies and pickles to sell and cakes for the café. Since we are neighbours and fairly isolated out here, I liked to keep an eye on her, which is why I always called round in the mornings. I used to check up on her in the evenings whenever I could – you know, just to make sure that she was okay for the night."

"Had you seen her the night before?" I interrupted. He looked uncomfortable.

"Well, no. I wasn't able to go round that night. I had to go out. I wish I had, it might have saved her."

He looked so upset that it was my turn then to put out a comforting hand to him.

"You couldn't have known."

"No, I suppose not. I had told her I was going out and she seemed fine. She was planning on trying out a new cheesecake recipe, she told me. I did call her later and she said she was fine and the cheesecake had turned out great. She promised me that I could have some the next day and everything seemed perfectly normal.

In the morning I went round as usual and was surprised that the house seemed quiet and was shut up. She was always an early riser and on most mornings her kitchen door was always open already.

I tried the door and it was locked. I was puzzled and tried to remember if she had told me that she had an early appointment somewhere that I'd forgotten about but I was sure she hadn't mentioned anything. Somehow, I felt things weren't right so I decided to go in the house in case she had been taken ill or something."

He stopped to take a sip of his water as if it would fortify him for what he had to say next.

"I knew where she kept a spare key for the kitchen door, so I found it and went in. There was no sign of anything in the kitchen; I opened the Aga fire door and it was almost out. I knew then that something was wrong because she never let the Aga go out, whatever the weather. She always baked her bread rolls in the Aga cooker; she said they tasted best from there – which they did, her bread was amazing, it always went like hot cakes in the café.

Anyway, I thought she must probably be in bed if she was ill, so I made my way through to the front hallway and there she was, lying on the floor in the hall. I could see she was dead but I checked anyway and then I called the police from her phone because my mobile doesn't always have a signal here and I waited for them. That's pretty much it really."

"It must have been awful for you. If it had been me, I think I would have been in pieces."

"Well," Ken looked across at me, then at his glass, took another sip slowly and then back at me. "I think I must have been a bit affected because while I was waiting for the police I went upstairs."

"Why did you do that?"

"I could have sworn I heard footsteps up there."

Chapter 8
Kenny

Footsteps! It wasn't long ago that I thought the same thing, was it? I stared at my companion and I heard myself give a little gasp.

His eyebrow went up slightly, making his face look a little crooked. I thought irrelevantly that it made him look rather comical but at the same time, quite attractive. I forgot the notion as quickly as it had come. I composed myself rapidly.

"Footsteps? Did you think there was someone upstairs?"

"I did. I went up very quickly and I looked into every room, even behind the doors but I saw no one. I thought I must have imagined it; nothing seemed to be touched and there was no way anyone could escape from up there. The windows are too small and in any case they were all shut."

"Well, I thought I heard footsteps up there earlier, although I'd just been up there. I decided it was probably the timbers in the house shifting or something because I'd just opened some windows."

"I expect you can hear all sorts of noises in a house as old as this. We get some in our house."

"I suppose you are right. The police said that Aunt Bea had been holding a poker and thought she must have thought she heard an intruder. Do you think it was the footsteps she heard upstairs rather than outside as had been assumed?"

He considered this and then said,

"Well, if the house regularly makes noises like that, I wouldn't think so, would you?"

"Perhaps not. I don't know what to think really."

"I suppose we will never know. Well, I should go, I have work to do."

He rose from his chair. I got up too; I was reluctant to see him go really. Although I was drawn to the house, I could see that it could get quite lonely out here.

"Oh, do you have any pickles that you'd like me to sell?" Ken asked, "I was due a new supply when she died."

"Well, there are loads of jars in the pantry; I suppose they must be for you. Come and see."

He followed me into the house and we looked in the pantry.

"Yes, I would say that is my order; or at least, some of it is. She used to supply the village shop too and would donate to any church bazaars."

"A busy lady, wasn't she?"

"She was indeed, she was always doing something. Have you found all her business logs yet? She used the lean-to room as her office."

"I haven't got that far yet," I replied. "I only came here today just to look and try to get the feel of whether I wanted to stay here."

"Have you decided?"

"Not yet."

"It can be lonely living out here." Ken unconsciously echoed my thought of a few moments ago. "Do you have anyone who would come and live here with you?"

"Well, no, not really. My dad has his own place on the King's Acre Road; I can't see him wanting to be out here except for the odd night. I have a fiancé in London but he won't want to bury himself here either."

"I heard you have a fiancé. It's going to be a hard decision for you, I think. Now, I really must go."

He turned and exited the back door and I walked with him to the driveway.

"If you are going to be here tomorrow, I could come to fetch my order. I would need to bring my van to transport them; I'm on foot now."

"I don't know when I shall be here tomorrow."

"Well, I'll give you my phone number and perhaps you can call me if you come over. I can also deliver the order for the village shop if you like."

"That might be helpful, thank you."

He handed me a card and gave me a nod. I watched him walk across the garden in the direction of the river. Then I went back to the patio, picked up the glasses and the plate of biscuits that were left and took them into the kitchen. I rinsed out the glasses, found a tin to put the biscuits in and then wandered into the lounge. I sat down on one of Aunt Bea's squashy comfortable chairs. Somehow, I felt restless and the place seemed suddenly lonely now. Getting up again, I went back into the kitchen, gathered my bag and the big bunch of keys and left, carefully locking the door behind me. Then, as I looked up at the house, I realised I'd left some windows open so I unlocked the door again and, dumping my bag on the table again, hastened through the house shutting the windows downstairs.

Heart thumping a bit, I made my way up the winding staircase to shut the windows up there. Fortunately, I neither heard nor saw anything. This done, I retraced my steps to the kitchen where I picked up my bag, went out and locked the door again. I gave one last look at the house and then got into my car and negotiated my way back down the narrow lane onto the wiggly village road.

****

Dad agreed to come and spend the weekend at River View Farmhouse with me. With that in mind, I went shopping for groceries so that we would have plenty of supplies to keep us happy. Butch would come too, of course, so we had to take his food, bowls and bed. I had checked that there was plenty of bedding at the farmhouse; I just needed to get there early enough to make sure it was properly aired. I sent a message to Ken Baxter, telling him of our plans.

We lost no time in getting out to the farmhouse; we were there before lunch and as usual, I went round the house throwing open the windows and then dug out the sheets and duvets to hang out on the line that was at the side of the house outside. The spring sun was working hard and it was quite warm. I must not forget to get them in before the evening damp started.

Dad got busy lighting the Aga; we'd decided we would put it on to make sure everything was working properly. Butch wondered around outside leisurely sniffing at various corners and doing general doggy things. He was familiar with this garden and he was reacquainting himself with all his favourite places. Then he followed me in to investigate the corner of the living-room where his bed had been put. As I was a food-safety conscious chef, I wouldn't allow a dog to sleep in the room where food is made, even though he would be in there with us quite a bit. There was a small alcove in the living room and his bed fitted perfectly. He seemed happy with it.

I cooked us a light meal on the gas cooker. As we were finishing our meal, Butch woofed and walked to the kitchen door, tail wagging.

It was Ken. When I opened the door, Butch greeted him effusively, his whole body waggling with his tail. Ken made a fuss of him.

"Hello, old fella. You're a beauty, aren't you?" He looked at me. "What's his name?"

"This is Butch, he's my dad's dog. And this is my dad, Tom Dixon."

I watched while the two men shook hands.

"I understand it was you found my sister, Ken?"

"I did, sir. I am sorry for your loss. Bea was a good friend of mine, as well as my neighbour."

Dad nodded. "Thank you."

"Dad, Ken has come to take the last consignment of jars that Aunt Bea made for him. They are all in the pantry."

"Oh, very well. Come on in then, young man. We will help you take them out."

"I'll just bring my van down to the door if I may?"

"Of course; that will make it much easier."

I watched while he loped off up the drive and, not many minutes later, he reappeared in a small van which was white with a design of flowers around the name of 'River View Nurseries, J. Baxter & Son' on the sides. He stopped right outside the kitchen door.

It didn't take long for us to load up the trays of marmalades and pickles into his van. I was sorry to see them go really, although I noticed there were still a couple of odd jars left in the pantry so I assumed they could be for my consumption.

"I have to take two trays of these to the village shop; the rest will go on sale at my nurseries," Ken explained.

"Actually," I said suddenly, "Could I come with you? I'd like to meet the owner of the shop and see your nurseries. I think I should know a bit more about Aunt Bea's business. What do you think, dad?"

He nodded. "Yes love, I think that's a good idea. Butch and I will go for a walk and we will head over to the nursery and meet you there."

"Great. I will clear up later."

"I'll do that," dad said quickly. "Go on love, don't keep Ken waiting, I expect he's busy."

I grabbed my jacket, gave him a quick peck on the cheek and hurried to get into the passenger seat of the van. Ken held the door open for me; I was glad I had jeans on because it was difficult to do and still be ladylike. He shut the door and went around to the driver's side. Moments later, he had expertly turned the van round on the forecourt and was heading back up the driveway.

It didn't take long to get to the village and he pulled up outside a very picturesque shop, called 'Sutton's Olde Village Shoppe'. We both got out and went round to the back of the van and Ken pulled open the doors. He wouldn't let me take a tray; he said they were very heavy. Not believing him, I started to pick the other up and very quickly found what he said was true, so I put it down again, grinning sheepishly and followed him into the shop.

A woman with a friendly smile came up to us.

"Hello, Ken, hello dear. You are Bea's niece, aren't you? I saw you at the funeral. I am so sorry about Bea, my dear."

"Thank you, Mrs...?"

"Whatton, Madge Whatton. Call me Madge, dear."

"Thank you. I'm pleased to meet you. I do remember speaking with you at the funeral but I met so many people that it was all a bit of a blur, you know?"

"Of course, dear, don't you worry. I am pleased to get another delivery of your aunt's wonderful produce. Will you be taking over her business, do you think?"

"Oh, um, I haven't decided yet. I'm still thinking things over. I live and work in London and I have a fiancé there too so it would be a big thing to come here to live."

"Of course, dear. You must do the right thing for you, although we would be very sad for River View to belong to strangers. Also, of course, we would miss all her wonderful culinary supplies. If you made the decision to come here, at least you would have a business already in place to support you."

While we were talking, Ken had brought in the other tray of jars too and they were both set on the counter. I didn't want to keep him standing around so I made to leave.

"It's been very nice to meet you Mrs Whatton – erm – Madge. I'm afraid there are no more jars at the house."

"It would be the last consignment for the winter anyway; Bea would go on to produce summer fruit jams and jellies shortly – seasons, you know?"

"Of course. Well, I must be going."

"Shall I pay for these the normal way, to 'Aunt Bea's Pantry'?"

"Oh! I don't know. I will have to ask the solicitor. Leave it for now, Madge, I'll let you know, if that's okay with you?"

"Oh yes dear; I understand you must get things sorted. The money will be there ready once you know."

"Thank you. Goodbye for now."

I smiled at Ken, who nodded to the round, cheerful woman, and I turned toward the door. He hastened to open it for me and I smiled my thanks and turned to give a little wave to Madge, who stood watching us leave, her brown curls bouncing as she waved back.

"What a nice woman," I remarked to Ken after we had set off.

"She is indeed; in fact, most of the people in the village are nice, very supportive of each other. Sutton is a real community, the way villages should be. In some ways, it's a place frozen in time; people grow up and stay here, generations of people hand the same house down to one another. The village shop has been run by three generations of Madge's family; it was started by her grandmother. Madge was lucky to marry Len Whatton who was happy to come and live here and support her in her shop. It's a thriving business too and is the centre of village life. Madge is the driving force behind all sorts of village activities."

I was beginning to get a picture of how life was in this place and I have to say that it appealed to me.

Chapter 9
River View Nurseries

Being in the van with Ken was a strange experience. We sat in silence as he guided the vehicle round the winding road out of the village. It took only minutes to get to his nursery because it was closer than the farmhouse was. We didn't talk but somehow the air was charged; I could almost feel it crackling. I didn't know what to say to him really and I was glad of the thought that I would be walking back to the farmhouse with my dad. When he drew the van to a halt, Ken turned and gave me a grin that immediately dispelled the uncomfortable feelings I was having.

"Here we are," he said unnecessarily, "Welcome to J. Baxter and Son."

"Is J. Baxter your father?" I asked as I joined him outside.

"Actually, it was my grandfather, Joseph Baxter and the son, my dad, John Baxter. When it became John Baxter there was no need to change the sign."

"So, your dad owns the nursery now?"

"No. I'm afraid my dad died a few years ago. I'm the owner but I decided to keep the name in memory of my dad and granddad."

I was impressed by this; I thought there were many who would immediately want their name to be on the signs. I followed him in through the nearest door. The interior really surprised me; it was like a tardis in that it stretched away, long and deep. The whole impression of the place was that of cleanliness and order, light and airy.

We went through one of the side doors to the outside. It was huge; the grounds surrounding the building were set out to grassy paths and garden beds showing to best advantage the plants that they had for sale. People visiting here could see how these plants and trees would look in their mature form and in a proper garden setting.

In my experience, this was fairly unusual in garden centres that I had been to. Behind the commercial part of the grounds was an area of lawn, surrounded by more beds and to the side was an orchard with various mature fruit trees, laid out in cordons forming a hedge, or in bush form, or in espaliers against a wall to show how these things are done.

To our right was a house, which I assumed was where he lived. He nodded towards it.

"Our house, called very originally, 'The Nursery House'. Used to be four small farm cottages and they have been made into one house. It's quite quaint really. I'll show it to you another time."

"It looks lovely. Oh!"

My 'Oh' was because Butch suddenly appeared at my side, tail wagging as always, tongue hanging, and panting from his run. I bent to pat him and then looked up as my dad appeared.

"Sorry, Ken, I shouldn't have had him off the lead. He spied Lucy and took off. Come here, boy!"

"Oh, don't worry, Mr Dixon, I'm sure he hasn't done any harm. I was just showing Lucy around. Would you like to join us now?"

"Of course. Keep still, you daft dog!" Dad managed to slip the lead onto Butch's collar. Butch came to heel then and walked at dad's feet.

By the side of the cottage, there was a large kitchen garden, the soil brown and smooth with green shoots appearing. There were labels already in place to say what was growing in all the different areas.

As we walked back to the shop, I asked,

"What do you do with all the vegetable and fruit that you grow?"

"We-ell, we use a little of it and some of it is sold in Madge's shop. Some of it goes to the restaurant in the village, called 'The Wyeview Restaurant.' Much of it was used in Bea's produce; we had a working arrangement, you see, we pooled her produce and mine and she used much of it in her jams, jellies, chutneys, pickles, pies and cakes. She supplied us, Madge's shop and the restaurant with various things. A local farmer supplies the restaurant with meat and eggs; the restaurant is famous for its fresh, locally-grown meat and veg. I'm not sure what we will do with some of it now. Still, I'm not going to worry about that just yet. Come and meet my mother."

His mother! I hadn't given a thought to who the 'we' were that he referred to when talking about his house. Somehow, I assumed he meant he had a wife.

Mrs Baxter turned out to be a sprightly woman, very smartly but simply dressed. She wore black trousers and a pink overall with a logo of 'River View Nursery' and a flower on the top pocket. Somehow, she managed to look very elegant. Her brown straight hair framed her face and her smile was exactly like her son's as she greeted us with outstretched hand. I warmed to her immediately.

"You must be Lucy. I've heard so much about you from Bea. She was my best friend, you know."

"I'm sorry, I didn't know," I replied. I was trying to think if I met her at the funeral; I'm sure I would have remembered her.

"I felt awful when I heard about her death. I was away at the time, looking after my sister who'd had an operation. I missed the funeral and everything; I just couldn't leave my sister at the time. Poor Bea."

"I'm sure she understood. Please don't feel bad about it. This is my dad, Tom."

"We've met before, haven't we, Tom? We met at Bea's once."

"Indeed we did, Mrs Baxter."

"Oh please, do call me Sheila; I always feel about ninety when I get called Mrs Baxter, although I do miss my poor John, Kenny's father."

"I'm sure you do," replied my dad gravely.

"Kenny tells me that you are staying at Bea's place for the weekend?"

"Yes, Lucy wanted to stay there a while so she can get a feel of what she might do. You know the condition of the will?"

"No, I don't. Do tell me."

I quickly outlined to Sheila what the will was about. Her eyes grew round.

"My goodness, what a dilemma for you, Lucy – a big decision for you to make."

I nodded and a silence fell for a moment.

"Tell you what, why don't you come over to our house to have Sunday dinner with us tomorrow? We don't open the garden centre on Sundays, in spite of some public opinion that we should open. My father-in-law was strict about that and so was my husband. Keeping the Sabbath Day holy was important to them so we keep the same tradition. We have found that we don't suffer for it. Our customers know that we give a good service. Unlike other garden centres which are pretty much just plant shops, all our staff can give expert advice on everything, especially organic gardening, so our customers organise their lives so they can come here on other days. We stay open later in the evenings to help make up for it.

"Personally, I'm glad that we have a whole day off. No one can continue to work seven days a week indefinitely. My husband always felt that it's important for our workers to be able to spend a whole day with their families. There's not enough family life for people these days."

"I think I agree with you, Mrs - um, Sheila," my dad said. The rest of us nodded.

"Will you come to lunch with us then? Ken and I go to church first and we have lunch around one."

Dad and I looked at each other. He nodded slightly. I turned to her.

"We would love to come. Thank you."

"Bring your dog too, don't leave him behind." She bent down to fondle Butch and he fawned over her like a young dog. 'Someone is smitten,' I thought, watching him. I also had my suspicions about my dad too...

"Well," said Ken, "I'm afraid I have work to get on with."

This brought us back to where we were and what time it was. I turned to him.

"Oh sorry, Ken, I didn't mean to keep you this long. Thank you very much for taking me with you to the village."

"No problem, it was my pleasure. I will see you tomorrow." He nodded to dad and me, gave Butch a quick pat and off he went.

"Let me show you the way out of here that is quickest for you to get back to your house," said Sheila. "Bill, could you man the till for me for a short while please? I won't be long."

"Of course, Mrs Baxter." The man called Bill, a short, stocky man, came towards the till and Sheila beckoned us to follow her.

We walked back to the house and she took us around the side to the back of the house. There was a private area there and some outhouses. At the far end of the garden was a gate.

"This is our private path from our house to yours," she said. "It means we don't have to go all the way round but we just go alongside the river; it's more or less straight from here to River View Farmhouse. Of course, at one time, our cottage was part of the farm so they are quite near. It's useful to be able to go this way."

"That's great. Thank you." I realised this was the way Ken had gone when he left the house yesterday.

We said goodbye to her and set off. It was a lovely walk being able to look down upon the river as it meandered along on its way to Hereford from the mountains in Wales. It was very peaceful. Butch trotted along, stopping occasionally to nose around. The river curved around and that's why our house wasn't immediately visible from the Baxters' house, and there was a small spinney of trees between us. We also passed a picturesque small stone bridge opposite a wide gate that led into a meadow where cattle grazed peacefully. It was a very short distance; we covered it in about ten minutes. When we stood at the gate that led into our garden (I hadn't noticed it before) I could see the large house further along the river that was the nursing home, Sutton Court. The large, white building looked very elegant in its setting of trees – well, what I could see of it anyway.

Coming into the garden, I realised I needed to get the sheets and duvets off the line – what a good thing we had not been out longer. Dad helped me get them in and we immediately went upstairs to make the beds. By unspoken agreement, we avoided Bea's bedroom; dad went for the spare room down the landing and I went for the room by the stairs. Dad told me that Bea used this room as her 'quiet room', although why she needed a quiet room when she was the only occupant of the house was completely beyond me! However, I sensed that this room had a very peaceful atmosphere and was drawn to it.

By the time we had done that and got ourselves a meal, it was still light; the days were getting longer with the spring.

It was cosy sitting in the small living room with the television on, Butch lying on dad's feet. We didn't talk much; we were content to be in each other's company.

Jim called me around eight o'clock. I went into the kitchen to talk with him so dad could continue to watch his programme. In a way, it shocked me; I'd practically forgotten about Jim, so absorbed had I been about all that we'd been doing. I felt guilty then.

I told him about the house and the business but it seemed he just wasn't interested, until I mentioned going in Ken's van today.

"You did WHAT? You went with this guy, in his van? How could you be so stupid, Lucille? You don't know him! What is he after? Did he try anything on?"

I was annoyed.

"Don't call me stupid! It was quite safe; he is my neighbour and my aunt's friend, for goodness' sake."

"An old man? That's worse! Nothing worse than a dirty old man!"

"He's not a dirty old man, he's ..."

"Oh, you know, do you? How do you know?"

In the end I got angry – and I was annoyed that he called me Lucille, it always annoyed me.

"Jim, you're not listening to me! If you're going to be like that, I'm going. I'll talk with you when you can be reasonable."

"Lucille!"

"And don't keep calling me Lucille – you know I hate it! Goodbye, Jim! Call me when you can talk to me without treating me like a child."

With that, I snapped off the phone and stalked back into the living room to join my dad. I flung myself down in my chair.

"What's up, love?"

"Oh nothing! Jim can be so annoying at times. I couldn't stand talking with him any more for now. I told him I would talk with him again when he can talk with me as if I'm an adult and not a five year old."

"Oh dear," remarked dad.

At that moment, Butch got up and ran to the door to the hallway, ears pricked.

"What's the matter, boy?" asked dad, as Butch gave a low growl in his throat.

It was a moment later when we heard the soft sound of footsteps above our heads…

Chapter 10
Footsteps!

Dad and I looked at each other, alarmed. Butch was scrabbling at the bottom of the door, barking. Dad got up and opened the door to the hallway and Butch shot out. Dad followed him and I went after them both, my heart banging in my chest. Butch skidded to a halt at the bottom of the stairs; he knew he was not allowed to go upstairs, even though he now lived in a bungalow, he never went in the bedrooms. He stood, front feet on the bottom step, growling, hackles raised. Dad went to go past him.

"Oh dad, do be careful!"

"Don't worry, lass, I don't see how there can be anyone up there. Come on, boy."

Butch was reluctant at first but after a moment he bounded up the stairs, dad was just behind him. The footstep noises had stopped and all I could hear was the click-scuffle of Butch's claws on the wooden floorboards and dad's soft footfall because he was wearing his slippers. I waited on the third stair where the staircase curved round, anxiously peering round the corner. It wasn't long before they were back, Butch hurrying to get down again, his body wiggling comically as he passed me.

"Absolutely nothing there," dad reported. "We looked into all the rooms, behind all the doors and under all the beds. No windows open anywhere either."

We went back into the sitting-room and shut the door.

"What do you think it was?" I asked dad as we sat down again. Butch curled himself on the rug, tucked his nose in and went immediately to sleep. Obviously, he was no longer bothered.

"I have no idea. There was no sign of anyone having been up there."

I shivered.

"Do you think it could have been – a ghost?"

Dad considered this for a moment, tapping his fingers on the arm of his chair.

"I suppose it's possible," he said, slowly. "Bea did mention from time to time about 'the other occupants of the house' but I never paid much attention."

Other occupants! Did that mean there was more than one ghost? If I came to live in the farmhouse, how many others would be here with me? I shivered again at the thought of being alone in a house full of ghosts. How could I come and live here?

"It seems odd though, don't you think?" Dad was speaking again.

"How's that?"

"Well, it's reckoned that animals won't go where ghosts are. They sense them and will cower away. Butch couldn't wait to get up there."

"Yes," I agreed. "Now you come to say, that does seem rather odd."

"Well, whatever it was, it's gone now." Dad nodded at Butch who was still sleeping peacefully at his feet.

"I think I need a hot chocolate," I said and got up to go into the kitchen to put the kettle on. Butch got up and followed me and a moment later he was pushing a few of his dog biscuits around in his bowl and started crunching. I watched him while I waited for the kettle.

"I wish you could talk to me, Butch and tell me what it was upstairs."

He stopped his crunching to look at me, his tail waved slowly. I could almost believe he understood and would like to talk. The kettle clicked and I moved to get the mugs out and Butch resumed his chomping. He was, however, ready to follow me back into the lounge when I went through with the drinks.

I admit that I was a bit reluctant when it was time to go to bed but I went up behind dad and put my night things on in Aunt Bea's quiet room, now my bedroom, while I waited for dad to finish using the bathroom. When I heard him come out, I went to kiss him goodnight and then watched him walk down the landing and into his room. After I'd used the bathroom I went back to my room and shut the door.

Just as I was settled into the bed, which was surprisingly comfortable and cosy, I heard the sound of the stairs creaking and soft footfalls. My heart leaped up and started beating crazily; the stairs were just outside my room, part of my room was over the hallway. Was the resident ghost about again? However, I realised these footsteps were different and as I heard the lounge door being opened, I knew it was dad down there. My heart slowed down to its normal rate and a few minutes later I heard him coming back up, accompanied by the click-click of doggy footsteps on the wooden flooring, fading away and the soft sound of dad's bedroom door being shut. I smiled to myself; obviously dad was breaking his long-standing rule of never allowing Butch in the bedroom. I was glad; with Butch up here, I felt there would be little to worry about.

*****

I awoke in the stillness of the small hours, wondering what had awakened me. I peeped with one eye above the covers. The room was surprisingly light, considering it was night. The illumination was coming through a gap in the curtains and I could see the bright moon, large in the sky. It threw a column of silver into the room, its edges softened by the thin material of the curtains. In the dim light I could pick out the dark shapes of the furniture in the room. In the quietness it seemed the room was holding its breath; hard to describe really. Was something there?

Afraid of what I might see and yet somehow compelled to look, I raised myself up in the bed.

"Hello?" I whispered. "Hello, is there anyone there?"

I strained my eyes and ears into the room; my heart was surprisingly calm. I caught a slight movement out of the corner of my eye. When I looked again, I could see nothing.

"Lucy."

I thought I had imagined it, for it was barely a sound, so soft in my mind.

"Aunt Bea? Is that you?"

I strained my ears and my eyes. But, however much I listened and looked, there was nothing there. In the end, I gave up and settled back into my bed, making a mental note that perhaps I should get some thicker curtains for my room.

Although I heard nothing more that night, somehow I felt more peaceful than I'd been for a long time. Maybe this was the right place for me, in spite of my doubts. Feeling soothed, I drifted back into slumber.

Chapter 11
Discoveries

"I suppose we should be going to church this morning, dad, but I feel I need to start going through Aunt Bea's office. I'm only going to be able to stay here a couple more days and I need to find out as much as I can about her business."

Dad and I were sitting together in the kitchen of River View Farmhouse having our breakfast. It was another lovely spring morning but it was a bit chilly as yet.

"It's also a daunting thought about going to church here, I feel that people will be looking at me, they all know who I am because they were out in force for the funeral. Also, we are going to be at the Baxters' for lunch and probably some of the afternoon, we can't really rush away after they've given us a meal. Time is short, dad."

"I agree. I think you should stay here this morning. If you decide to come here to live, there will be plenty of time to get to know the church and everyone."

"Did you sleep all right?" I asked him.

"Surprisingly well. You know that I took Butch up to sleep in my room? I thought it would be best if he was up there, in case we heard noises again. But we heard nothing, did we, boy?"

Butch looked up at dad adoringly and thumped his tail on the floor. He always knew when he was being spoken to.

"How did you sleep, Lulu?"

"Like you, surprisingly well. I woke up at some point in the night because the moon was shining really brightly through my window and the curtains are not very substantial. It was a strange experience I had in a way."

"How do you mean?" Dad stopped his hand holding his toast on its way up to his mouth to look at me with a puzzled questioning look.

"Well, I sort of felt there was someone in the room and I thought I heard my name whispered but now I'm wondering if I imagined it. But I had such a feeling of peace come over me that I was able to go back to sleep."

"Strange," remarked dad as he resumed biting into his toast.

"It was rather. I kind of had the feeling that Aunt Bea was watching over me."

He nodded.

"Not impossible."

"But you're sceptical?"

"I'm not sure that I believe in that kind of thing," dad responded slowly, "however, I'll keep an open mind on it. Knowing my sister, I wouldn't put it past her to do it if it was at all possible."

I washed up the few crocks we had used. Dad said he would take Butch out for a walk, so I saw them off and then made my way through the house to the other end.

Bea's lean-to office was very light, it having a large window forming much of the long wall of the room, the sloping roof meant that the window was low and showed a lovely view of the patch of garden alongside the drive. Another window faced the front of the house. The other end had a door leading to the outside. No doubt Aunt Bea found it useful to be able to go in and out of the house through her office and also if people came to see her on business, they could come in this way instead of having to come all through the house. The inside wall had shelves full of books and files. A table under the window looked as if it had once been a kitchen table, it had a well-scrubbed look. The chair that obviously was Bea's chair was a lovely old polished wooden armchair with a colourful cushion on the seat. Two other chairs were also in the room with similar cushions on their seats. The floral curtains matched the cushions.

I sat in the chair by the table; it was positioned so that I could see through the big window. I could see the rose bed that ran alongside the drive that came down from the lane to the back of the house to right outside the door of the lean-to office and on to the kitchen door. As I sat there, I could just imagine my aunt, sitting here in the summer doing her office work with the door open and listening to the music on the radio that stood on the window sill, the warm air wafting in, bringing the sweet scents of the flowers in her garden.

Under the table I found an old sewing machine – and I mean 'old'. It was in a wooden case and was heavy. But it was obviously still being used because it had long bobbins wound with cottons in the drawer and the machine was threaded up with cotton the same colour as the curtains and cushions. There was also a carrier bag with scraps of the material. Obviously, Aunt Bea had made them and fairly recently too.

This was a happy workroom; it seemed to me that Bea had spent a lot of time here when she wasn't busy making her cakes, jams and jellies. I could see why; I thought this could become my favourite room downstairs.

Enough of this wool-gathering! I stood up again and started to look at the contents of the shelves. There were many cookery-books; some of them bright and new, some old-looking and well used.

Bringing one of them down, I noticed that there were coloured book markers in certain places. Aunt Bea had marked all her favourite recipes. I could see that all the books had coloured papers in them. I would look more closely at them at a later time. I reached for some of the folders. These were immaculately-kept records of everything she made and sold, where she sold them and the prices.

I was soon immersed in the records; I couldn't help but be impressed as I examined them with my professional eyes. I was astonished to learn just how profitable my aunt's enterprise was. If I decided to come here and continue with it, I would be taking over a very lucrative business indeed.

By the time dad and Butch came in search of me, I was deep in thought. My discovery of the details of my aunt's business had given me much 'food' for serious consideration.

He brought with him two mugs of tea which he set down on the table and then he drew up one of the other chairs and sat down.

"Have you been able to find out much?" he asked.

"Oh yes indeed. Aunt Bea was very meticulous in keeping all her records. She had a very good business – I'm quite surprised but pleased."

He nodded, unsurprised.

"I suspected as much. I know she inherited quite a lot of money from her husband when he died but a place like this would cost a bit for the upkeep and she's had the garden completely landscaped since she's been here. At one time it was very reminiscent of the farmyard it used to be. Your aunt was very creative and she had an eye for making things look good. The garden was done entirely with her vision of what she wanted. It's been done some years now of course, it's well-matured. It would be so like her to make a business profitable; she always made a success of anything she put her mind to."

I picked up my mug and held it with both my hands; I realised how cold I'd become while sitting here. I'd been so absorbed in my task that I had forgotten to put the heater on. I loved the warmth spreading through my hands and took a sip of the drink.

"The more I learn, the more I want to be here. I love this house and I love the surroundings and am intrigued with the successful business that's here. But then there's my job in London – and Jim of course. I don't want to let this place go but I don't know how I'm going to keep it without causing chaos in my life." I sighed and took refuge in my drink again.

Dad put his mug down and got up from his chair. Butch was immediately ready to move too.

"Well love, think about it carefully and pray about it. I'm sure you will soon get your answer. We will need to be going off to the nursery very shortly. I'll take these mugs through and rinse them out while you pop your files away."

I looked at my watch; it said 12.45 – goodness, I had no idea it was so late!

"You're right, it's time we were going. I'll be right there in a couple of minutes."

He picked up the two mugs and left the room, followed by Butch and I gathered all the files on the table and popped them back on the shelf. As I did so, my hand touched something that was lying flat on the shelf. I picked it up and looked at it curiously. It was a book that had obviously been made by Aunt Bea. It had a photo of the farmhouse on the front and as I flicked through it, I could see more pictures of the house and garden. Firstly, they were black and white photos, then later coloured ones. I could see it was a record of how the house and garden had changed over the years.

As the pages went by, some loose pieces of paper came out that had been folded and left inside. I picked them up, and unfolded one of them. It looked like part of a letter:

'A man came here today. I caught him wondering around the garden when I came back from visiting with Sheila. When I asked him what he was doing, he seemed flustered and said he was lost and had come to ask directions but hadn't been able to find anyone. He said he must have taken a wrong turning, he had asked directions in the village but he must have misunderstood and arrived here instead.

'Fair enough' I thought. But then he asked if there was any chance I might be thinking of selling. Of course I told him no and he said 'pity.' He then bade me goodbye and sorry for disturbing me and went off up the drive to his car which was parked by the gate. I realised afterwards that he'd never told me where he was trying to get to or asked me directions. Perhaps he thought me too old or senile to be able to tell him anything.'

I turned the page over but there was no more. I was going to look at the other pages but, upon looking at my watch, I hurriedly put them back into the book and put it on the shelf where it had come from. I would look at it more closely another time, I thought.

Chapter 12
A Wonderful Dinner

The door was opened almost before we knocked and there was Sheila, all smiles and welcoming.

"There you are! What great timing, Kenny has just started to carve the roast. Come away in; let me take your coats."

She took our coats and hung them on an old-fashioned coat stand in the hall. She patted Butch.

"Hello there, my lovely boy – I've got something nice for you! I have a nice, juicy bone for you in the kitchen."

Butch treated her to his best smile and tail-wag, then we followed her through a door into a room that had a gorgeous, polished dark wood table, all set out for dinner with five places. The table had a lovely centre piece of a spring flower arrangement which enhanced the appearance without being too dominant. Someone obviously had a talent for floral arranging.

An elderly man was sitting at the table, he looked like a much older version of Ken

"This is my father-in-law, Joseph Baxter, Ken's granddad."

I smiled at him. "Hello, Mr Baxter, I'm happy to meet you."

His eyes twinkled at me as he smiled. "I'm happy to meet you too, young lady."

At that moment, Ken appeared, carrying a big serving dish with a lid which he set down in the middle of the table.

"Hello, Lucy, Mr Dixon, welcome. You've come just at the right time."

"Oh, do call me Tom; Mr Dixon is so stuffy."

"Tom then." Sheila tucked her arm through his. "I love making new friends and I love having friends to dinner – or lunch, whatever you care to call it. Sunday dinner is my favourite meal of the week."

"Mine too," dad smiled at her as she led him to a chair.

Ken pulled out a chair next to dad and I sat down. Ken and his mum were opposite us and Joseph was at the head of the table; obviously he was still looked upon as being the head of the family.

The food was delicious; the beef was cooked to perfection, the Yorkshire puddings were light and airy; the vegetables just right. As a chef myself I couldn't fault it but in any case, I was always happy to eat a meal cooked by someone other than myself.

The conversation was lively and interesting; Sheila turned out to be a great mimic and she regaled us with stories of the locals, imitating their voices and mannerisms so that one could almost see them. I felt I would recognise them when I saw them and looked forward to doing so. It seemed that the village was full of colourful characters. Ken and Joseph were quieter but obviously they enjoyed Sheila's performances and laughed along with us.

Dessert was a perfect apple pie with cream. I felt so satisfied that I felt I could easily sit down somewhere and go to sleep. Instead, I got up to help Sheila clear the things away. In fact, we all helped carry the dirty dishes through to the beautiful kitchen. It had been created out of the whole of one cottage's ground floor and was an amazing room, so spacious, full of shining worktops, modern fitted cupboards and sparkling windows with tiny vases of primroses on the sills.

"What a pretty kitchen!" I exclaimed upon first seeing it. Sheila smiled at me.

"I'm glad you like it. We only had it refitted last year and I love it. I enjoy cooking for my family but this is not my favourite room of the house. After we have finished eating I will show you and Tom the rest of it. It has been a work in progress for many years. The cottages were amalgamated by Joseph when he started the nursery business. When I moved in with my husband, it was a charming house but very rough round the edges; it was rather dark and full of the heavy dark wood furniture, which was available then. The kitchen had a big wooden scrubbed table where my mother-in-law did all her baking; she was a great cook and of course, electrical equipment was at a minimum then. My word, you should have seen her stirring a cake mix with a wooden spoon! She could stir it like the clappers and her sponges were so light. And pastry! I used to love to stand and watch, listening as her wedding-ring clicked on the rolling-pin as she rolled out the pastry; her pastries would melt in your mouth. Every time I roll pastry now I think of her. She was a lovely woman."

"Has she been gone long?"

"Oh, about fifteen years. I'm afraid she became very ill with cancer and it took her quite quickly. And you know that my husband, John, died last year. But Joseph is amazing; he just keeps on, even though he is nearer to eighty than seventy."

"He doesn't look that old," I remarked.

"No, he doesn't. I think it's because he keeps fit; he still does a lot of work around the garden centre although he's passed it over to Ken. I have a daughter, too, called Angela, but she is married with two children. They live in Ross-on-Wye; her husband is a solicitor there. They come over some Sundays; they couldn't come today because they were going to his parents' house to visit them. They live in Cheltenham."

"Ah, right. In that case, it was good of you to have us over; I would have thought you'd be glad of a break."

"Oh, it's no trouble. I have to cook for the three of us anyway and including two more is nothing. Anyway, I wanted to have a chance to get to know you better, in case you end up coming to live here. Have you had any more thoughts on the matter? It will be a big decision for you, won't it?"

"Yes it will. I'm still undecided really. I can feel the pull of the house and the challenge of running the business but there's so much to leave behind in London. It's not going to go down well with Jim, my fiancé."

"I heard you have a fiancé. Wouldn't he come up here to be with you?"

"Well, he might but somehow I don't think so. His life is very much tied up with London."

"Oh, that's nonsense really; with the internet you can run a business just about anywhere from anywhere."

"Perhaps you're right. We'll see."

"Well, if we are all finished, would you like to see the rest of the house? I think Butch is still happy with his bone in the kitchen. Shall we leave him there for now? Dad will take care of him if he wants to come through."

"Yes, that sounds fine. I'm longing to see the rest of this gorgeous house."

Sheila led the way out of the dining room and across the hallway. We entered a lounge that was large and sumptuously furnished with brown leather sofas and chairs. There was a large cream rug in front of the enormous brick fireplace that had an old wooden beam across it. There were wooden stanchions along the sides where once they had supported walls which had been taken out. On the one long side the stanchions were supporting an upper landing which was open to the room with a very attractive wooden balustrade. The room was 'olde worlde' and yet modern too. I was very taken with it.

This house reminded me of my farmhouse in the way the rooms led through from one to the other with a central hallway, but the farmhouse was much older than these cottages had been and it was obvious that the cottages had been opened up in such a way to maximise the space.

The stairs went up from a corner of this room. There were four bedrooms and a bathroom upstairs. All were beautiful rooms and two rooms had their own shower rooms en suite.

I was very impressed with the house. It was obvious that Sheila had a very good eye for décor; her room was so elegant, very feminine. Kenny's and Joseph's rooms were very manly but still managed to be attractive.

Downstairs, there was a utility room off the kitchen and beyond that was another room that was used as an office. These had once been outhouses of some sort and had been converted later than the rest of the house.

"What do you think of the house, Lucy?" Ken was close behind me as we made our way back to the lounge where Joseph was taking a nap in a chair.

"It's wonderful; your mother is a very talented lady."

"Isn't she just?" he grinned. "She's made this a lovely place; she has really thrown herself into it since dad died. Mum needed something else to think about. She made big changes to the garden centre too, planning and setting things out in there to make it its best. Granddad and I are good with plants but mum is the one who makes it all come together in an artistic and attractive way within the building. We have a lot to thank her for; there is so much she can do and she makes such a difference. She has a natural flair for what works."

I agreed. Was there anything Sheila couldn't do, I wondered?

"Is there anything you can't do?" dad echoed my own unspoken thoughts. Sheila's laugh tinkled joyously.

"I'm sure there's lots I couldn't do," she answered, "In fact, although I have planned and designed the garden centre, I'm no gardener! Oh no, I have always left that to my menfolk; they have all been obsessed with gardening and so I decided I would just leave them to it! Angela loves gardening too; you should see her place."

We settled down in the lovely comfortable sofas in the lounge and Sheila brought a tray through with mugs of tea for us all. As I took one, I said,

"Thank you. So, how long were you friends with my aunt?"

"Oh, I first met her many years ago when she and her husband first bought the farmhouse. But I only became close friends with her when she came back to live here. We saw a lot of each other and she was wonderful when my John died."

She sank down on the sofa beside me.

"I still can't believe she has gone. I'm grieved that I wasn't here. I had only been gone a couple of days when it happened."

"I found something strange today," I offered. "I was looking at her papers in the lean-to office…"

"Oh yes, she called it her den. Quite why she needed a den when she had the whole house, I'm not sure. I can understand her using it as an office but she spent hours in there sewing and doing other things. If it was me, I'd be doing that in more comfort in my lounge."

"I thought that about her 'Quiet Room'. Why did she need a quiet room when she had the whole house?"

"Oh well, I suppose she liked to have a room where she could sit and commune with God. I know she loved to be up there because the view from the window is lovely. It being higher up, she could see the entire garden, river and the countryside beyond that. She said it inspired her."

"It certainly has a lovely, peaceful feel about it. Anyway, as I was looking through her things in her office, I came across a paper. It seemed to be part of a letter and it was saying about a man who came wondering onto her premises and tried to persuade her to let him buy it."

"Oh yes, I remember that! She told me about it. She'd just been here and she got home and found him in her garden. She phoned me as soon as he'd gone and she was quite agitated about it; for some reason it had really upset her. I came round to see her because she was really worked up about it. She seemed okay when I left though. I wonder who she was writing it to?"

"More to the point, why didn't she send it?" I turned to look at dad, who had said nothing until now on this point of conversation.

"Where was the paper, Lucy?" Ken asked me, frowning.

"It was in a book she had made herself about the house. There were pictures of the house going down through the years she'd been there. The paper was folded and tucked in among the pages."

"Hmm, almost like it was part of the record of the house," mused Ken.

"I'd say it was almost like it was something she meant to be found."

Chapter 13
Suspicions

We stayed a while longer, until dad said that Butch really needed to go out and I said that I had to do some more at the farmhouse as I would have to go back to London very soon.

Ken went to fetch our coats and Butch's lead. Dad shook hands with Joseph and I gave the old man a kiss. He patted my hand.

"I hope you decide to come back, young lass. It would be nice to have you around."

I smiled at him. "We'll see."

Sheila insisted on kissing both me and dad and I noticed he didn't object at all!

Kenny shook hands with dad. Then he turned to me.

"Do what you feel is right for you, Lucy. Of course, we all want you here but it's your life. Remember that."

His hand was warm on my shoulder as he spoke and his brown eyes gazed intently to mine. Inside, I felt a little flutter as I tried to gauge the meaning in his look. I nodded. In a moment that look was gone and I knew I'd imagined it.

On our walk back to the farmhouse, dad's words that Aunt Bea's description of finding the man who'd wanted to buy the house was meant to be found, went round and round in my head. As soon as I got in, I made my way back to the den and took down the file about the house. As I did so, a paper fluttered to the ground. It was another piece of notepaper like the first one. From it I read:

'There was something about him that reminded me of a weasel'

I frowned at the paper; those eleven words were the only ones on it.

I looked for the other paper, which was still tucked in where I had left it. I could see that these were both in Aunt Bea's distinctive scrawl but the first one was written in her usual black ink and the second one was written in blue. Not written at the same time then, nor was the second a follow-on from the first. How strange.

*****

As I sat at the table in the den reflecting on Aunt Bea's strange words, dad came through, Butch at his heels. He held something out to me. It was a card with Detective Chief Inspector Cooke's name and a number. On the back was written:

'Sorry to have missed you. Please call me asap.'

"Oh bother! He came all the way out to see me and I wasn't here. I'd better call him now. Where's my mobile? Oh, it's in my bag in the kitchen."

I called the D.C.I. and he said could he call in tomorrow morning about nine, would that be too early? I said it was fine.

"Dad, I really need to get back to London. I will wait and see the police tomorrow and then set off. Is that okay with you? I don't think I can do any more here for now anyway."

"That's fine with me, love. Of course you need to get back and I want to get back to my house really, I don't like to leave it too long, although the neighbours are very good, keeping an eye on it."

"That's settled then. I'll go and do some packing and then I'll make us some tea."

When I went up to my bedroom, I went over to the window and gazed out.

It was indeed a beautiful view across the garden, over the river and beyond. It gave me a tranquil feeling in one way but in another I was far from calm. I had a big decision to make and didn't know how I was going to make it.

"Oh, Aunt Bea, why have you done this? What shall I do?"

As I breathed the words quietly to the room, I listened intently as if I expected an answer. However, none was forthcoming. I went to the bed, put my small case upon it and started gathering up my things. I couldn't put everything in; some things had to wait until I was nearly ready to leave. The job was soon done. I left my case on the floor at the foot of the bed and went back to the window. As I looked out, I thought I caught sight of something that moved along the lawn, then it was gone. I continued to watch but saw nothing else. I sighed and turned away; it must have been a rabbit or something – and yet I could have sworn it had been the figure of a woman.

*****

Detective Inspector Cooke was as good as his word. He turned up promptly at nine, just as I'd made a pot of tea

He accepted my offer of a cup of tea and even took some toast as he sat at the kitchen table with me. He seemed very relaxed and patted Butch, who sniffed at him and then settled down on his feet, a sure sign that the dog approved of him.

"Mm, I love toast and jam; is this home-made?" He picked up the jar. "Aunt Bea's Pantry," he read. "It's good. My wife would like that."

I smiled; I liked this man.

"Yes, Aunt Bea was a wonderful cook. Now, Inspector, what can I do for you?"

"As you know, your aunt died of natural causes. Obviously, she had been worried about something outside, given that she was holding a poker at the time the heart-attack struck. Officially, there is no enquiry about the circumstances of her death because of the post-mortem results. However, off record, I'm not happy about it. There's something about this that smells nasty. I have a nose for suspicious things, Miss Dixon, Mr Dixon, and my nose is saying that your aunt's death was not right. We couldn't find any traces of a possible intruder outside the house but that doesn't mean to say there wasn't one. Having no clues means there's no trail – except for this nose." He pointed to the said appendage, which, I have to say, was actually quite a nice nose.

"I've been in the business a long time and I know when something isn't as it seems. Can you help me at all? Do you have any thoughts on this?"

"Excuse me a minute please, I just need to get something." I got up and hurried out of the room. I went to the den and picked up the file about the house and took it back to the kitchen.

"I was going through my aunt's office yesterday and I found these." I handed the Inspector the two pieces of paper. I watched them as he read them and saw the frown come over his face as he looked from one to the other and then put them side by side.

"So, who is she talking about in the second one? Who reminded her of a weasel – the man who wanted to buy her house?"

"No idea. It just seems a bit random."

"They obviously were written at different times; you would have thought that if she was talking about the man prowling around here as reminding her of a weasel, she would have written that at the time. It seems rather strange that she should have kept this paper with the one sentence on it. It looks like she was keeping a record of her thoughts about things, although quite why she would keep this in her file about the house, I don't know."

"I think in some way this last little bit is connected with the house, otherwise why leave it in the house folder? Do you think she wrote it when she was thinking about the man at some point much later?" I mused.

"That may well be the case, although as we have already said, you would have thought she would have added it to the same piece of paper that she wrote the first bit on if that was so."

"Yes. My aunt was always a bit random except where her business was concerned. She was meticulous in her record-keeping for that."

"Was it a good business?"

"Yes, it was, very good indeed. I could see she made a lot of money; she must have done to be able to keep this place going, it's in good condition."

"And are you going to come and live here, Miss Dixon? I understand that you've been left this house? Did you know she was leaving it to you?"

"No, I don't think I really thought about it. I never imagined a time when she wouldn't be here you know. I was busy with my life in London."

"Ah yes, I understand you have a good job down there," he stated. I realised that I was being investigated as the beneficiary of the will but somehow it just felt like normal friendly interest the way he was asking.

"I do. Now I have to decide if I am going to leave it to live here."

"Why should you do that?" he frowned. "Can't you just keep it and rent it out or something?"

"Oh, you obviously don't know the conditions of my aunt's will, inspector. If I want the house, I have to live in it for a year. If I decide not to do that, it will be sold and the money given to various charities. You see, my aunt knew that I am engaged to a man who is very well off and if I marry him I won't need this house, or the money from the sale of it. My aunt was a great one for supporting certain charities. She left me a letter explaining her reasons, which the solicitor gave me when I saw him on Friday."

"Indeed? I don't suppose you would let me see that letter?"

"Of course; I'll fetch it for you."

I went upstairs to my bedroom and took the letter from my case where I had put it ready to take with me. Coming back downstairs, I handed it to the detective and watched while he read it. He handed it back to me.

"A very nice letter, Miss Dixon. May I ask how you feel about the conditions and her explanation?"

"To be quite honest, although I understand her reasons, I am a bit upset by it. I would rather she just left the house to dad or directly to the charities rather than make me make a life changing decision, which it will be if I decide to come here."

"Yes, I can see that. Do you know yet what you will do?"

"No I don't. While I'm here, I feel I want to stay here. How I will feel when I'm back in London, I don't know. I only have a couple of months to decide."

He stood up then.

"Well, you must do whatever you feel is right. But please let me know when you do decide. This nose of mine tells me there is more to your aunt's death that meets the eye and I intend to find out what is it."

He held out his hand.

"Thank you for the tea and toast and have a safe journey back to London, Miss Dixon. Please keep in touch."

We shook hands and I saw him out of the kitchen door. I watched him drive away in his car and then turned back into the house.

"Well, what do you think of that, dad?"

"I think he is a very astute man. I also think there's more to Bea's death than meets the eye. But I don't know how he will ever find out what."

Looking back, I think that was the moment when I decided to come and live in Aunt Bea's house. If there was any way of finding out what had gone on, I had to be here. I dreaded telling James; I knew there was going to be trouble.

Chapter 14
The Move

"Darling, if you feel this is something you must do, then I'm with you, you should go and live in your aunt's house."

I couldn't believe my ears! Was this really Jim, my fiancé talking to me? I think my disbelief must have shown on my face because he wrapped his arms around me and said,

"Don't look so surprised! Surely you know that I only want what will make you happy? I know you want to keep your aunt's house. I thought a lot about it while you were away and I realise that if that is something you want to do, then I will support you in it. It's not as if it's a million miles away, I can soon zip up the motorway to see you and I'll come whenever I can."

He took hold of my hand and drew me down on the sofa beside him.

"Are you sure about leaving your job? I know you love it."

"Well, it won't be easy because you're right, I do love it. But I think I like the challenge of taking over my aunt's business, 'Aunt Bea's Pantry'. I'm sure I can do it and even expand it."

I had told him that I was going to Hereford in order to take over Aunt Bea's business; for some reason I didn't mention that I was going because I wanted to find out more about why Aunt Bea died the way she did. Nor did I mention the strange footstep noises dad and I had heard and Kenny mentioned. I didn't want anything to stop me going.

His arm tightened around my shoulder and he gave me a quick hug.

"You'll be brilliant. It is great to run a business; I thoroughly enjoy being in business myself, as you know."

"I do. And I have no idea what sort of business you have, even though we've been together for ages."

"Oh, it's a sort of import/export and we deal with some other things too. We don't want to talk about business, darling. How soon do you think you will get away?"

"Well, I shall stay at work until they find someone to take over my job but I shall write to the solicitor to let him know my decision. I'm hoping that I can go in about six weeks."

"Six weeks – my goodness. We'll have to make the most of the time we have.

Not many moments later, I was enveloped in his arms once again.

*****

Leaving work was so hard. I recommended my first assistant, Sue, to take over my job and they moved everyone up and appointed a new kitchen assistant who would eventually work his way up.

On my last day, as I was preparing to leave, they threw a party for me and gave me cards and gifts that they had collected for. They gave me the latest state-of-the-art Multichef and a gorgeous, sumptuous afghan throw, because Sue somehow imagined that I would be very cold, living in the country!

A week after I left work I was back at River View Farmhouse. I had brought all my personal stuff with me and some favourite pieces of furniture, most of it small bits. Sue's husband has a large van and he very kindly drove up to Herefordshire with my things. He stayed overnight with dad and then went back the next day, which I thought was very good of him. I did pay him of course but it was still good of him to sacrifice his weekend.

Dad came over to help me get sorted. Sheila popped over with Kenny in the van, bringing me a wonderful casserole and some cut flowers which she arranged and popped on a table in my living room. It made the room feel very welcoming.

In fact, when I arrived at the farmhouse and I opened the kitchen door, call me daft but it felt like the house was wrapping arms around me and welcoming me to where I belonged. Dad helped me to bring the things in from the car and he and Kenny and another man from the nursery unloaded the van when it arrived. I knew it would be chaotic for a while until I decided where some things were going but I didn't care; I knew that eventually I would get it the way I wanted it. Once all the things were in, dad stayed on to share the casserole with me because we were both more than ready for food. Kenny and Roger had gone home. After we had eaten, dad went back to his bungalow too, because he had left Butch behind and the dog was probably bursting to go out by now.

When everyone had gone and I had cleared up after our meal, I went to sit in the living room. I didn't have phone or internet services yet but I still had my mobile. Aunt Bea had – guess what – a radio-gram! Wow –a real, old fashioned one too, not a reconstruction, and a whole collection of records. Many of the records were classical music but she also had records from the fifties, sixties and seventies and it seemed that she had a wide taste in music, which somewhat surprised me. From the Beatles to Dolly Parton; she had something of everything. This I liked; I loved the sixties' classics.

I spent a very enjoyable twenty minutes looking through all the records that were there. I had a music stack – again, a bit old fashioned but not as old as the radio-gram. I had intended to have it in this room, but maybe I would have it somewhere else, perhaps the kitchen, and keep the radio-gram in this room. For this evening, I would enjoy listening to some of Aunt Bea's records.

Finally, I looked at my watch; it was getting quite late. Jim had text me a few times during the day asking me how things were going, so I decided I would call him for a chat and then make myself a warm drink and settle down to some music.

Jim and I talked quite a while. I told him all about the move and the help I'd been given and the meal Sheila had brought. He seemed in a good mood and listened patiently to everything I had to tell him. Apparently, he had gone home to visit his parents as he couldn't be with me; he was concerned because his mother wasn't too well.

"I'm sorry, Jim, my darling, my phone is running out of battery and I'm not sure where I've put the charger so I'm going to have to go in a moment," I said at last.

"That's alright, sweetheart. I hope you get sorted during the week. I'll try to come up next weekend, see how you're getting on."

"That would be lovely. I'll speak to you during the week. Bye for now."

The phone went dead just as I spoke, in fact, I wasn't sure if he heard it all. I thought I would go and put the kettle on then look for the charger. This I did and thankfully I found the charger in the case with my laptop; which of course was the sensible place to put it. I had no recollection of putting it there but I must have done of course and I was glad I'd followed logic.

I left the phone to charge in the kitchen and carried my hot chocolate into the living room. I put on a record and sank back into Aunt Bea's favourite armchair.

As I sat there, feeling the comforting warmth of the electric coal-effect fire that I'd switched on and serenaded by the dark velvet tones of Scott Walker, I felt a deep sense of contentment and somewhere in the depths of my soul I knew that this was where I belonged, I had come home.

Chapter 15
Settling In and a New Discovery

It pains me to say this because I loved living in London and enjoyed my job down there, but it took me no time at all to feel completely at home at River View. I loved the old-fashioned-ness of it and there was no doubt that the house had a welcoming atmosphere about it and I could feel Aunt Bea's presence. Having said that, sometimes I could sense something else, something I couldn't quite put my finger on, depending on where I was in the house. There were times when I felt reluctant to go upstairs and at other times I was fine. It was odd to me and if anyone had asked me about it, I would have had difficulty trying to explain what I meant.

Even in the 'quiet room', which I had chosen to be my bedroom, I sensed other presences around. Fortunately, I did not mind this because I didn't feel threatened by it. When dad came up and brought Butch with him, the dog seemed quite happy wherever he was in the house or grounds so I thought that was a good indication that there was nothing to worry about.

I spent a few days organising and reorganising my things until I was happy with where I'd put them. I also spent time in Aunt Bea's den, sorting through things there, to do with her business and otherwise and deciding what needed to be thrown away. It seemed she was something of a hoarder, which surprised me because she had always come over so efficient and orderly in our home. I supposed it was because she knew she had the space in her own home to keep the things she didn't want to be rid of.

The den wasn't the only place she hoarded things; I found materials, wools, knitting needles, crochet hooks and cottons, embroidery threads and sequins, beads and all sorts stuffed away in cupboards or boxes in the spare bedrooms. I thoroughly enjoyed myself sorting it all gradually and discovering her 'treasures'.

I found I learned more about her, the hidden side of her that I didn't really see although we'd been very close. There were remnants of material from dresses and other garments she'd made for me when I was little and I found myself going back in time and remembering things I'd forgotten for a long time.

I loved it and I loved her for keeping these things; sometimes I would find an actual dress or hair ribbons and little things that had been mine and they were carefully labelled: 'Lucy's hair ribbon when we went to the seaside and she lost one in the sea' or: 'I made this dress for Lucy when she was three and she soon grew out of it. She used to look so sweet in it'. It brought a lump to my throat when I realised that she'd kept them because she loved me so much. How sad that she never had her own child.

I found that I just couldn't bring myself to throw out all these, Aunt Bea's treasures. I wasn't ready yet; I wanted to hold onto her and I'd found a way of keeping her close. I put them all back where I had found them. Maybe one day I would be able to get rid of them, or maybe I would find a way to use them, perhaps I would learn how to make quilts or something.

I was sitting surrounded by some of these things one day when a knock came at the door. I left everything where it was and went to open the door. It was Kenny.

"Oh hi, Kenny, come on in," I said and left him to follow me into the small sitting room where everything was on the floor and armchairs.

"Goodness! Whatever are you doing?" he asked, gazing around at all the things.

"I'm sorting through Aunt Bea's cupboards," I grinned. "I'm discovering what a sentimental person she was and I'm finding I'm just as bad; I can't bring myself to get rid of half of this stuff." I smiled at him sheepishly and he laughed.

"Well, I suppose it really doesn't matter. Are you settling in well?"

"Oh yes, I'm really at home here. I feel as though I have always been here and it's only been a few days."

"That's great, I'm happy you feel that way. Have you looked around outside at all?"

"Well of course I have been outside to hang washing but I have been busy in the house, getting sorted. There's not a lot going on out there just now, is there?"

"Well, no, not really. I just wondered if you've taken a look at the walled garden yet?"

I frowned. "Walled garden? What are you talking about, Kenny?"

"Haven't you looked at the deeds?"

"No, I don't have them. They stay with the solicitor until I've been here a year. Conditions of the will and all that, you know."

"Ah yes. Well, pop on a jacket or something and I'll show you."

Feeling curious, I hurried to get my fleece, leaving everything where it lay. A few minutes later, we were outside, crossing the lawn in the opposite direction to that which I take to go to the nursery. We passed through a gate, which I had not noticed before and it led to a short path and through another gateway. We were, indeed, in a walled garden. I looked around at the paths and beds laid out before me. I looked enquiringly at Kenny.

"This used to be part of the gardens at Sutton Court. Your aunt bought it a few years ago because the grounds there are extensive and they couldn't manage it all. They also needed to sell the garden in order to make some improvements to the house."

"This is where most of the soft fruits and vegetables are grown that your aunt used for her jams, jellies, chutneys and other things she made. I helped her with it as it's a lot for one woman to manage. My workers are always happy to garden here; they are great people. We all benefit from it because of what the produce is used for."

"It's amazing! I had no idea that this was part of my property; in fact I didn't even know it was there. Aunt Bea just gets more like Superwoman to me." I chuckled.

"You do know that she owned all the grassland between your house and the road and my nursery, don't you?"

Now I was even more surprised.

"No I didn't. Whatever for?"

"She said it was to protect the area. She was always afraid that someone would want to build on it, which of course would ruin the whole feel of the place."

"It would indeed. I would hate to see it built on. I'm glad she was such a thoughtful person; I had no idea she could afford to buy so much land. Is it used at all?"

"Well, a local farmer hires some of it to graze his cows. The two fields nearest the road are often used for village fetes and sometimes a travelling fair comes."

He laughed at the look on my face; I was thrilled that so much went on here and that River View was the hub of so much activity. I felt that life in the country was not going to be dull.

"I have to get back to the nursery. Why don't you have a wonder around this garden and say hello to it, see what's here?"

"Yes. I'll do that. Thank you so much for coming to show me. I do appreciate all your help you know."

"We aim to please, ma'am!" He doffed his cap and flashed me his charming lop-sided grin. I watched him go back through the gate before I went in the opposite direction. I chose to go straight down the middle. The garden was beautifully set out in a style that I would say was true Victorian or Edwardian or something. It had three sections, divided by hedges. Each section had a round bed in the middle, surrounded by a path and then the beds splayed out on each corner and in between with paths running between them, so each section had six beds surrounding the middle round one.

The first section had obviously once been a rose garden, for the middle bed was planted with rose bushes, now showing new green leaves and tiny buds. The surrounding beds had all kinds of vegetables, some just beginning to show, others still under the earth.

The middle section was full of soft fruit; the redcurrant bushes were full of flowers and my heart leaped with excitement that I would soon be picking juicy currants here. I could already smell blackcurrants. My mind was a whirl of thoughts of summer puddings, jams and jellies. The third section was an orchard with an abundance of fruit trees, kept small for easy picking; all looked healthy with their leaves fresh and green. I thought it was wonderful.

I wandered down a path that led to the outer pathway which followed along the walls. The outer beds were packed full of herbs just beginning to leaf and other things that I had no idea what they were. Halfway along, I came across what appeared to be an alcove, all overgrown with honeysuckle, which smelled delicious. I spied through the tangle a statue and I gently pushed away some of the foliage to get closer. It was obviously old and had been there a long time, for it was quite green. I decided that once the honeysuckle had finished flowering, I would cut it back and then see if it was possible to have the statue cleaned.

As I turned away, I caught a movement down the path that was opposite the statue. I hastened along the path to see who was there, but I couldn't see anyone.

"Hello? Hel-loo! Were you looking for me? I'm here, hel-lo!"

I looked all around me, listening but I heard and saw nothing. In the end, I shrugged my shoulders and started to make my way back to the gate. When I reached the gate, I looked back along the path that I'd just come down and caught my breath – I glimpsed, just for a second or two, a woman. She wore trousers, a jacket and gardening gloves. On her head was the disreputable old hat that was hanging on the back of the door in the den and she carried a basket that seemed to have foliage of some sort in it, not that I could see clearly at that distance.

"Aunt Bea!" I gasped. She smiled at me, but as I started towards her, she was gone.

As I made my way back to the farmhouse, I felt light in my heart; Aunt Bea knew I was there and was glad.

Chapter 16
Sutton Court

Instead of going back to the house, I diverted towards my favourite place – the seat in the garden. Now, it was covered in sweet-smelling honeysuckle and intertwined with it was a rose, although I couldn't yet tell what sort as it was only in bud. By the looks of it, it was a miniature climbing rose; I could tell by the leaves which were small. I vaguely recalled a rose that Aunt Bea called 'The Fairy', which had small pink flowers, many on a stem, and they flowered prolifically all summer. I was surprised that my aunt had allowed it to grow so much but I suppose she hadn't had a chance to prune it before she died. So it had gone mad. I would soon get it sorted; I decided to have a go at it now and went in search of secateurs.

I found gardening tools in the barn, and on the wall hung a large bag which had small tools in it. I found what I wanted and made my way back to the seat. I tried to tackle the rose but found that I couldn't do it without harming the honeysuckle. Not wanting to cut off those flowers, I decided reluctantly to wait until it had finished. My seat would have to wait a while longer.

As I took the secateurs back to the barn, I suddenly realised that I'd left all Aunt Bea's things from the cupboard strewn over the sitting-room, so I thought I'd better go and clear up. As I did so, I thought with pleasure of the walled garden; what an amazing thing! And all that land – I suspected that Aunt Bea's Estate was actually worth a lot of money, never mind her business.

I experienced a moment's guilt at depriving so many worthy causes so much money and I made a mental note to ask Mr Gamble if he knew what charities would have received money if I had not claimed the estate. Maybe I could give them donations in remembrance of my aunt – and salve my conscience a little. As I thought about it though, I knew that Aunt Bea had really wanted me to have her home for my own; I had no doubts about that at all. I allowed myself to imagine this as a family home with me at the hub and children running joyously in the garden. Yes, I knew I wanted my children to grow up here.

Once I'd cleared up, I got myself some lunch. As I ate, I thought about what I should do for the next few days. The garden wasn't yet ready to provide me with ingredients to start making things so I decided to start ordering in more jars and other things I would need in readiness for when I could start. I would also go and visit Aunt Bea's past customers. I already knew Madge in the village shop but I had yet to meet the owners of the Wyeview Restaurant or my neighbours who owned Sutton Court. I thought I might also search on the internet for other local, but a little further afield, possible outlets for my produce. Weobley wasn't far away and I bet there were places there that would sell local produce. In fact, I had an idea I had seen some information in Aunt Bea's files. I would go and take a look and tomorrow I would go out to start getting acquainted with the neighbourhood.

Happy with my plans, I washed up my few bits of lunch crocks and headed back towards the den to see what I could find.

****

I went to bed that night, having compiled a list of places to go the next day, beginning with the Wyeview Restaurant. However, in the morning I lay in my bed with the sun glinting through the curtains, thinking back to the dream I'd just had. It featured a large white house, which I recognised as Sutton Court and I heard my aunt's voice saying 'you must go to Sutton Court first'.

How strange, I mused. Now, why should I dream that? In fact, Sutton Court had been quite low on my list of intended visits but if Aunt Bea thought I should go there first, who was I to argue? Of course, I realised I could be barking up the wrong tree, or just barking mad, doing what I'd been told in a dream – who did I think I was – a Wise Man or something?

I giggled at my own joke and got up.

An hour or so later, I set off for Sutton Court. I decided to take the car as I intended to go on to other places. I didn't feel I should take the short cut from the walled garden into their grounds so I'd have to go the long way round.

I parked the car in the visitors' car park and made my way round to the front door. A man answered my ring at the doorbell. He was casually dressed, was around fortyish, I guessed, with a pleasant face. He had a harassed look. I quickly said.

"Oh hello. I'm Lucy Dixon and I'm living next door at River View Farmhouse."

He stuck his hand out. As I took it, he said,

"Hello, Miss Dixon, I'm pleased to meet you. We heard you might be coming. Do come in. I'm Neil Milton, the owner of Sutton Court. I'm sorry, I'm in a bit of a flap so I can't keep you long. I'll take you to meet my wife."

"Oh? Do you have a problem? Anything I can do?" I enquired as I followed him inside.

"No, no. Our chef has had an accident this morning and hasn't been able to come in. Her under-chef is away on holiday. I've been trying to get a temporary replacement from an agency but as yet I've had no luck; everyone is either away on holiday or unavailable for other reasons." He unconsciously ran his fingers through his hair in his frustration, making it stand up on end and having the effect of making him look very vulnerable.

"Well, it seems my aunt was right," I remarked.

"What's that?"

"Oh, er, nothing. It seems I have come at the right time, Mr Milton. I can help you."

"You can? How?"

"I'm a chef, Mr Milton! I've just left my job as top chef to a firm in London. I have all the right qualifications and if you are worried, you can contact my old boss."

He grabbed my hand.

"My dear, you're a wonder, a miracle, a Godsend, a –"

"What's this Neil? Who is this?"

We both turned to the sound of a woman's voice as she came towards us. She was a bit taller than me with dark hair and she wore a dark blue nurse's dress.

"Oh, Cessy, darling, we have been rescued!" Neil said, holding his arms out to her. "This is our new neighbour, Miss Dixon, and guess what – she is a chef!"

"Is she indeed?" She came towards me, hand held out and smiling warmly. "Hello, Miss Dixon, I'm very happy to meet you. But we can't possibly expect you to help us, you have your own business to see to."

I shook her hand and smiled at her.

"I can't do anything with regard to that until the garden starts to yield things that I can use. I was only going to go round meeting with people today who will be my customers and hopefully meet other residents of the village. Somehow, I felt to come here first and now I know why."

"Oh!" She seemed flustered for a moment.

"Why don't you take me to see your kitchens?" I suggested gently.

"Yes. Yes, of course. Please come with me."

I followed her down a long hallway and into a large kitchen which was light and airy. A couple of women were working there; one was scrubbing vegetables, the other was getting a trolley of drinks and plates of biscuits ready.

"We managed breakfast alright; Emma here got that organised; thankfully, our chef's husband called her to ask her if she could come in earlier than she usually does. Everyone knows everyone else around here, as you will soon find out."

I nodded and smiled at Emma and she nodded back and returned the smile and continued her scrubbing.

"And this is Dot; she is preparing the trolleys for the mid-morning drink and snack. The others will be along in a moment, Dot."

I cast my eyes around the kitchen, my professional side kicking in. I was impressed by the cleanliness and was thankful; I didn't want to antagonise anyone by immediately ordering a scrub-down and was also gratified for the sake of the residents.

"Do you have details of the residents' dietary requirements?"

"Oh, yes of course. Emma knows the ropes, she can show you anything you want to know. I can't tell you how grateful we are to you, Miss Dixon. How soon can you start?"

"How about now? Do you have a clean overall for me and a cap? Oh, thank you, Dot." I took the proffered items held out to me. "Do you know how long your chef will be off?"

"I believe only a couple of days. I can't tell you how grateful we are to you, Miss Dixon."

"Just one thing, Mrs Milton."

"Yes?"

"Please call me Lucy, after all, we are neighbours."

She smiled. "Of course, and I'm Cessy, I'm Cecelia really but I prefer Cessy. I hope you enjoy it here. Thank you so much."

I did indeed enjoy my time at Sutton Court. The 'couple of days' turned into a week and during that time I got to know all the staff and residents at the home. We are always hearing about sloppy care at such places but there was none of that here. The residents were very well looked after; Sutton Court had carers who were just that – carers. They cared and went out of their way to make sure everyone was looked after properly. It was a happy place.

As it turned out, this was a good place to start getting to know the village. It seemed that everyone who worked here either lived in the village or was related to someone there. Dot, for instance, was Madge's sister and Emma was niece to Sheila. Peter and Kay, two carers, were brother and sister to Alex who owned the restaurant.

Neil Milton, I discovered, had inherited Sutton Court from an uncle because the uncle had no children. He and Cessy had then just got married and, as she was a qualified nurse, they decided to come and run the place as a care and nursing home.

That had been twenty years ago. The house had needed quite a bit of work in order to make it suitable, especially as it was rather run down in some areas. The uncle had only lived in part of it and the other rooms had been shut up, the furniture shrouded in dust sheets. They had found some wonderful antiques in those closed rooms which had really helped with the cost of the renovations, although they had kept some favourite pieces which they had in their private apartment.

In the meantime, Cessy gave birth to two daughters, Penelope and Silvie, aged eighteen and sixteen respectively. Penny was about to go to university to study to be a nurse like her mother. Until then, she was helping at the home.

Silvie also helped out sometimes, taking the drinks trolley round and other such tasks. She enjoyed helping me in the kitchen and loved watching me making the dishes or mixing the cakes for tea.

"I think I want to be a chef, Lucy," she told me one day. "I love being able to make nice things to eat for the residents. They really like your cooking, Lucy, it's a pity Elsie has to come back. Can't you stay here always?"

I laughed. "I don't think so, Silvie. I have my own business to run. Perhaps when I get it going you'd like to come over sometimes to help me? There are all sorts of things a chef can do and you might be interested in the other side of things that I will do."

Her eyes shone. "Can I really? That would be so cool."

"Yes of course. If you give me your mobile number, I'll send you a text when I have work to do and you can come over if you feel like it."

"Thanks very much. I'll look forward to that. I'm going to tell mum. I'll see you, Lucy!"

Off she went to find Cessy and I looked after her, loving her enthusiasm. It looked like I'd got myself an assistant.

Chapter 17
A Snippet of Information

On my last day at Sutton Court, everyone was so sweet and said they will miss me. I said I would pop in from time to time to say hello to the residents and no doubt I would see the carers around the village. When I hung up my apron for the last time, Cessy came and asked me if I would mind just having a cup of tea with her in her own small lounge?

"Dot, would you bring some tea and biscuits to my lounge please?" Cessy said pleasantly.

"Of course. Won't be a tick," was the reply.

We left the kitchen and I followed Cessy along the corridor and up some stairs. I was familiar with the layout of the house now. Cessy, Neil and the girls had their own flat on the third floor. With the money they'd got when my aunt bought the walled garden, they had an extension built on the back of the house for more residents. They were the ones who needed nursing care and it had been purpose-built for this. It had spacious rooms to allow for hoisting and low windows so that their patients could see the gardens; they felt it was important for bed-ridden people to be able to see outside. The river was on the other side of the house so they couldn't see that but, as the house was surrounded by gardens, there was still plenty to see. An old pond with a fountain was in the centre and the gardeners always made sure it was working. There were some very beautiful old trees so there were birds and squirrels and even the odd brave rabbit could be seen.

Thinking of other 'homes' that I had seen that had practically no garden and the residents had little view of anything outside, I was very impressed by the consideration of these owners for the people they cared for. What a refreshing change; many who owned such places were only doing it for the money.

"Here we are," Cessy's voice interrupted my thoughts. "Take a seat, Lucy."

Thankfully, I sat down. I'm used to being on my feet but the moment I sit down I realise how tired I am. She sat too, then we both looked up as Dot came in with a tray.

"Goodness, that was quick!"

"The tea was already made so I just poured it out and got the biscuits." Dot put the tray on a small table and handed me a cup and saucer.

"Thanks very much, Dot. I'm ready for this!"

"We are going to miss Lucy, Cessy, she's been wonderful."

"We are indeed, I agree. We can't thank you enough for stepping into the breach, Lucy."

"No problem at all, it's been great, I've enjoyed it immensely. It's been good to get to know so many people and I've quite fallen in love with some of your residents."

I smiled at Dot and she left the room with a little wave.

"That's understandable. Each one of them has their qualities. Some are a bit-erm-shall we say, challenging? Others are just sweethearts, very grateful for everything we do for them or help them with. We encourage those who can do things to keep doing them. Once you let an elderly person sit about and allow things to be done for them, the quicker they deteriorate. As you know, we let them help with small jobs, like putting the cakes out for everyone, laying the tables and putting their own things away in their rooms. Of course, they don't have to, the carers will do it but they like to help. We encourage them to get together and play games or talk and in the summer we take them out into the gardens where we can stroll around or just sit and enjoy a drink."

"Can I book my bed now?" I asked, smiling. "I think if I need care when I'm elderly I'd love to be here. Some places are just abysmal, you know. Talk about 'Waiting for God'."

Cessy grimaced. "I know, I worked in a couple of them – down near London, not up here. It's one of the reasons why we set this place up; I wanted to run a *good* care home, where the elderly are treated like human beings, which they are of course. Mind you, on tough days I sometimes find myself wishing we'd accepted the offer made to us last year. Then, not long after, I'm glad we didn't."

Startled, I put my cup in the saucer with a little clatter.

"You had someone wanting to buy Sutton Court?"

"Yes. A man came here last year. He actually rang our doorbell and asked to see the owner – imagine! Then, when he saw Neil, he said this would make a wonderful place for luxury apartments as holiday residences for business people and was he interested in selling? Neil called for me to come down and the chap explained he was looking for potential properties in this area and he named a jaw-dropping figure for Sutton Court. We couldn't do it though – this is our home! And what would happen to all our residents? It would kill some of them to have to move and they might end up a long way from their families. No, I couldn't do it."

"What did this man look like?"

"Oh! Just ordinary really; dark hair, going a bit bald on top, which I noticed when he took his hat off. Medium build; nothing that really stood out, you know? Why do you ask?"

"I was just curious. Apparently, a man came last year and asked my aunt if she would sell River View Farmhouse."

"Oh yes? I bet it was the same man. He didn't have much luck around here then, did he?" she laughed. "Anyway, as it's your last day, I must give you this; it's what an agency chef would have got. I realise it's not as much as you would have earned at your London job."

"I'm not worried about that and I didn't particularly want to be paid, Cessy. I did it because you needed a chef and I was there! It was the neighbourly thing to do."

"Well, we are glad you were there! And we must pay you, keep our books straight. I don't want to get into any trouble with our accountant! But you have our grateful thanks and if you need help with anything we can do, we will be happy to do it."

"Well, thank you very much. I'm happy that I've got off to a good start with my neighbours!"

I stood up to leave and she did too. As I did so, I looked out of a small window near me.

"Oh, you can see the walled garden from here."

"Yes indeed." She came and stood beside me to look out of the window with me. "That was the best thing we did for that garden, selling it to your aunt. It was a mess; we just couldn't keep up with all the tending it needed. It always reminded me of that story, the Secret Garden, you know. I used to feel that if I could peel back the foliage on the walls I would find a magical garden behind it."

"Well, I suppose it is a magical garden, all gardens are because nature is wonderful. But it's even better with people like my aunt and Kenny Baxter to tend them. I'm sure I'd never manage to look after all my garden on my own without his help."

"Ah yes, our Kenny. He helps us too, you know. We only have two gardeners and this is such a large garden. He and his workers at the nurseries are really great."

As I walked through the walled garden from their garden to mine, I thought about our conversation. It seemed I had come to live in a fairy-tale place where everyone was nice and helped each other – could that really be so? As for Kenny Baxter, surely he was just too good to be true?

Chapter 18
Making a Start

As I was on my way home from Sutton Court, instead of just walking through the walled garden, I decided to go and see what progress the soft fruit bushes were making.

"Hello! What's that I see? Gooseberries!" I spoke out loud as I headed towards the bushes.

I jumped when a voice said,

"First sign, you know!"

"Eh?" I spun round and there was Kenny coming up behind me. "Oh, Kenny, I never saw you there. I'm afraid I often talk to myself. Comes of spending so much time on my own."

"Hmm, not good. Anyway, I see you've noticed the gooseberries. Here, try one."

He picked one deftly and handed it to me. I took a bite; it was surprisingly sweet.

"I must get out here and start picking tomorrow; my first crop! Or rather the first crop since I came."

"I'll pick them; you need strong gloves for protection; gooseberry bushes are vicious."

"Oh, I don't mind doing it, it will give me lots of pleasure. Perhaps I can buy a good pair of gloves from you and a protective apron too."

"I'll pop some over to you. I agree, it is exciting to pick! I guess you have the time just now. When the fruit bushes really come on, you will need help because it's a race again time to get the jam made while the fruit is in good condition."

He joined me as I walked on through to the farmhouse and then he touched his cap at me in an endearingly old-fashioned sort of gesture and left me at my door.

I thought about the gooseberries as I got my meal ready. I needed to look in Aunt Bea's records to see what she did with them. I thought about the residents at Sutton Court and how they might enjoy having some gooseberry fool.

Without much thought, I picked up my phone and called Cessy.

"Hello Cessy, how would you feel if I made some individual gooseberry fools for your residents? I have some lovely gooseberries ready to pick tomorrow and they are actually quite sweet. I could whip some up and bring them over when they are ready. You could freeze them and use them when they are wanted. What do you think?"

"Lucy, I think that's a lovely idea. It would be something different for them and I'm sure they would love it."

"I'll give you a call before I bring them over. Bye for now, Cessy."

"Bye, Lucy."

If I was going to make individual desserts, I needed something to pack them in. Tomorrow I would go into Hereford to see what I could find. Then I would pick the gooseberries. Or maybe the other way round...

That night I went to bed very happy.

"Making a start, Aunt Bea! The gooseberries are coming on, some are ready for picking, and the first thing I'm going to make is gooseberry fool for my elderly folk. I'm looking forward to really getting on with things at last."

I didn't see her or hear her but I felt that Aunt Bea was smiling down on me.

As it happened, I didn't need to go to Hereford to search for containers. I found a number in Aunt Bea's files that I called and ordered containers for individual desserts; they would be delivered the next day. The telephonist recognised my address when I gave it and upon her enquiry, offered her condolences on Aunt Bea's demise.

"I had been wondering why we hadn't heard from her in a while. I am so sorry to hear of her passing, she was such a nice lady."

"It was a shock. None of us knew she had a heart condition."

"So, you are now running her business?"

"Yes, I am her heir. She left everything to me. Now I am excited to carry on where she left off."

"I hope you do well."

"Thank you. I'm going to give it my best shot."

As I put the phone down, a knock came at the door. Upon opening it, there was a man standing there with some things that he held out to me.

"Hello miss. Kenny sent me over with these. He says he's sorry he couldn't come himself."

"Oh, thank you, erm, it's Joe, isn't it? I remember seeing you at the garden centre."

"Yes miss. Well, I'll be away then."

"Oh, but I must pay for these!"

"Kenny says no charge, miss."

And with that, he nodded and turned away.

"Please thank him for me!" I called after him.

"I'll do that, miss."

Excitedly, I went into the house to find something to put the berries in. I went into the den and spied Aunt Bea's basket on the table – that's funny, I'm sure it wasn't there before – but I picked it up, and her old hat hanging on the back of the door caught my eye. Yes, I would wear that too, it was quite warm today.

Donning the heavy protective apron, and gathering the other things I needed, I went out of the house, locking the door behind me – after all, the house was out of range of the walled garden. I slipped the large key into the spacious front pocket, jammed on the hat and made my way across the lawn to where I could get through to the walled garden.

I spent a wonderful and peaceful hour or so picking gooseberries; very glad of the thick gloves and apron. I filled the basket easily and when I came away there were still loads to pick. But I was well pleased with my first cropping. When I couldn't get any more in the basket, I took off the gloves and went back to the farmhouse.

I thoroughly enjoyed making the gooseberry desserts; the cream had arrived from the farm in Kington that Aunt Bea's records showed she used for supplies. I also made some that were good for the diabetic residents.

I delivered them as soon as they were made, late in the afternoon and returned to the farmhouse, tired but happy with my achievements. Tomorrow I would go and meet with the proprietors of the Wyeview Restaurant.

****

Not being quite sure where I should approach the restaurant, I rang a bell that I found by the side of their front door. The place was closed, it being ten o'clock in the morning. It didn't open until the evening.

I heard the sounds of bolts being pulled back and a lock being turned and I came face to face with a welcoming smile.

"Oh my! I think you must be Lucy, Bea's niece. Come on in, I've been wondering when we would meet you."

I instantly warmed to this blonde whirlwind as she caught hold of my hand and drew me inside. Somewhat bemused, I allowed her to almost drag me at speed through the restaurant, which I only got a fleeting impression of, it not being lit and the vertical blinds at the windows being shut.

"Alex! Alex, we have a visitor!" shouted Stephanie Hunter, as we went through a door at the back, marked 'private'. As we entered through another door, I heard a deep, manly voice answer,

"Oh yes, who's that then?"

Then the owner of the voice appeared by our side, having come out of another room, which I guessed was an office.

"Alex, this is Lucy, Bea's niece who has come to live at Riverview."

"Well, hello, Lucy."

To my amazement, he took my hand and bent to kiss it and then stood and gazed at me soulfully, still holding my hand.

"Oh, stop it Alex! Let her go; don't use your imagined charms on her, stop teasing her, she doesn't know what to do, poor girl!"

He smiled ruefully at me and let go of my hand.

"Sorry, Lucy. I just like to wind the missus up sometimes, you know? Keep her on her toes! Ow!"

That was in answer to the playful punch Steph landed on his arm.

"You hit me, woman!"

"Oh stop it, you daft thing!"

Alex looked down at his petite wife and grinned, his dark eyes soft. As we laughed, I gazed at these two, so obviously still in love with each other and I wondered wistfully if Jim and I would still be like this several years after we'd married. I chased the thought away because the lanky spider that was Alex was speaking again.

"Seriously, Lucy, we are pleased to meet you. Come on in and sit down."

I followed Stephanie into a cosy room that was obviously their own private sitting room, Alex followed us.

"I've just made some scones, would you like one?" Stephanie offered.

"Oh yes, I'd love one, thanks. I never turn down an offer of something that someone else has made!"

"I'll be right back. Talk to Alex – and don't let him embarrass you again! Alex, be good!" She pointed her finger at him in mock severity and he looked at her as though he was a naughty child. I couldn't help smiling, they were quite a duo.

"So, Lucy, tell me about yourself."

"Well, what do you want to know?"

"Oh, you know, all the usual things like, erm, where do you live – oh, I know where you live, silly me! Where did you grow up, what have you done in your life, you know, all the things that are interesting about you."

"Well, I'm not sure I'm that interesting really. I grew up in Hereford, Bea helped my dad raise me because my mum died. I went to the Hereford Catering College and I've been working in London until recently when I inherited Aunt Bea's house. I'd like to know about you and Stephanie."

Stephanie arrived with a trolley on which she had put a teapot, cups, saucers, cream jug and sugar. There was also a plate of delicious-looking scones.

As we ate, we talked a lot. It was a very pleasant visit indeed. When I came away, I felt I had made a couple of friends as well as making sure they would still be my customers. Onwards and upwards; I was making progress.

Chapter 19
An Unexpected Invitation

"Who are you? Go away!"

Hmm, it seemed I had found someone who wasn't friendly amongst my neighbours.

"Mr. Price?"

"Yes, who's askin'?" I could hear the scowl in his voice as he glowered at me over the fence. His blue eyes seemed at odds with his ruddy face as they glared at me beneath bushy eyebrows.

"I'm Lucy Dixon and I own the land by the river that you graze your cows on, Mr Price."

"Oo-ar? And what do you want wi' me, then? I pays me rent."

"You do indeed, Mr. Price. I just wanted to make your acquaintance, seeing as we are more or less neighbours, or at least, your cows are."

"Well, you've met me now so I'll bid ye goodbye."

"They are fine creatures; are they Herefords?" I was determined to persist. He looked at me quizzically.

"Don't ya know a Hereford when ya see one? Fine beasts they are, yes indeed."

"Have you farmed for long, Mr. Price?"

"All my life, gal, and my father and grandfather afore me. It's a hard life but a good one." His ruddy face seemed to soften a bit for a moment. Then he picked up the bucket and shovel he'd been carrying but had set on the ground when I spoke to him. "And that bloke had better not come back trying to persuade me to sell up. This is my home and I aint leavin."

"Has someone tried to make you sell, then?"

"Oo-ar, a fella came last year and wanted to buy my land. Nice lot o' money 'e offered but I wasn't 'aving none of it. I'll be a-stayin' 'ere until they carry me out in a box. Now, if ye don't mind, I 'ave to be getting on."

"Of course. I have work to do too. One thing though, Mr. Price," I answered and he stopped and looked at me again. He didn't speak but was obviously waiting for me to finish. "Would you mind letting me know if you get another offer to buy your farm please? Or if you see that man again?"

"O-ar, I'll do that."

"Thank you."

I watched him for a few moments as he stomped off over his farmyard, his bucket and shovel in hand, and into a barn. I turned and made my way back to my car and, fairly thankfully, drove away.

*****

Kenny laughed when I told him about my encounter with the farmer.

"Yes, I should have warned you but I never thought about you going to see him. He's a bit taciturn but he's alright really. He's a good farmer."

"Does he have a wife?"

"Oh yes, and they had six kids – two of them have left home now. The other four, two sons and two daughters are still at home and the lads help on the farm. The youngest girl is only fifteen or sixteen so is still at school."

"Perhaps Sylvie will know her? They are about the same age and I bet they go to the same school."

"Of course she does – everyone knows everyone around here – and they know everyone's business too! If you like to be private, Sutton's not the place to live." He laughed heartily and I smiled and nodded thoughtfully. That was something to take into consideration, I supposed. He caught my eye and stopped laughing. He took hold of my hand and looked into my eyes. I felt for a moment that I couldn't breathe.

"Don't take me seriously, Lucy, this is a wonderful place to live. I wouldn't think of living anywhere else and I feel you are beginning to love it here."

I nodded, not able to speak for a moment. He let go of my hand and turned away and I was surprised that I felt disappointment.

"Must go and get some work done. I'll be seeing you." He walked away as he spoke and gave me a brief wave, which I didn't return because he wasn't looking.

'Don't be daft, Luce, my girl. Of course he wants you to stay because if you go he will lose all my extra garden and all the stuff I will make for him to sell. That's the only reason, get real. In any case, you are engaged, don't forget.'

Having given myself a good ticking off, I turned and set off back to my house. I had seen Sheila in the distance at the nursery but she was busy so I gave her a wave which she returned and then turned to deal with her next customer.

I went home, feeling a little bleak.

Later on that day, I had a phone call from Jim.

"I find that I'm free this weekend, darling," he said. "Shall I come up and view the inheritance?"

"You make it sound very grand," I giggled. "But yes, of course, come up. You know I'd love to see you. I'll take you around and introduce you to my neighbours. Actually, it's a good idea for you to come now because it won't be long before the fruit is ready and I'll be run off my feet."

"I'll see you tomorrow then, Luce. Gotta go, work calls. Love you, bye for now."

"Love you too," I said to the phone but he'd already gone. He didn't stop long, did he? Still, he'll be here tomorrow. I must get things ready for him and plan food. Oh, perhaps it would be nice to take him to the Wye View Restaurant. That would be a good way to introduce him to Alex and Stephanie.

****

Not long after Jim called, I had another call. This time it was from Cessy. I hoped she wasn't going to ask me to work...

"Hi, Cessy," I answered my phone brightly, keeping my fingers crossed. "I didn't expect to hear from you."

"No. I'm doing my usual last-minute arrangements! It's Penny's birthday tomorrow and she says she would like to have dinner at the Wye View Restaurant with us and a few friends."

"Oh! Oh, that's very nice. I'm afraid my fiancé is coming down for the weekend."

"Bring him too – the more the merrier! I have already booked a big table, I'll just give Alex a ring when I know how many are coming. I will look forward to meeting your man."

"Do you mind if I just contact him to ask him if he is alright with that? He will have travelled so he might not be up to it. Can I let you know?"

"Of course! I'll wait to hear from you."

"Thank you for the invitation though, Cessy, it's lovely to be thought of."

"Of course you are! You're one of us now. Talk with you later then. Bye for now."

"Bye."

When she had gone, I sent a text to Jim: *'We have just been invited to a birthday dinner at our local restaurant tomorrow night. I was going to suggest we had dinner there anyway but we don't have to go. What do you think, would you like to go or don't you feel like meeting the neighbours 'en masse'?*

It was well over an hour when the message came back:

"*Yeah, sounds fun. Accept the invitation.*"

Cessy was very pleased when I called her back to accept. And so, at the end of what had been quite an upsetting day because of Mr. Elwyn Price, I ended the day with an unexpected but quite a pleasant problem – what to wear at a posh dinner party.

Chapter 20
The Birthday Dinner

Give Jim his due; he behaved impeccably during the birthday dinner. Considering the only person he knew was me and he could have been withdrawn and morose as he has been sometimes when we have been with my friends, he went out of his way to be as amenable and pleasant as possible. Any onlooker who didn't know would almost have thought he was the host, so easy was he with everyone. I have to admit he looked so handsome in his dinner suit; the dark colour highlighting his silvery-blonde hair to perfection.

I wore a black dress, fitted at the top with a flared skirt. It had diamante embroidery on the skirt which caught the light as I walked. The top was plain but it was a perfect setting for the neat ruby and diamond pendant that I put around my neck. A matching pair of earrings sparkled as my long dark brown hair rippled and danced. I felt good and Jim's eyes told me so, even though he said nothing.

Upon our arrival at the venue, we gathered in the lounge, a private room set aside for special occasion parties such as this one. Here they served drinks while we waited for everyone to arrive. I introduced Jim around to the people I knew, which was most of them. Neil and Cessy and their daughters were already there, waiting to welcome their guests. Penny was looking gorgeous in a red satin cocktail dress which showed up her blonde hair and figure to perfection. Jim's eyes were almost on stalks when he saw her until I nudged him and reminded him that I was there! Sylvie looked lovely too in a blue dress, obviously expensive and a beautiful cut that made her look grown up.

"You have two beautiful daughters, Mrs. Milton," Jim said to her, at the same time looking with admiration at the woman before him who was wearing a gown of the palest salmon pink, almost white, which draped elegantly around her slim figure. "And I can see where they get it from."

Cessy giggled girlishly and turned to me. "You have quite a charming young man there, Lucy. You will need to keep a close eye on him, I think!"

"Mm, I think you might be right there, Cessy. All the women are looking glamorous this evening and Penny looks stunning."

"She does, doesn't she? I think my babies are all grown up." A wistful sigh escaped her lips and I put my arm around her briefly. She smiled at me, then looked at Jim.

"But don't you think our Lucy is looking wonderful? I quite envy her figure and that dress looks amazing on you, my dear. You must be so proud of Lucy, Jim, she has already achieved so much since she came here. We quite think of her as one of us."

Jim put his hand lightly around my shoulder and smiled at me.

"I'm glad to see how well she is doing here. If anyone can make a success of her aunt's business, she can."

"Oh, I absolutely believe that. Oh, at last, here comes the last of our guests."

I turned to see who had arrived, to see Sheila, followed by –

"Dad!"

I made my way over to them to embrace first Sheila and then dad.

"I didn't expect to see you, dad."

"No, well, I thought I would surprise you," he grinned. "Sheila invited me."

"Dark horse," I grinned. "Sheila, this is my fiancé, Jim."

"How do you do, Jim? So you're the lucky man I've been hearing about."

"I hope you've been hearing good things," he said gravely, taking her hand and kissing the back of it. The gesture immediately reminded me of Alex. Was he around? I wondered. We had not seen either him or Stephanie as yet.

As I watched them speaking, the door opened again and in came a young woman, followed closely by Ken Baxter. I watched as he took her wrap and gave it to the member of staff at the door. He then guided her forward towards us.

"Oh, er, this is Glynis, Ken's um, current lady-friend," remarked Sheila. For some reason, she seemed embarrassed but I couldn't for the life of me work out why she should be. "Glynis, this is Lucy, Tom's daughter and her fiancé, Jim."

"Hello Glynis, I'm pleased to meet you," I held out my hand to her but she ignored it and passed me, heading for the tray of drinks. I raised my eyebrow slightly and looked at Ken. He looked annoyed.

"Oh, Jim, this is Ken Baxter. You know, the man who found my aunt?"

The two men nodded at each other. For some reason, the air seemed suddenly cold as if the door had been left open. As they shook hands, I noticed it was brief, barely hand-touched and, although I couldn't see Ken's face properly, I could see Jim's. His eyes had narrowed and his 'pleased to meet you' sounded tight-lipped.

"Excuse me, I have to keep an eye on Glynis." And Ken was gone. For a moment, amid all the buzz of conversation, there seemed to be a sudden quiet amongst the people I was with, until Sheila brightly said.

"Oh look, doesn't Penny look simply wonderful? We must go and wish her a happy birthday, mustn't we Tom?"

And Jim and I stood and watched as dad followed Sheila through the crowd.

"Well, that was a surprise, wasn't it, my love? It seems dad and Sheila are becoming an item – what fun!" I giggled brightly, hoping to see the dark cloud across Jim's face pass away. It seemed to do the trick, for he looked at me and smiled.

"Yes, the sly dog! Do you think they'll hitch up together?"

"Well, I don't know. We'll have to wait and find out. They might beat us to the alter!"

Jim was saved a reply because at that moment, Alex came into the room and announced that our table was ready and would we all like to follow him through to the dining room?

I couldn't fault the meal, it was gorgeous. Obviously, their chef was of the highest calibre. Cessy had gone old-fashioned and seated partners opposite each other. I found myself seated next to a young man who turned out to be Sylvie's boyfriend, Jake, and on the other side, Dot's husband, Dick. (Dick and Dot? They sounded like a stage double-act ha ha!) I actually had a great conversation with them both because Dick was part of a band in his spare time and Jake, who was Dick's nephew, had just joined the band because he was a great vocalist and Dick was the lead guitarist. They told me all about the places they played and what sort of music they did. Jake was studying music at school, apparently.

Once I looked up to see Ken looking at me but when I smiled at him, he smiled briefly and looked away. I looked across at Jim, who was glowering in my direction and I thought 'oh-oh' and hastily turned back to Jake. Jim had Sylvie on his side, opposite Jake and Dot on his other, opposite Dick and, to be fair, he did his best with both of them. Actually, he gave Sylvie a bit too much attention and I could see Jake giving the odd smoulder across the table.

"Don't mind him, Jake. He's not really interested in Sylvie, he's mad at me and wants to get back at me, trying to make me jealous."

"Oh really? That's ok then, as long as he's not after my bird. He's an old man anyway."

He shrugged and continued with his narrations, telling me about how he came to join Dick's group, which apparently rejoiced in the name of 'The Haymakers'. He said they were thinking of changing the name because it made people think they just sang country songs. I solemnly agreed, while at the same time having a giggle at Jake's observation that Jim 'was an old man' at thirty five while this kid's uncle Dick had to be forty at the very least! Still, obviously, Dick wasn't going after Jake's 'bird'. I wondered what Cessy would think of her daughter being called that.

After the meal we all gathered in the lounge again, where coffee and mints were served and where we all sang 'happy birthday' to Penny, who blushed nearly as crimson as her dress and laughed prettily as she blew out the candles. I could see that Jim was devouring her with his eyes and thought that it was certainly not Sylvie who would interest him! Still, after today he wasn't likely to see her because she would soon be off to begin her studies to become a nurse. I wasn't worried anyway, because he wasn't the only male in the room to be giving Penny lascivious looks; I saw a few wives giving their husbands nudges and a few shamed looks on the said husbands' faces! At a guess, most of these men had known Penny since she was born, except for the younger ones who had married into the village and this was the first time they had seen her 'brushed up' like this. It was enough to turn any man's thoughts and I really didn't blame them, I suppose...

****

"I don't want you to have anything to do with him, Lucille! I don't like the fellow."

We were home now and barely inside the house; things between Jim and I were strained. I was actually quite angry and was having difficulty keeping it in. How dare he tell me who to be friends with!

"It would be hard not to have anything to do with him, Jim. He is my nearest neighbour and not only that, he does most of my gardening."

"Pay someone else to do it; I'm sure you have enough money now."

"Why should I when we have a good system in place?"

"Yeah, a good system that allows him to see you whenever he likes."

"Oh grow up, Jim! He's a neighbour. He's one of my customers too. So, how come it's okay for you to goggle obscenely at a young girl, years younger than you but it not okay for me to have a neighbour come and garden for me?"

"I was not goggling obscenely!"

"Oh, you were, you should have seen yourself! If you could have had her on the floor in front of everyone you would have done it!"

"Now you are being obscene – as if I would do such a thing."

"Perhaps not but you wanted to. In fact, almost every man in the room wanted to, except her dad and my dad."

"There you go then! I'm just a red-blooded male like the rest of them. We just appreciated beauty in front of our eyes."

"The way she was almost squeezed into that dress, I'm not surprised! And the red was almost asking for it." I was ashamed as soon as I'd said it, because Penny had actually looked wonderful and not 'squeezed in' to the dress at all. It fitted her perfectly. But I was getting really riled up now. I knew I had to stop before I said something really bad.

"I'm tired. I'm going to bed. I'll see you in the morning."

"I hope you'll be more reasonable in the morning."

I left the kitchen, slamming the door behind me before I said anything else.

Later, as I lay in bed listening to his movements as he came up the stairs and into his bedroom, then the bathroom and then his bedroom door shut, I wondered why I was so upset at his insistence that I shouldn't have much to do with Ken Baxter.

Chapter 21
Busy, Busy!

"Oh hi, Sheila, how are you this morning?" The phone had rung about eight-thirty, to my surprise. I was actually still in bed, although awake and reading. I knew Jim hadn't yet got up, I would have heard him moving about.

"Oh, just fine, love. It was a great party last evening, wasn't it?"

"It was indeed. Everyone looked lovely and Penny looked like she was having a good time."

"I'll say she was, she had plenty of attention from her young men friends and the older ones too," said Sheila drily.

"She did indeed." I remarked.

"Don't take it to heart; men are all the same, see woman in a red dress and that's all they can see!" she laughed.

I couldn't help laughing too; a very shrewd woman was Sheila.

"How would you and your Jim like to come over for lunch today? Your dad is going to come over too."

"Well, thank you very much Sheila, it's very sweet of you but we have other plans for today," I lied. Inwardly, I cringed at the thought of Ken and Jim being together across such a small dinner table! I didn't know what we would be doing today but it wouldn't be going to lunch at the Baxter house, I was sure of that.

"Oh well, another time then," Sheila said brightly. "I hope you will come again, Lucy dear. My father-in-law has been asking to see you again."

"Oh, has he? In that case I'd better come. Shall I give you a call during the week?"

"Yes, do that. I hope you have a lovely day, dear, whatever you decide to do. Bye for now."

When she'd rung off, I didn't see much point in staying in bed any longer so I got up.

Jim came into the kitchen, tousle-haired, looking like he'd just got out of bed, which of course he had. To me, he looked every bit as attractive standing there in t-shirt and pyjama trousers as he did last night wearing his posh dinner suit. I eyed him over my tea mug, wondering what sort of mood he would be in today.

He came over and put his arms around me.

"Sorry about last night, Luce, don't know what came over me."

I snuggled up to him.

"I'm sorry too. I think jealousy got hold of both of us. Tea or coffee?"

"Coffee please. What do you fancy doing today?"

"I thought it would be nice to go out into the country somewhere; do a bit of exploring. What do you think?"

"Sounds good, although I don't want to go too far as I'll have to drive back to London later. But I tell you what, I realise I've neglected you lately; I will have to come up more regularly."

"That would be good," I replied, although I admit to a little sinking feeling inside because I knew I was shortly going to be very busy. I didn't really want to have to feel I had to take time away to entertain him. I shook the feeling away, thinking how ungrateful I was.

Almost as if he could read my thoughts, he said,

"I know you will be very busy soon, love but if I come and you're doing something I can always just take off somewhere for a bit and let you get on. Then we can have the evenings together or whatever."

"You would do that? Come up from London just to spend an evening with me?" I admit I was a bit incredulous.

"Of course. You're worth it, aren't you?" He nuzzled my face and we ended up kissing. Then, reluctantly I broke away.

"Well, if we are going to do anything today, we'd better get on with breakfast. I'll cook while you get dressed."

"You really should have a shower fitted, you know."

"Yes, I know. I'll get around to it."

We did have a good day, or about half a day. We went up to Hay Bluff and had a walk up there and then drove down into Weobley and had a light lunch in a tearoom there. We returned mid-afternoon and we relaxed in the garden for a while. Then we had drinks and some quiche and salad that I'd made yesterday and Jim packed his flashy Merc, gave me a kiss and off he went.

****

The summer passed in something of a blur; when I look back, all I recalled was a flurry of either picking fruit or making the jam with it. It started off gently enough; soon after the gooseberries the redcurrants were starting to be ripe enough to begin picking. I loved to be out there picking the fruit and found great peace as I stood among the bushes gathering the succulent, fat berries. In fact, I often found it difficult to stop picking once my allotted time was over, being seduced into reaching for just one more string of plump redness that caught my eye and yet another and another until I couldn't balance any more in my containers.

Then it would be back to the farmhouse to deal with the task of making redcurrant jelly. Once I had strawberries and raspberries too, I made summer puddings, individual ones to send over to Sutton Court and to the café at the garden centre. I kept a few for myself because I loved them. I even sold some at Madge's shop; once the villagers spotted them, they went like hot cakes – I could barely keep up with the demand!

Picking the strawberries was a back-breaking task; I was glad that some thoughtful person, probably Kenny, had planted them in raised beds so the bending wasn't quite so arduous. Sylvie loved to pick for me and sometimes Kenny would come and help, as would Sheila or Joseph. Sometimes Kenny would send one of his workers over to pick. Often there would be quite a gathering in my walled garden!

Sylvie was a great help to me; she loved to watch what I was doing and was also excellent at putting the labels on the jars perfectly centralised.

"You have a good, steady hand, Sylvie," I complimented her, holding up a jar for inspection. She glowed at my praise.

I also bought extra fruit from growers nearby; after all, I couldn't grow enough to meet all my orders and I saw that Aunt Bea had done the same.

The blackcurrants were just amazing; they were big and juicy and smelled oh, so delicious. The aroma was there in the plants even before the fruit was ripe and being out there was a delight to all the senses as I enjoyed the warmth of the sun as I picked.

Rainy days were more of a challenge as the fruit still needed to be gathered. I would wear a big raincoat, heavy duty, and waterproof trousers and shoes. Even so, I would come into the house absolutely wringing wet and have to get dried off before I could begin cooking. It was at times like this that I wished I'd had a shower fitted as Jim had said. However, I was far too busy to see to it just now. It was a race against time alright, to get the fruit picked and jammed or made into puddings or whatever while the fruit was still fresh and good.

Jim formed the habit of coming up every couple of weeks and I have to say he was pretty good, helping with the picking and assisting me in the kitchen.

He was surprisingly efficient at washing up. I noticed that when Jim was there, Kenny didn't come and I was quite thankful for that because when or if the two did come across each other you would swear you could cut the atmosphere in half. I noticed that Sheila never issued a dinner invitation again either, although she was always very friendly whenever I happened to see her.

****

I got a big surprise one day when I was just coming back to the farmhouse from the walled garden, to see that I had a visitor. It was on a Saturday and I wasn't expecting Jim that weekend.

"Mr Gamble! How nice to see you! Excuse the attire; I've just been picking some of today's fruit."

"Oh, don't you worry about that, young lady. I just thought I'd call and see how you are getting on."

"Come on in, would you like a cup of tea?"

"I'd love one. Thank you."

Fortunately, the kitchen was fairly tidy because I hadn't started the day's jam-making, although I had bread loaves rising on the Aga. My bread was also popular with the locals and I made a delivery to Madge's shop every day. I'd already delivered to her and these were for my own use; every now and then I made an extra batch for my freezer. It saved me some work and made sure I always had some to use.

"Excuse me a moment," I said, and whipped the cloth off the risen bread dough and popped the two trays into the Aga oven, shutting the door firmly after them.

"I will just make the tea; would you like to stay in here or sit on the patio?"

"Oh, I'm fine here, don't you worry about running around after me, I know you're busy." He sat down on a chair by the table, looking surprisingly at home there. But of course I recalled that he was used to visiting Aunt Bea.

"I am indeed," I replied, pouring water into the teapot. "But I love every moment. I do tend to drop to sleep immediately at the end of the day though, it is very tiring work some days, especially when it's very hot."

He nodded understandingly.

"Your aunt said the same. She used to say that in some ways she wished that the fruit came on in the winter as she wouldn't mind having to slave in a hot kitchen so much when the weather is cold!"

"Yes, I can certainly relate to that," I said, feelingly. Sometimes when it was very hot, making jam and cooking was the last thing I wanted to do.

I poured the tea and, remembering his sweet tooth, pushed the sugar bowl in his direction and he began to spoon in the sugar and then stirred his tea in an absent-minded fashion.

"I often used to sit here like this with your Aunt. I do miss her." He sighed, and before I thought was I was doing, I reached across to lay my hand on his.

"I'm sorry, I know you were good friends. I realise it's not the same, but you are welcome to call whenever you feel the need."

He looked up and looked into my eyes; I noticed his were a little watery. He gripped my hand for a moment, then let go.

"Thank you, my dear. It's hard to lose someone you love."

"I know it is; I miss her myself. Sometimes, when I'm working in here, I feel like I shouldn't be doing it, it should be her here making the jam and kneading the bread dough. I love this place, I am so at home in this house but I still feel like it's not quite right sometimes."

I got up and reached for the oven gloves. I took out the bread, now golden and smelling divine.

"Tell you what, how about sampling one of my rolls and some strawberry jam? Tell me if you think they come up to Aunt Bea's standard."

His eyes sparkled at the thought and sat there like an expectant schoolboy while I put a plate in front of him with a roll on it, still fresh and warm from the oven. Then I put the butter and a knife there and a jar of jam that I'd just made the day before. It was a part-jar, so I couldn't sell it.

Mr Gamble buttered his roll and I did likewise with one and then I waited while he spread the jam and took a bite, watching for his reaction. He closed his eyes briefly. 'Mm.' He opened his eyes and looked at me.

"They are wonderful, both the bread and the jam. Bea would be proud, young lady."

I smiled.

"I'm so glad. I'm happy that I come up to her standards – and you were the best person to tell me, Mr Gamble."

"Do call me Paul, I'm out of the office – and especially now we are friends."

"Paul," I said, "thank you. I'm happy we are friends."

We ate our rolls in silence then, although it was a friendly silence as we enjoyed our food. Was there anything quite as gorgeous as bread fresh from the oven and newly-made jam?

When we had finished, we chatted a while about how the business was going and how settled I was in the house, my period of helping out at Sutton Court and the villagers I now knew. At last, he got up.

"Well, lass, I know you are probably chomping at the bit to deal with that fruit you have brought in so I will leave you to it. I've already stayed here longer than I meant to. You are good company, my dear. You have really helped this old man today. I might be a solicitor but I'm human too you know."

I laughed and kissed him on his cheek.

"I know. Go on with you then, I do have to get on. But I meant it when I said you can come whenever you feel like it. Or when you feel like some new bread and jam." I smiled mischievously. He laughed and gave my arm a pat.

"Oh no, I've been rumbled already!"

We were both chuckling as I watched him amble down my drive. As I turned to go back into the house, I thought I saw a faint figure in the garden, watching and I was sure, smiling. Then, as I tried to get a better view of her, she was no longer there.

Chapter 22
Conversations

"Oh, hello, Sheila."

I was in the middle of a jam-making session; the two huge jam saucepans were boiling away merrily on the stove and I was busy taking the hot jars out of the oven in readiness to receive the hot fruity liquid. It was rather a warm day and so the kitchen door and the two windows were wide open in my efforts to get something of a through-draught in order to help me keep from boiling over myself. I turned at the sound of a knock and a cheery voice calling

"Hello Lucy, can I come in?"

"Of course! Excuse me though, I'm just about to fill my pots. Sit down, I'll not be long."

"You carry on, don't mind me, I've plenty of time."

I hastily set the hot jars on a tray by the side of the cooker and started to ladle the jam into the jars. It took me a while, having two cauldrons to empty but I couldn't stop; the jam has to be jarred just at the right time. After I'd done that, I popped a waxed circle in the top of each jar and then put all the tops onto them. Doing that while the contents are still hot helps the jars to seal properly. Later, when the jars had cooled, I would wipe them over with a hot wet cloth to make sure they weren't sticky and tomorrow Sylvie would come and put the labels on for me.

I popped the first cauldron into the sink and poured hot water into it and then, after I'd heaved it onto the draining board, did the same with the other. Hot water was the only way I was going to get them clean again but I would do that later once Sheila had gone.

Now, I was ready for a drink and a sit down.

"Sorry about that, Sheila, you just got me at the wrong moment! Would you care for a cool drink? I'm going to have one, I need it."

"Oh yes please."

I poured some home-made lemonade into two glasses, popped some ice in and a straw each.

"Shall we have them outside? It's so stuffy in here."

We went out onto the front patio where my table and chairs were out all the time now. I sank gratefully onto a chair, took a sip of my drink and looked expectantly at Sheila.

"It's really good to see you, Sheila, but you don't usually call on me. What can I do for you?"

"I feel bad for neglecting you, my dear but you know the garden centre is very busy this time of the year. Also, I realised that inviting you over for dinner is something that is not going to go down very well with your Jim, is it?"

I must have blushed, for she leaned forward to touch my hand.

"Don't worry about it, my dear. I sense some rivalry between him and my Ken."

"I don't really understand why, Sheila. Ken has always been more brotherly towards me than anything else and I've never given Jim any reason to think otherwise. In fact, I told him that he had nothing to worry about with regard to Ken."

"Is that so?" I couldn't see her expression because her face was shaded suddenly by her hat. "Well, don't worry dear, I can see that you want to be left alone when he's here. But that doesn't mean to say that we have forgotten about you. Joseph is always asking about you."

I was suddenly stricken by guilt; I remembered she'd said that before and I hadn't yet been to see him.

"I'm sorry, I really should come over and see him. It's just that I'm so busy right now. If I'm not picking, then I'm making the jam or cooking something else. There seems no let up. I can see that I shouldn't neglect others though. Now I come to think of it, I haven't seen dad for ages, not since Penny's birthday party dinner."

"It's okay, he understands. He is so proud of you, he talks about you so much. I hear you had a visit from Paul Gamble."

"I did, it was about three weeks ago now; he's quite a sweetie, isn't he? He sat and sampled my bread and jam and said it was as good as Aunt Bea's."

"Yes, he told me. I think he's quite taken with you, Lucy. He often comes into the café and loves to eat your bread or scones with your jam. I'm sure he can't be far off retirement age you know. He is so pleased that you love being here."

"Oh yes, I love the village. But mostly I adore this house and garden; sometimes I can hardly believe it's mine, or going to be mine."

"It's certainly a great place to live, I wouldn't want to live anywhere else now. Anyway, I've come to talk with you about the Village Fete."

"Village Fete? Oh yes, what's that then?"

"Well, it's a fete! It's usually held on your field, the one nearest the road and the one opposite across your service road is used as a car park. It's held on August Bank Holiday Monday and is very popular with the people who live in the surrounding area, even as far as Hereford itself. A few fair rides for the children come and we have stalls selling things like cakes or books and we have tombolas and other games and competitions. We also have ring events, such as marching bands and dancers and other things. There is usually a big marquee with refreshments, drinks and so on."

"It sounds wonderful."

"It is. It's the village's biggest event of the year, although the Christmas Fair comes a close second."

"Christmas Fair?"

"Yes, that happens all through the village; the main street gets closed. But I'll tell you about that nearer the time. Now, we need to think about the Fete. I've been sent by the Fete Committee to ask you if we can use your fields again. You should have been asked before really but the committee wasn't sure whether they should ask you as your aunt has died; we might have to cancel it for this year."

"Well of course, there's no question! If it's a village tradition, then it must happen. I'm sure my aunt would have wanted it to go ahead."

"That's my girl! I knew you would say that. Now, someone from the nursery will mow the fields a couple of times before the event and everything will be done that needs doing. You won't have to concern yourself with the arrangements. However, I did want to ask you a big favour too."

Although I suspected what this might be, I encouraged her to carry on.

"Many of the villagers contribute refreshments and your Aunt Bea used to make cakes for the marquee and also she gave a certain number of her jars of jam to be sold. Would you do that too? And maybe do an hour helping in the refreshment marquee? I'm in charge of it and other women help me in shifts so that everyone gets a chance to go to the rest of the fete. What do you think?"

"I'd love to! I want to try to do everything my aunt did; I would like the village to be able to carry on as it always has, I'd hate to stop any traditions. It seems to me that my aunt kept that ground not only to stop development but also to give the village a fairground when needed." I laughed. "That's so like her!"

Sheila laughed along with me.

"It is, isn't it? But I don't want to force you to do anything just because your aunt did."

"Oh no! I think it will be fun. You must let me know how much you need me to make. I'm sorry to hurry you away, Sheila, but I really must go and pick some more fruit. I have to do as much as I can before it gets too ripe. The raspberries need picking every day or it gets out of hand."

"Of course." She stood up. "That's one of the reasons why we have the fete near the end of August – because the soft fruit season is almost over then and before the winter fruits come on. Hopefully, in a couple more weeks you won't be rushing quite so much."

"I'll certainly be glad of a break by then," I said ruefully, pushing a stray lock of hair back from where it had stuck to my face. I needed to go and re-pin my hair before I did any more. Sheila and I hugged briefly and I waved as she crossed the garden to the river path and I turned back towards the house.

****

It was the week leading up to the Village Fete and already preparations were being made. The field had indeed been mown twice and was looking pretty good for a field, surprisingly smooth really. Of course, Mr. Price's cows never went into this one. The car park field had also been cut and rubber stuff had been laid out on it, roll by roll, to stop too much mud being churned up by the vehicles. Every day as I drove past, making deliveries or just going to the village, something else had been done. I was very impressed by the organisation.

I was also busy making cakes and freezing them, although there would be many that I would make the day before the fete and even on the morning – I intended to make lots of scones which would be served with fresh cream and my jam.

On the Saturday the marquee was erected and tables and chairs were brought in from somewhere. I wandered down the lane to take a look at it.

"Hi there, Lucy!" A voice hailed me as I drew closer to the great tent. I knew immediately who called me and ignored the little jump I felt inside me at the sound of his voice.

"Ken."

I walked towards him.

"I suppose you are overseeing all this?" I made a wide sweep of my hand, taking in the whole expanse of green around us. He grinned at me.

"Of course. Mother would flay me alive if I didn't."

"I don't believe she would do such a thing!" I retorted.

"Oh, you don't know mother! Well, she wouldn't flay me but she'd certainly nag my ears off! This Fete is planned more precisely than a military operation. So, here I am, doing my duty."

"Are things going according to plan?" I asked, ignoring his joviality.

"Oh indeed they are. Nothing will be done tomorrow, it being the Sabbath Day, you know – can't risk the wrath of Our Lord; we want Him to smile on us and send us sunshine on Monday! Then, on Monday morning, all the stalls with their various canopies or tents or whatever they are using will be shipped in and the whole thing will be in full swing by midday."

"I think it will be wonderful; I've never been part of something like this since I left school. We used to have something like this there, but not on such a large scale."

"I just have to supervise the erection of the ropes for the ring events, then I'm done here for the day."

"Right. Well, I'll let you get on with it then." I started to move away.

"Erm, Lucy?"

"Yes?"

I watched him as he hesitated. He shook his head. "No, it's ok. I'll see you here on Monday, then? Is your – erm – Jim, going to be here?"

"No, he has to be somewhere else this weekend. He was going to be but I think his father wanted to see him or something. Anyway, he's not coming."

"Ah, right. I see. Well, I'll see you on Monday – somewhere, then."

He went away from me then and I saw him waving his arms and shouting to a couple of men, who set about putting up the ropes for the ring.

I made my way back up the lane to River View, pushing down sudden feelings of – what? Disappointment? Over what? That Jim wasn't coming? No, I admitted to myself that I was actually glad he wouldn't be here; I would be able to enjoy the fete without worrying. I had to admit to myself that country fetes probably weren't my fiancé's scene.

Chapter 23
The Village Fete

The Sabbath Day observance must have worked, for the Bank Holiday Monday dawned bright and clear – at least, I assumed it did but I didn't get up *that* early. I was up quite early though, baking bread, scones and small cakes for the refreshment tent. Sylvie turned up to help me, which was a pleasant surprise but I knew she was keen and she was indeed a great help. She was particularly good at icing and so she did a lot of the piping on the fairy cakes and made them very attractive and inviting.

We filled my pantry, laying large trays across the jars of jam that still sat in there; most of it was for the fete anyway. We also utilized the rest of the house, laying covered trays on any horizontal surface.

By eleven, we had just about done and I reckoned we deserved a rest. We took cool drinks and some bacon butties outside and collapsed on my garden recliners.

"Phew! I'm tuckered," said Sylvie as she flopped down. "and very hot! I think I'm melting all away. No wonder you're so thin, Luce, even though you make gorgeous food."

"That is one drawback about cooking for a living, Sylvie. Whenever you work in a kitchen, unless you happen to get lucky with air conditioning, at times it's going to be hot work, especially in the summer. In the winter, it can actually be quite nice. But if you go to the catering college, you will experience that for yourself and you will be able to judge. But for me, there's nothing quite as satisfying as producing culinary works of art that are enjoyed and appreciated."

"So how do you feel about mostly producing jams, chutneys and pickles as the biggest part of your work now? Do you miss making meals? I remember some of the meals you did at Sutton Court, they were wonderful."

"Thank you. In some ways I miss it but in other ways there is just as much skill in producing a good jam or chutney and I do like having my own business. I still make some specialised desserts for Sutton Court and bread and small cakes for Madge's shop and for the café at Baxter's Nurseries."

"Kenny is sweet on you, isn't he?"

Sylvie shot a sly look at me; I was a bit startled.

"No, he isn't; he has a girlfriend. Anyway, I'm engaged."

"That doesn't mean he can't fancy you. I've seen the way he looks at you when he thinks you're not looking. I watched him at Penny's party, he could hardly take his eyes off you. No wonder your boyfriend was mad at you."

"How do you know he was mad at me?" I was even more taken aback.

"I could see it in his eyes when you left and the way he hussled you out."

I frowned but didn't answer. I couldn't help wondering how many other people had noticed.

We ate our butties and sipped our drinks. I searched for something else to talk about.

"So, when does Penny start her nursing? Where has she decided to go to train?"

"I think she's going to Nottingham. She hasn't mentioned it lately. I've been wondering if she's changed her mind about it you know."

"Oh really? I wonder why that is."

"I have no idea; she's become quiet, not like her really. She can be quite vicious at times if something riles her so I stay out of it."

"Oh dear, it's sometimes so hard to know exactly what to do at that age. I feel for her."

"Hmm. I suppose I should go home and have a shower and freshen up before the fete this afternoon." Sylvie remarked but she didn't make a move. Instead, she looked like she was going to drift off. I sympathised; I felt the same. I sat back and allowed my eyelids to droop.

I started kind of floating around, half asleep. Images of Kenny and Jim drifted before me, along with Aunt Bea, who seemed to be trying to tell me something. I heard a voice saying, 'Lucy, Lucy' and eventually realised it wasn't in my dream but someone trying to waken me. I opened my eyes to find Sheila smiling down at me.

"Come on, sleepyheads! We have work to do! I've come to help take the cakes down to the refreshment tent."

"Already?" I struggled to wake up – somehow, my body still thought it was asleep. Sylvie looked like she was having the same trouble.

"Oh yes indeed! It's twelve and the fete opens in half an hour! Come on, lass, get yourself moving!"

I got up reluctantly and led her into the house. She sniffed appreciatively.

"It smells wonderful in here. Oh, my goodness!" She had seen all the trays of cakes in the pantry. As I led her further into the house, she was even more overcome at the sight of all the culinary delights everywhere. "I never expected all this, Lucy, you have worked miracles."

"I couldn't have done it without Sylvie; she's been amazing."

"Don't listen to her, Sheila, Lucy has done all the hard work; I just did icing and the nice decorating stuff."

"They look wonderful, you have a good eye and hand, Sylvie," said Sheila admiringly. "I can hardly bear to load them without eating them!"

A sharp knock sounded at the door.

"Ah, that'll be Kenny, he's come to help."

I quelled the heart-jump I felt when he came in and we all got busy loading the produce into the two vehicles; Sheila's Mondeo and Kenny's sturdy Freelander. He took the cases of jams and all the bread and wedged some trays of cakes on top of the jam. Sheila managed to take quite a lot of the cakes and I said I would bring the rest.

"But first, I'm going to just run this young lady home so she can shower and change," I said.

"Better not," remarked Kenny, "It's conglomerated at the bottom of the lane, it will take you ages to get through."

"I never thought of that," I said. "I'm sorry, Sylvie."

"Oh, that's okay, it's only a few minutes going through the walled garden. Don't worry, Lucy. I'll be off now, I'll see you later down on the field."

She gave a cheery wave and was off, running across my lawn. Where did she get her energy? I wondered. Not long ago she was so weary she was falling asleep.

Anyway, I had no time to lose; I needed to run down in the car with the rest of the cakes then come home, wash and change into something more suitable for a summer fate. Yet again, I wished I had a shower.

****

An hour or so later, I was back on the field again, this time more coolly dressed in a sunshine yellow sleeveless dress with dainty white daises all over it. I had fallen in love with the dress in Black's in Hereford. It would have looked entirely out of place in London but was perfect for a country fete. I had scooped my hair up in a ponytail and would have worn strappy sandals but, upon thinking about the field, decided instead to wear white socks and trainers. It spoiled the look a little but it was sensible under the circumstances, I felt.

My field, usually so quiet, was teaming with people of all varieties. It was obviously a popular event. The field opposite was chock-full of vehicles of all shapes and sizes. I was glad my car was safely at home. Cars were already parking up the lane, although I recognised Ken's Freelander and Sheila's Mondeo; they obviously felt it more sensible to park up the lane to leave spaces free on the field. I wondered around the field, looking at all the stalls and games. As I did so, I saw many faces I knew and received shouts of greeting or waves. Besides the stalls selling just about everything from sweets to cakes to meats, cheeses, nuts and plants, there were ice-cream vans which were doing a roaring trade and hot-dog and Donut stalls.

All sorts of games had been set up, from a coconut shy to finding the treasure, from 'drop the penny on the pound' watery game to guess how many beans there were in a jar. Tombolas and other fund-raising stalls, bran tubs and so on were there. I don't think I've ever seen so many games, stalls and competitions in a field! When I arrived, a marching band was performing in the ring; people were sitting around the outside of the ropes on bales of hay or folding chairs; many sat on the ground on rugs or even plastic bags. A small carousel for children was there, along with other rides for children and a bouncy castle.

Once I'd done a complete round of the field, I made my way to the marquee, where Sheila was in charge of proceedings. It was full of people taking refreshment. Many of the residents of Sutton Court had been brought down and were comfortably seated around tables in their wheelchairs and were happily supping tea and eating cakes.

They greeted me cheerfully when I came towards them and I spent some time chatting with them and their carers. They told me that they try to bring all the residents down in rotation, except for those who are bedridden. When these people were taken back to Sutton Court, others would be brought down. How lovely for them to be able to come out, I thought.

"Lucy!"

I turned at the sound of a male voice calling my name and flung my arms around my dad, who had come up to me.

"Dad! It's lovely to see you. I haven't seen you properly for ages."

"Why don't we sit down at one of these tables and have a drink and one of those wonderful-looking cakes and have a chat?" he suggested. I nodded, and followed him to a table. Sheila came bustling over.

"Hello, you two! Shall I come and join you? I could do with a break. Dad said he'd be here just now – oh, there he is!"

Joseph Baxter saw us and waved cheerfully and made his way carefully towards us through the throng of people.

"I'll go get us some drinks and cakes," said Sheila. "Come and sit down, dad, and join us here. I'll be back in a jiffy.

I hugged Joseph and he and dad shook hands. Dad helped the older man to a chair and we all sat down. I couldn't help wishing that Ken would join us. I had seen him outside, keeping an eye on things and going to give a hand wherever help was needed. I wondered who was looking after the garden centre, since I'd seen everyone I knew who worked there either on this field or directing car parking.

"Oh, we don't open on this day!" Joseph smiled at my question. "Everyone around knows that Sheila and Ken will be here running things, and just to make sure, we leave a notice telling any stray customers where we are and to come and look at our stall here on the field! That way, we pick up any unknowing people and get them here! All in a good cause, you know. Or rather, several causes as we give to a few charities from our proceedings."

"I think it's a great thing to have something like this in a village; villages should have traditions. It's good to have fun and do good for others at the same time."

Sheila came back at that point with a tray with four cups of tea and a plate of cakes. We helped ourselves to which we wanted and we sat together companionably.

"I hear you're getting on very well with your business, Lucy," remarked Joseph. "Are you enjoying it?"

"I am, rather. I wasn't sure at first if I would miss actual catering too much but I have found that I enjoy making products that come up to Aunt Bea's standard so that my customers are still satisfied with their orders. I also like to make specialised desserts for the residents of Sutton Court; why should people who have certain dietary requirements not be able to have the things others are able to enjoy? I make bread for Madge's shop and the café at the garden centre and also cakes and scones for both. But the cream on the cake, so to speak, is the garden; the peace I feel when I'm picking the fruit is special and to be able to grow the fruit, pick it and make it into a finished product is something that I haven't been able to do before."

Stopping for breath, I looked around at my companions. Each one had stopped eating and was looking at me, their eyes sparkling, on the edge of laughter. I smiled, sheepishly.

"I suppose I was getting a little intense."

Sheila leaned forward and touched my hand.

"It's so good to know that you are enjoying what you are doing, my dear. We all hope it means you will decide to stay after the year is up."

"There is little doubt," I assured her.

"What about the footsteps?" asked Joseph. "Have you heard them at all since you have lived at River View?"

"I was going to ask you that," said dad. "I have been quite concerned, you know, but you're always so busy that I've not really had a chance to speak with you."

"Oh dad, I feel so bad, hearing you say that! I am ashamed that I haven't made time to see you or Joseph here since the fruit started my race against time!"

It was dad's turn to take my hand.

"Don't you worry about that, Lulu. So, what about those footsteps?"

"There's been nothing. I've heard nothing. Mind you, I've been so busy right into the evenings and I fall into bed so tired at night that I probably wouldn't have noticed anyway. But I'm pretty sure there hasn't been any. I have seen Aunt Bea a few times, briefly, but usually in the garden. I've never seen her in the house, only felt her sometimes."

"Well, I'm pretty sure those footsteps are not connected to her. Not in the way we mean. But inside I think there is a connection between them and her death," dad mused. The other two and I looked at him questioningly.

"Oh, there you all are! Look who I found wondering around like a lost sheep."

We looked up, startled, to see Penny and, behind her, James.

"Jim!" I exclaimed. "I wasn't expecting you today. You said you couldn't come." I got up and went towards him and he kissed me coolly.

"Hello Luce. The business I had finished early and so I thought I'd pop up and surprise you."

"Well, you've certainly done that. Would you like a drink? And a cake?"

He nodded. "That would be very nice. Do you have coffee?"

Sheila got up hastily.

"I'll get you one."

Dad and Jim shook hands and I introduced Jim to Joseph.

"How do you do, young man? Your young lady here is a superb baker, sample one of her cakes?" John pushed the plate forward. As Jim took one, I happened to look up and caught sight of Ken and Sheila speaking. She waved her hand towards our table and he looked in our direction. He said something – and I could swear that he said 'bugger' and he turned round and walked out of the marquee.

'Bugger,' I repeated in my mind and reluctantly turned back towards my company, to see Jim pulling up a chair for Penny. She giggled and sat down.

"Excuse me," I heard myself say, before I realised that I was going to speak. "I have to go outside. It's a bit too stuffy in here, I'm getting a headache."

The others started up and I held up my hand.

"No, stay here and finish your drinks and cakes. I just need to be alone for a while, perhaps find some shade. I will see you later, Jim. I'll be around somewhere."

He sat down again and smiled at Penny. I turned and hastened towards the entrance of the tent. Upon hearing Sheila call my name, I stopped.

"I'm sorry, Sheila, I have a headache. I can't stop to help you. I think it must have been all the cooking in the heat and the early morning; it's been a long day. I need some quiet and coolness somewhere."

She patted my arm.

"Don't you worry, my dear, I understand perfectly. Better than you think," she glanced towards the table I just left. "You go. Why not go down the path to the river? It will be cool down there and will soothe your headache. I go there when I need soothing; the rippling of the water and the calmness helps me sort my head out. I'll keep the others busy for a while; keep them away from you."

"Bless you, Sheila. Thank you."

And without a glance backwards, I left the marquee.

Chapter 24
Too Much Heat

Coming out into the sunlight, I squinted a bit and brought my sunglasses down from the top of my head and put them on properly. The field was teaming and in the ring there were a lot of ducks and geese being herded by a couple of sheepdogs. 'Strange', I thought, but I was in no mood to stay here. The shine of the day had gone and I just wanted to get away. I couldn't explain this feeling to myself, nor understand why I was just seething mad. No wonder I had a headache, so mad was I. I rushed out of the field entrance and up my lane to my house. I just wanted to be away from all the noise. The nearer I got to River View, the more the noise receded. I walked down my driveway; it was green and cool because of the trees that were along the edge of the drive.

Should I do what Sheila suggested and go down by the river? Or should I go and sit in the walled garden, I loved it there and it was sheltered by the fruit trees. Or perhaps my favourite seat in the garden?

I imagined Jim coming up here to find me and decided I didn't want to be found. I would go down to the river and just walk around the bend out of sight. I let myself out through the gate as if I was going to take the river path to the garden centre. A little way along, there was a set of steps, disguised somewhat by the undergrowth, although I knew they were there. They would be quite hazardous in wet conditions but today they were dry and safe.

I made my way slowly down there and walked alongside the river. Around the bend was a seat under a weeping willow tree that drooped and dangled over the water.

It was a lovely place to sit, so green and cool with the song of the river as it rippled and danced over stones. The water was so clear here that I could see little fish swimming under the surface. I watched a dragonfly, its body and wings shimmering as it dipped and glided over the water. I felt myself relaxing and closed my eyes and just enjoyed the sounds of the river and the occasional gentle twitter of a bird.

I felt the seat move slightly and opened my eyes with a jump. Beside me sat Ken, looking at me with concern in his eyes. I quelled the flutter I felt in my chest.

"Hi."

"Hello there. Are you okay, Lucy? Mother told me you weren't feeling too good."

"I just have a headache, that's all. Too much heat and noise, I think. I've got used to the quiet life, you know. I'll be fine."

"Are you sure?"

"Oh yes. It's lovely here, isn't it, so peaceful."

"It is. My dad had this seat put here and it's a place that mum likes to come to when she needs to get away. Not that she does it often now. She did it a lot when dad was ill and when he died. But I think she is finding a new happiness these days."

"Could my dad have anything to do with that?" I smiled at him sideways.

"I think that's likely," he answered with a return smile.

Silence fell between us, but it was an easy silence. As we sat there, his hand reached out and took mine. I looked at him and he gave me a shy smile.

"I think there is something, isn't there, Lucy?"

I sat still and looked down, saying nothing.

"If you need someone to talk to, you can talk to me, you know."

'You're the last person I could talk to,' I thought.

"If you can't talk to me, you could always talk to mum," he said, as if he had read my thoughts. "She's a very good person to talk to and very astute. Although she works in the garden centre, she'd always make time for you, you know. She's very fond of you, and granddad is too."

"I know and I'm fond of them too."

He patted my hand.

"I need to get back to the show. Are you sure you're alright? I don't really like to leave you."

"Oh no, don't worry, I'm fine. I am just a bit worried that Jim will come looking for me though."

"Tell you what, have you got your phone?"

I nodded.

"I'll go back to the fete and see if he's still around. If he comes up to look for you, I'll send you a message."

"That's great, thank you. I'd like to stay here a while, it's so soothing but I don't want Jim to know about this place, somehow. I'd rather be at home if he looks for me."

"Leave it with me. If you don't hear from me, don't worry, just wander back when you're ready."

I nodded again and he started to leave.

"Ken?"

He turned to look at me. However, what I wanted to say wouldn't come out, so I just said, "thank you."

He smiled and turned away and I watched him go regretfully. I leaned back on the seat again but somehow the charm of the place had dimmed. I waited for a while to give him time to get back up the steps and along the path and then started to make my way slowly in his wake.

****

"I can't believe you left me like that, when I'd just come!"

Jim's face was red with anger and the vein in his neck stood out.

"I had a headache."

"You had a headache. Is that all you have to say? After I'd driven all that way on a Bank Holiday just to be with you and you go off because you had a headache?"

"I came back, didn't I?"

"Oh yes, when I'd been left to entertain your father and a senile old man."

"Joseph is far from senile! And there was the luscious Penny of course. Could hardly miss her, could you? Couldn't bring yourself to leave her to come with me. If you had cared that much, you would have brought me home and looked after me."

"Ah, so that's what this is all about – Penny? I might have known you would be singing that old song!"

"Very convenient that she was the one who found you, wasn't it? How did that happen then?"

He wiped his hand across his hair in a familiar, aggravated gesture.

"I don't know; I just happened to see her and I asked if she'd seen you. She said you were likely to be in the Marquee."

"I see. So you then had to insist that she sat down next to you and eat a cake."

"Well, why not? I was only being friendly, to thank her for helping me find you."

"But you were still with her when I got back, over an hour later, well over an hour in fact."

"Well, she was someone I knew and I needed company."

He obviously thought I was being churlish, but so was he. Why was he so cross at me still, so long after the event? I'd gone back to the show and found him; he seemed to be having a great time helping Penny to throw coconuts. I was pretty mad about that; he'd obviously spent all the time I was away with her.

I told myself that anyone who really cared wouldn't have stayed but would have come looking for me the way Ken had…

"I think I will go find a place to stay in Hereford tonight. I don't think we're in the right mood to be companionable this evening. I'll be in touch."

With that, he picked up his jacket, slung it over his shoulder and went out, slamming the kitchen door behind him. Moments later, I heard the familiar sound of his Merc starting up and listened to it moving away.

I couldn't bring myself to be sorry he'd gone. Not for the first time lately, I was pretty glad to see the back of him.

Making myself a pot of mint tea, I took it into my small lounge ready to relax the rest of the evening, happy with my own company. Glad for the peace and quiet, I reflected on the day. It had been a mixed bag indeed. I realised that perhaps Jim had reason to be jealous of Ken for I had to finally admit to myself that I felt a definite pull towards the owner of the garden centre. He showed qualities that I had to admit that Jim was sadly lacking that I wanted in a man. Could it be that I was falling out of love with my fiancé?

Chapter 25
Ponderings

After a disturbed night, I got up and went downstairs to put the kettle on. A brisk knock came at the door, making me jump. It was Jim. I opened the door reluctantly and he came in. He put his arms around me and was all contrition.

"I'm sorry, Luce. You were right, I should have been more caring of you yesterday. I feel really bad about how I treated you last night. Will you forgive me please?"

Feeling the familiarity of his arms about me and looking into his handsome, troubled face, I did forgive him. He couldn't have known what a busy day it had been for me, could he?

"I suppose I do forgive you. But I'm not sure that I want to continue with our engagement, Jim. I feel like we're growing apart."

Shocked, he stood back.

"You can't mean that! Of course it's difficult with you up here and me having to be in London, it's bound to put a strain on our relationship, don't you think? I'm doing my best, I come up here whenever I can."

Looking at it that way, I had to admit he had been putting in a big effort. Driving from London to Hereford wasn't an easy or quick journey, I knew. Perhaps I was being too hard on him.

"Okay," I relented, "you have been good. And you're right, it's not easy with the distance between us."

"You have no idea how much I miss you back in London. It just doesn't seem right without you. When this year is up, we will get married. Next summer. Once you have secured this house as yours, we can do what we like – we could get married in the South of France, or in Canada, or Hawaii or wherever you fancy! What do you think of that?"

"It sounds lovely."

"Well, you have plenty of time to think about what you would like. I have to get back to London now but I will be back in a couple of weeks."

"Don't you want anything before you go?"

"No, I just had breakfast. Must run, I have meetings later today."

He kissed me briefly and he was gone.

Well! I sank down on a chair by my kitchen table without making my drink or anything. I had tried to finish the relationship between me and Jim but instead I'd allowed myself to be talked round. Not only that, he'd actually said we would be married next summer! Perhaps things were looking up with us? Perhaps he had needed me to give him a jolt.

****

Jim came again the very next weekend and went out of his way to show me that he was serious. He helped me by washing up and so on and also worked with me in the gardens.

I had discovered that I enjoyed gardening. I didn't know much but I was learning. At this time of year, weeding was the most pressing thing to do and I found it quite therapeutic being out there, with the noises of the country around me, the song of the river, more distant here but could still be heard and the birds as they sang their joyful songs as they flittered about. The lowing of Elwyn Price's cows in the field beyond the house, added to my feeling of peace and at the end of my work there would be a tidy bed on display.

I dead-headed the roses and other flowers in the garden nearest the house and loved to watch the moorhens and ducks on the pond at the far end of my garden.

I preferred to work alone but as there was so much to do, I didn't turn down Jim's offers of help. I knew that the more I did in the garden, the more it freed up Kenny's workers to be at the garden centre; I felt I really couldn't keep putting upon him or them, not that they seemed to mind a bit. I got to know them all as they seemed to take it in turns. There was Joe, who I already knew, then there was Eddie, Roger, Patch, Gerry, Mike and Ron. There were also a couple of women, Mavis and Janice, who came sometimes and I enjoyed their company.

Ken came quite often and busied himself in the garden and he always helped me when I had trays of jars to deliver.

August slipped into September and September into October. I was working on the tree fruits now; the plums had been and gone and so had the cherries and I actually had a Damson tree, not in the walled garden but in the house's own garden, something that's not often seen these days, so of course I made Damson jam.

It's easy to make, damsons are so rich in pectin that it sets easily. Of course, the stones are a pain but I have a good sieve that soon sorts them out. I found they sold very quickly; Madge told me that she has customers from as far away as Kington who made special journeys to her shop to get my jam, in particular the damson because it's so hard to get.

I actually had a special request from one of her customers who particularly asked if he could have some damson jam with some of the stones left in! I did them as a special favour without my 'Aunt Bea's Pantry' label and in ordinary jars, not like my business ones and told him that if he does himself any damage on the stones I would deny all knowledge! Fortunately, he never had any accidents, to my relief.

I had an abundance of apples; of course for Aunt Bea's Pantry I made many jars of apple sauce; these were smaller jars than for the jam but were the same octagonal shape with red and white squared patterned lids. With the apples I made pies, large and individual, to be sold at Madge's shop and at the nursery and also kept the nursing home supplied too. I hit upon the idea of making pie fillings in jars so I ordered large jars and filled some. I made fillings suitable for diabetics with agave sweetener instead of sugar. This experiment turned out to be a good one; there was demand for them in the village so of course I made more.

Picking the apples was easy because Ken had made sure that the apples trees stayed short; many of them were espaliers along strings or the walls of the garden. The pears were also grown like that. There were not so many pear trees because it was hard to know what to do with the pears but I found that the shop and the garden centre were just able to sell them as they were. I did make some flans with glazed pears. I have to admit that I ate quite a lot of the pears myself; they were my favourite fruit and to my mind there was nothing I liked better than to have a couple of fresh pears for breakfast. Pears are notoriously difficult because they ripen and go off so quickly. I resolved to do some research about how I could make better commercial use of my pears.

At the request of Madge and Sheila, I made toffee apples in readiness for Halloween.

One day when I was making deliveries at Madge's shop (bread rolls, cakes etc.), Madge said;

"I expect they've started making preparations for the bonfire, haven't they?"

"Have they? I have no idea. Where do they do that then?" Even as I asked the question, I had an idea that I already knew the answer!

"Why on your field of course, Lucy! Hasn't anyone asked you about it?"

"No."

"Oh! Well usually, we have a big bonfire on your field and a firework display. Everyone in the village comes. We reckon it's safer to do it that way than to have children playing about with fireworks at home. Fireworks are dangerous and so expensive! Even if a family buys some fireworks they won't get much for their money. So, we all come to the field and pay the entrance fee and that money is then kept and spent on next year's display."

"Sounds like a good idea," I said.

"A fair comes and we have that on the field too and we have roasted chestnuts and hot dogs and all sorts."

"Sounds like fun," I said again, wondering who was going to approach me about all this, as if I didn't know...

I have no doubt Madge was on the phone the moment I left the shop, for later that day, Sheila arrived on my doorstep.

"Don't tell me, I can guess!" I laughed, when I opened the door and saw her there. She stepped into my warm kitchen and sniffed appreciatively.

"Mm, I do love coming here! There's always such a delicious smell and your kitchen is so warm and inviting. It's beginning to get a little chilly, isn't it?"

She took off her coat and sat down on a chair. I put a cup of tea in front of her.

"So, you're a bit late with coming to see me about the Firework Night, aren't you?"

"To be honest, my dear, I'm a little distracted just now! And I was convinced Ken would have spoken with you about it already."

No, he's not said a word; in fact, it's been a while since I saw him."

"I've noticed he's not himself at the moment."

"Why? What do you think can be wrong with him?" I asked, feeling concerned.

"I really couldn't say. My son is not very forthcoming. I have my own ideas of course but since they are only ideas, I can't really say what I think. He has to sort things out for himself. So, are you alright with us holding our bonfire evening on your field?"

"Of course! You don't really need to ask, you know. I think my aunt bought that field so it could belong to the village really."

She nodded and took a sip of her tea. While she did so, I popped a small apple pie on a plate and some whipped cream on the top and put it before her.

"Oh my! That looks gorgeous!" I waited while she took a bite. "Mm, it's a lovely as it looks! The pastry is so light it melts in the mouth and I just love the apple and cinnamon taste. You're such a good cook, Lucy."

"Thank you."

"As you were saying, I think you're right, your aunt did mean that field to be for the village. But it's still your property and it's only right that you should be asked."

"Just take it as read that the village can use my field for anything that it's usually used for. Are there any other events I should know about?"

"Well, we have a winter fair in December but that is held actually in the village. It's a lovely event and we will certainly be asking for culinary contributions from you for that!"

I nodded and smiled. I didn't mind that.

"We also hold a May Day event on the village green. The children from the village school dance round the May Pole and we have a May Queen. It's a smaller event than the Bank Holiday Summer Fete and the Bonfire Night but we do use your field as a gathering place for the May Queen and the other 'floats' because it's a sort of carnival.

"They gather in your field where they are judged, they drive around the villages and then park up around the green. They parade through this village and the two neighbouring villages, Sutton Field and Long Sutton and floats come from other places too. Actually, come to think of it, it's quite a big event!"

We laughed at that and she took another bite of her pie.

"So," I said. "What preparations need to be made for the Bonfire Night?"

"Don't you worry about anything, Ken and the lads at the nursery will do that. The fair will arrive during the day. Ken will be there to open the field for them. The men will build the bonfire; the villagers bring stuff for it too so you may well see people around there in the days leading up to it."

"No problem; it's far enough away from here not to disturb me. What do you want me to do?"

"Actually, I don't think there's anything really, so just come down and enjoy the evening. The firework display is usually pretty good."

"Okay, that sounds all right to me."

"It will be a little break for you."

Sheila finished her pie, drank the last drops of her tea.

"Just as well I don't come too often or I would soon get fat!"

"Oh, I don't think so, you work too hard to get fat."

"Has Paul Gamble been to see you lately? He really should have one of those pies."

I laughed. "No, he hasn't. I'll get on the phone and invite him over."

"You do that, he'll love it. Poor man, I bet he's lonely nowadays. He spent a lot of time here, you know."

"Well, I don't know how much time he spent here but I did gather that he and Aunt Bea were pretty close."

"Very close, I'd say. Well, I really must be off. I forgot to ask how things are with you? Is your fiancé still managing to come over quite a bit? Do you think you will stay the year out?"

I nodded my head.

"Oh yes, my mind is made up. I'll be staying here. I am hoping that Jim will decide that we can live here, perhaps, although I'm doubtful, his work is in London. Still, we have time to decide yet, I suppose. Jim has been coming here regularly; sometimes every weekend. He's very helpful and considerate towards me. He does go for a walk sometimes if I'm in the middle of a load of cooking then he comes back and helps me to clear up. I can't fault him really."

"Oh well, as long as you're happy. Must be off. Thank you for the wonderful apple pie. It has been lovely to see you. I know that Jim is here most weekends but don't be a stranger! If you can't come over for Sunday lunch, come over during the week, we all love to see you and I'm sure your dad would like to see you more often."

"That's a good idea, I'll do that."

"Bye for now then."

I reflected when she had gone that she was right; I should spend more time with them, especially if my dad was thinking of marrying Sheila, they would become my family.

Chapter 26
An Exciting Invitation

It was about the second or third weekend in October. Jim was staying with me. It was the Saturday evening and we had eaten at the Wyeview Restaurant and were later watching a film on television. It had finished and so we turned the television off and Jim was pouring us a nightcap before we retired for the night.

"Did you hear that?" Jim stopped and listened, glass and bottle held in mid-air. I paused and listened too. Then I heard it – the unmistakable sound of footsteps above us! I felt the blood drain from my face and if I hadn't been sitting down already my legs would have let me down I'm sure.

Jim put down the bottle and glass.

"What is it? It sounds like someone is upstairs!" He picked up the poker and made for the door, wrenched it open and I heard the sound of his shoes on the stairs as he hurried up there. I couldn't follow; I felt too shaky. I hadn't heard those sounds for months now – why had they started again? Was it a ghost that only haunted on dark evenings? Did the light summer evenings keep him/it away?

I looked up questioningly as Jim came back into the room. He put the poker back in place.

"Nothing there. I looked in every room but there was nothing at all, no windows open, no doors swinging. Can't think what it was."

He must have noticed my expression then because he came and put his arm around me.

"What is it, Luce? Has this happened before?"

I nodded, slowly.

"Yes, but not for quite a long while. It happened once when dad and I stayed that weekend before I moved in. He and Butch went upstairs to look and found nothing. It's not happened since then."

For some reason I didn't want to tell him that Aunt Bea had obviously heard it too, and Ken.

"What can it be? Ghosts? I don't believe in ghosts. There has to be some other explanation for it."

He went back to the table where he had been pouring our drinks. He finished pouring and handed me a glass.

"Here, get this down you, it'll make you feel better."

I took it from him and drank. He was wrong, it didn't. In fact, I realised I didn't care to drink really and Jim was far too fond of it for my liking. Of course, he'd grown up with it but I hadn't. I admit I do quite like a glass of wine if I'm eating out but otherwise I don't bother. But hopefully this one, plus what we'd had at dinner, would help me to sleep.

When I got into my bedroom, I had the distinct feeling that someone, or something, was there. However, I didn't feel frightened; rather, I felt reassured. Once into bed I was very soon asleep.

****

In the morning, it was obvious that Jim hadn't slept well at all. He said that he'd heard the footsteps again and they sounded as though they were right in his room with him. He looked pale and tired and so I persuaded him, later on in the day, to have a nap in the lounge before he drove back to London. He was sensible enough to heed my advice and he slept in the chair for about an hour and a half, during which time I went into the den in order to not make any noise and wake him.

To my surprise, I found that some files had fallen on the floor, one of them being the book Aunt Bea had compiled about the house. I picked them up and as I did so, I noticed a folded sheet of paper that had slid under the table.

Puzzled, I unfolded the paper to find it was a computer printout. It had a picture of my farmhouse and underneath the words: 'Curious death of a young girl at River View Farm, Sutton-on-Wye, 1952'. My attention caught, I read on: '*The body of a young girl who apparently drowned in a farm pond was found by farm workers early in the morning of yesterday, March fifteenth as they arrived for work. The girl was identified as Hannah Jones, daughter of Frederick and Agnes Jones, owners of River View Farm. Mr Jones and his wife said that they had last seen their daughter, Hannah, aged seventeen, when she was supposedly on her way to bed the previous night. It appears that Hannah walked into the pond fully clothed after her parents had retired to bed. A police spokesman told our reporter that they are not looking for anyone in connection with this incident and fully expect the coroner to record a verdict of suicide.*'

Oh! How sad! I had no idea that anyone had died in my beautiful pond. I wondered if Aunt Bea had known about this and then realised that of course she had because it must have been in her folder. It was a copy so obviously she had found it somewhere. It was strange though because I was sure it hadn't been there before.

So, was Aunt Bea trying to tell me something? Could this be something to do with the mysterious footsteps? Could it be the footsteps of Hannah as she crept out of bed with suicide on her mind? It made me feel 'funny' in my stomach when I thought of it.

Thoughtfully, I tidied the room, put the paper with the newspaper report on the table and settled down to read for a while.

When I heard Jim moving around in the house, I put my book down and went through.

"Ah, there you are, darling. I'm going to have to get moving I'm afraid. I feel better for my nap though. What did you do while I was asleep?"

"I went through into the den and read a book," I replied. "Do you want anything before you go?"

"Just a coffee. I'm not hungry, that dinner you made was excellent and will keep me going for a good while. I'll just go and get my things from upstairs."

"I'll make your coffee while you do that then," I said and I moved towards the kitchen as he went through the door on the opposite side of the room.

I waited in the kitchen for the milk to boil; I knew Jim liked his coffee made with milk. He preferred percolated really but I didn't have a percolator as I didn't really drink coffee.

It wasn't long before he was back with his overnight bag and his coat, which he put over a kitchen chair and sat down to drink his coffee.

"Darling, I nearly forgot to mention this, with all the goings-on last night. My parents have been asking after you and they would love to see you. How would you feel about coming to spend a couple of days in London and then out to the old home to see my mater and pater? They are going to have a big 'do', a sort of Halloween party combined with fireworks. Do come, it's going to be fun, loads of people will be there and I want to show you off, my darling. You will come, won't you?"

I nodded slowly. It would mean missing the firework night here but I'm sure I wouldn't be missed. It was true, I hadn't seen Jim's parents for ages and they were nice people. It might do me good to have a few days away from here and have a couple of days in London. I felt quite elated at the thought of those wonderful London shops which I used to love – and perhaps I could see some of my mates while I was there.

"Yes, I'd love to. In fact, I would really enjoy a few days in London; maybe we could see a show? I haven't been to anything like that for ages and I could do with a wander down Oxford Street. It would make a nice change and I'm not so busy now, nothing I can't leave for a few days.

I also feel that maybe I should do something about my flat. If we are getting married next summer, I won't be living in it again, perhaps I should arrange to sell it. What do you think?"

"Well, that's up to you, my darling. You might want it again, you never know. Perhaps you should just keep renting it out for now. No sense in doing something in a hurry."

"Perhaps you're right. I'll leave it for now, then."

"Right. I really must be off now. As it is, I'll be driving pretty much all the way in the dark."

"Do be careful."

"I will, I promise." He kissed me and I saw him out, watched his Merc slide away and shut the door hurriedly to keep the warmth from escaping.

Despite the fact that I loved living here, the thought of a few days in London was exciting and something I now looked forward to.

Chapter 27
Family

Following Sheila's invitation, I went over there a couple of evenings later. I knew dad would be there and I wanted to tell him I'd be going to London for a few days the following week.

Sheila's cooking as usual was wonderful. She dished up a creamy lasagne and it was jolly to sit round the table with dad and this family who he'd practically joined. There was much joking and laughing and it was a very happy time.

"I wanted to let you know that I am going to London next week, dad. Jim's parents want me to visit them and I thought I'd have a couple of days in London as well. I might be able to do some Christmas shopping while I'm there. It's a bit early but it's a good opportunity."

"Oh right, love," he replied, "when are you actually going?"

"I'm going to take the train down on Thursday, then go with Jim to his parents' house on the weekend when they are going to hold a party, apparently. Not that keen, I don't really like 'High Society' parties but they have been asking to see me again. We will stay the weekend, then I might stay in London a few days more, depending on what we decide, or what I decide – whether I can bear to be away from here for long."

I looked around at everyone and they smiled and nodded as if they understood perfectly – which I'm sure they did.

"Erm, I was wondering if you would watch over River View for me while I'm away, please?"

"Of course we will," said Sheila warmly, "Kenny will make sure everything is okay, won't you, love?"

"Of course. No problem. It's a pity you're going to miss our Halloween do though, Lucy. It's one of the highlights of the year in our village."

"Oh." I felt stricken. "I didn't know about that. If I'd known..."

"Do you go round with your eyes shut?" laughed Sheila.

"Why?"

"Well, there's notices all over the place; certainly one in Madge's shop window."

"I think I must do, I've not seen it and I go there nearly every day. Oh, I'll have to let her know that I'll be away. I can't be away for long, can I? I can't let her have no bread or cakes to sell for too long."

"No, that's true."

"Hmm, I'll have to give her extra things to have in her fridge and freezer to tide her over. Damn, I never thought of that. It's not so easy to leave a business, is it?"

"No it isn't."

"Shame about the Halloween party though. If I'd known about it – oh, I can't let Jim down now, can I? He'd never understand if I said I had to go to a village do as opposed to his parents' event. Oh dear, I am sorry."

"Never mind dear, we have one every year!" said Sheila brightly. "Mark the date on your calendar and come next year."

"Yes. Yes, I'll do that. Consider it marked down."

"If you're here next year." The remark was so soft, I almost missed it. I looked sharply at Ken.

"I will be here."

"Okay, if you say so." He got up then and started gathering up the plates. There was a suggestion of an atmosphere but I couldn't work out why but then it was gone as if I'd imagined it.

****

I made sure that Madge had plenty of pies and cakes to sell while I was going to be away. Dad took me to the station and I enjoyed the train ride down to London. I contacted Jim to tell him where I was and he came to meet me. I stayed with him in his penthouse flat. That evening he took me to see Les Miserables which was fantastic.

The next day, after a leisurely breakfast, we set off for his parents' mansion in Surrey, not far from Wokingham. It was a beautiful place; it had about sixteen bedrooms and several reception rooms (what on earth does anyone need sixteen bedrooms for?) and was in grounds that were just like a park. They had a team of gardeners and servants because they were stinking rich. I supposed any girl wouldn't mind marrying into such a family. However, I didn't want this kind of life. More than once I wondered if I would really fit in.

However, I did like James' parents, Harry and Caroline and so I would be on my best behaviour while I was here.

Caroline greeted me graciously.

"Hello, Lucy, it's so good to see you. It's been too long since we saw you! I have been pestering our son to bring you to us for ages."

"Thank you. I am very happy to be here at last. I'm afraid I've been very busy lately."

"Oh yes, I've heard all about your lovely farmhouse in the country and the business you have undertaken. What a clever young woman you are! And lucky you to have inherited a beautiful country retreat! Herefordshire is a much sort after location these days, so I'm given to understand. It would be worth quite a bit if you decided to sell."

I decided I wanted to be non-committal so I just said,

"I will have to see how I feel at the end of the twelve months I have to be there. Jim and I will have to decide what to do then."

"Of course. Come with me and I'll show you to your room."

I followed her up the elegant sweeping staircase. I reflected that you could probably get most of my farmhouse in the hallway of this house. However, it still managed to be warm and welcoming somehow. It was far from being a draughty mausoleum that many old estate mansions were. It had been well-maintained and looked quite modern in most rooms. It was obvious that Caroline had excellent taste. I knew she had been a designer before she retired and I also knew it was her ministrations that made this place what it was now. I still couldn't get my head around the sixteen bedrooms though. Could they really have enough guests to fill that amount of rooms?

"You're in your usual room," she was saying, "but I wanted to bring you up because I have something to show you."

I was curious and couldn't think what she wanted to show me. When she opened the door, I saw that my case had already been brought up but there was something on the bed that caught my eye. I gasped. She went to hold it up for me. It was a dress and it looked like it had come out of a Jane Austin novel. It was gorgeous, made in heavy brocade, gold and green. It sounded like it would be garish but it wasn't. It had exquisite embroidery down the front and the sleeves. There was a headdress fashioned in pearls and a matching eye mask of the same material as the dress, edged with pearls.

"Do you like it?"

"It's wonderful," I replied, fingering the material lightly.

"I'm glad you think so. Would you like to wear it? Tonight we are having a fancy-dress, masked ball. When I knew you were coming, I thought of this dress. It is a copy of a real dress in my possession. That dress is an heirloom, passed down through the generations. Of course, that one is too delicate now to be worn and so I had this one made and I thought you are about the right size to wear it.

"I have worn it several times, although not of recent years because I'm not quite as slim as I used to be," she said, laughing a little.

I had difficulty believing that because she still had a good figure. I was overwhelmed that she wanted me to wear it. I could hardly wait to try it on.

Caroline must have read my mind.

"Would you like to try it on, see if it fits you?"

"Can I?"

"Of course!"

She was as excited as I was as she waited impatiently for me to take off my clothes down to my underwear and helped me lift the dress over my head. She did the buttons up down my back and then did the laces for me. Fortunately, she didn't pull them too tight; I needed to breathe after all!

"Look at you." She turned me so I could look at myself in a full-length mirror. Wow! I was impressed; even with my modern hairstyle I looked a different person in the dress.

"Oh Caroline! It's superb, can I really wear this tonight?"

"Of course. That's the whole idea. It will give me a lot of pleasure to see you in that this evening. You will be stunning. I will send Melissa up with you to do your hair; she is a genius with hair. Now, let's get that off you for now and then you come on down. You haven't seen Harry yet."

She helped me off with the dress, then she left me to get my clothes on and I made my way back downstairs to join the family.

Chapter 28
Hob-Nobbing with the Elite

It was quite a mild day for October, so Jim and I took a stroll around the garden and then hopped in the Merc to visit the local pub. I say, 'local', it was at least five miles away! We sat by a roaring fire, drinking large fizzy soft drinks and watching football on the wide-screen television.

It seemed that Jim was quite well-known down here for a few men came and slapped him on the back and had a word and I was introduced to them too but I'm afraid their names went in one ear and out the other, if I heard them at all.

"Sorry we're on soft drinks, Roy," said Jim to the barman. "I'm driving and later there's going to be a big do at the old homestead. Mother would skin me alive if I started the evening drunk!"

"Oh tha's orlright, son. I know as how you lords an' ladies live!" Roy gave me a broad wink and I smiled at him. "Is this your missis? A right pretty filly she is an' all; you've got a cracker there, my lord!"

Jim slung his arm around me.

"Yes, this is my intended."

"Intended what?" shouted one of Jim's mates and this remark was followed by raucous laughter. I laughed a bit with them but I wasn't amused really. I was seeing a different side to Jim. He was on his home patch, away from London and his usual crowd there and away from work. It seemed he had a few different faces. Still, I comforted myself that I was not likely to come here much, even after we married because Jim liked being in London too much.

We'd had strict instructions to be back at five, although quite why, I wasn't sure, because they had plenty of people to do everything; we only had to get ready. I think it was so that Caroline would be sure that Jim would be there, on the spot, and not down here drinking with his mates.

Anyway, we were back in time and we were served a light tea in the small dining room. The party would be held in the ballroom, which, I remembered, was magnificent. Caroline had maintained the room in its original Regency splendour; when she had decorated it, she had kept it exactly as it had always been, with the gold leaf around the huge mirrors and the colour scheme the same as it was before.

When it was time to go up and get ready, I couldn't help having a little thrill of excitement run through me at the thought of coming down that stairway. A maid came to help me get dressed. She was an older woman and she chatted away, telling me how she used to help her mistress to put on this dress and enthused about the balls that had been held here. It seemed kind of out of place in the twenty-first century somehow, kinda 'Upstairs, Downstairs' sort of stuff but hey-ho, I was going to enjoy this, I felt.

When Rachel had finished helping me on with the dress, she told me to wait in my room and Melissa would come to me. She was just dressing Madam's hair and would come when she was done there.

Thankfully, a spacious armchair was in the corner of my room and so I was able to sit there quite comfortably while I waited for the hairdresser. I had a book to read and was quite happy waiting.

A knock at the door and a call of 'hellooo' told me of her arrival and I called 'come in'. A small woman, not much older than myself, bounced in, carrying a case which I assumed was her hairdressing equipment.

Watching her turn my long hair into ringlets and fitting the pearl coronet on was fascinating. Fortunately, the mask clipped at the back so I didn't have to put it over my head. It had a soft lining under the brocade so it was comfortable to wear. A little pouch purse in matching material completed the outfit.

"There! You look just wonderful," Mel was enthusiastic. "You look like you just walked out of an Austin novel. You are going to turn heads when you go down those stairs."

"I don't know about turning heads, I'm going to have to be careful I don't trip and land on my head!" I giggled. She laughed.

"You won't. A dress like that automatically turns you into something elegant and aware of yourself and your posture. Walk across the room," she ordered.

I did so and found she was right. I seemed to have a built-in awareness of how to handle the way I walked and hold up the dress just the right height.

Quite a few people had already arrived when I left my room to go downstairs. As I walked, as elegantly as I could, one hand resting lightly upon the polished wood banister, I allowed myself a moment to dream that I was coming down to Mr. Darcy, who would step forward and take my hand and dance with me all evening.

"Madam, may I escort you?"

At the sound of a male voice, I came back to earth swiftly. Before me stood a masked male wearing s doublet and hose, finished with ornate leather boots and holding a top hat in hand, bowing. Not quite Mr Darcy but not bad at all.

"Jim?"

"At your service, ma'am."

He put out his arm and I took it in the manner of those Austin Days and together we walked towards the ballroom, where a string quartet was playing Mozart. There were already many people there in various costumes, all of them extravagant; they obviously knew what sort of ball they were coming to, even though the ballroom was decorated in a discreet way that suggested Halloween.

That was pretty much where the 'Halloween' began and ended, except perhaps for the rather lethal punch that was served later in the evening. The buffet, which was served in an adjoining room, was sumptuous beyond belief.

In spite of my reservations over the extravagance of the evening, I did enjoy it. I loved ballroom dancing and didn't often get the chance to do it. Jim was a good dancer too. I danced with quite a few other men, most of them I had no idea who they were, except for Jim's dad, Harry, who didn't dance much but made an exception to do a slow waltz with me. He was a very accomplished dancer and had a polish in his execution of the moves that Jim didn't have. It was a pleasure to dance with him and I told him so. He beamed with delight and complimented me on my light step.

At eleven o'clock, we all donned coats or cloaks and stepped out onto the wide patio that ran along the whole length of the ballroom outside and there we watched an extravagant firework display which went on for quite a while; I was not sure exactly how long it was but I know I was feeling pretty chilly by the time it was over. We all came in and were served with hot punch which helped us to thaw out after being outside. It warmed our hands as we held it and inside as we drank it. It was actually a bit too warming; I felt somewhat woozy after drinking mine.

The whole thing finished at midnight. Apparently, in the past, it was not unusual for such evenings to go on until two or even three in the morning but Harry had declared to his wife that midnight was quite late enough for him now and instructed that the end time be put on the invitations so that no misunderstandings would occur. I have no doubt that those who had to clear up afterwards were glad that it would not go on as late as they used to – also those who had to chauffeur guests home were relieved too. Some guests were to stay there for the night because they lived too far away.

James escorted me to my room and very chivalrously bowed rather unsteadily and kissed my hand. He took so long over it I thought he'd gone to sleep for a moment! In fact, I ended up giving him my arm to walk him safely to his room and I left him there after depositing him on the bed and untangling myself from his arms as he tried to persuade me to stay. He was already snoring when I left the room a few moments later and I giggled quietly to myself as I made my way back to my own room. I managed to get out of the dress and took off the headdress, gave my face a token wipe-over to remove the worst of my makeup and cleaned my teeth before falling into bed and I went to sleep almost before my head touched my pillow.

****

I slept in late the next morning but so did everyone else. It was ten o'clock by the time I came to sufficiently to get myself out of bed. I wandered into my bathroom and had a shower, making sure I cleansed my face properly after the hasty ministrations the night before. Thus scrubbed and polished, I put in an appearance downstairs getting on for eleven. Jim's parents were in the small dining room, Harry behind his newspaper and Caroline nibbling half-heartedly at a piece of toast. They looked up and greeted me as I came into the room rather hesitantly.

"I'm sorry I'm so late up," I began.

"Oh, don't worry, my dear," said Caroline. "We are late this morning, aren't we dear? And James hasn't put an appearance yet. Do help yourself to whatever you want." She waved a hand vaguely towards the sideboard, on which a variety of covered dishes and plates were. "Our other guests are all having breakfast in their rooms."

I went to investigate and, upon lifting the lid of some bacon as the delicious smell hit my nostrils, I discovered that I was actually hungry, so helped myself to bacon, scrambled eggs, a sausage and some toast. How lovely to have a breakfast that I hadn't got ready!

As I carried my plate to the table and sat down, Jim appeared, looking a bit dishevelled, in pyjama trousers and a t-shirt.

"Oh James, look at the state of you!" reprimanded his mother gently. "Come and have some coffee."

He came over and kissed her on the cheek and then kissed me on my cheek and sat down next to me. He helped himself to some coffee from the pot on the table and sat, languidly supping his drink. I looked at him drooping over the table and thought what a far cry he was from the romantic figure he cut last night. Was this the sight I would be seeing at the breakfast table when we were married?

"Mother! Whatever was in that punch? It was lethal! Look what it's done to me!" groaned Jim.

"I really couldn't say, dear," answered his mother, mildly. "We left that up to the caterers. We didn't have any, did we, Harry?"

"Just a drop, I dare not have any more. It was a trifle strong," replied her husband, lowering his paper. "You do look a sight, lad. You look like you need more sleep."

"Oh no, no more sleep! I just don't know how you can eat a breakfast like that, Luce," Jim said to me.

"Well, I only had a little of that punch too! I think you had rather more of it than you should have done. I had to take you to your room because you weren't capable of getting there yourself without falling over the banister or something."

"Oh thank you, that makes me feel tons better! I have to drive back to the city later. I think I'd better go have a shower, see if that will help."

"You won't go until after lunch, will you?" asked his mother.

"No, we will leave about the middle of the afternoon I should think."

"Maybe you will feel more like eating later. You can't drive back without having something in your stomach."

"Ugh!" James pushed back his chair and walked carefully away, one hand still clutching his head.

"I'll send someone up with some Alka-Seltzer!" Caroline called after him and we heard a distant 'thanks' come back. Caroline and I looked at each other and laughed.

"So much for a dashing 'Regency Buck'! The cold light of day and all that!"

There was no doubt I did like this woman; I appreciated her humour and the fact that she could laugh at her own son while still loving him.

After we had finished breakfast, she took me to the conservatory; a gorgeous glass oval furnished tastefully with light basket-weave furniture and big leafy plants. It really made you feel like you were in the garden but of course with the warmth of the indoors.

"I thought you'd enjoy being in here while you wait for my son to recover. This is one of my favourite parts of the house. I enjoy pottering around the plants or I just sit and read or do some knitting. It's wonderful to be in here and watch the outside, the birds flitting about and the fountain when it's on. I must get someone to switch it on for you so you can see it."

"I'd like that," I said and sat down on a seat. She sat down in a chair near to me.

"Tell me more about what you are doing in your lovely farmhouse."

So, I spent a pleasant hour or so talking with Caroline and telling her about my business and she told me some things about her family. Eventually she said that she had to go and pointed to where there was a book shelf with books and magazines.

"Feel free to read anything," she said. "I think I should go and see if my son has recovered and find out if we are almost ready for lunch. Someone will let you know when lunch is served if you haven't seen James by then. It's been lovely talking with you. I do miss female company sometimes."

"Thank you, it's been really nice to be here and have the chance to spend some time with you. Thank you for having me here."

"It's been a pleasure," she said and I could see that she meant it. I decided that Caroline would be good to have as a mother-in-law.

Chapter 29
Bonfire Night

I came home on the Wednesday following the weekend in Surrey. Two days shopping in London was quite enough for me. I did call in to see everyone at my previous work and spent a happy half an hour with them; I was quite surprised that I didn't feel any pull towards coming back, even though they said they wanted me to. Even if I went back to London, I would look for some other place to work but I didn't tell them that.

Coming home on the train I mused that I must have changed quite a bit because I used to love shopping in London; now, I couldn't wait to get back to my Herefordshire village. Just what would Jim say if I said that? He would be horrified, I knew.

Dad met me at the station and I rushed to hug him. I petted Butch, who was wagging his tail nineteen-to-the-dozen.

"Oh my! Anyone would think you'd been away for months! Did you have a good time, my little Lulu?"

"I feel like I've been away for ages – I couldn't wait to get home! I am longing for my own bed in my own beloved farmhouse and the quiet peacefulness around it. I've fallen out of love with London in a big way!"

Dad chuckled.

"Becoming a country bumpkin, are you? Just want to be surrounded by ducks, moorhens and cows! Or perhaps it's all those men you get coming over to tend your garden?"

"Oh you! Of course not, although they are a nice bunch. There's women too, you know. I just love the whole Sutton-on-Wye community, that's all."

"So, how did you get on at your future in-laws' place at the weekend?"

"It was good. I have to say, although they are stinking rich, they are nice people. They certainly know how to put on a 'do'. James' mother gave me this beautiful costume to wear; I felt so grand – and half afraid to wear it in case I did something to it! I felt like I'd just stepped out of a Jane Austin novel and Jim looked dashing in his matching outfit. He didn't look so dashing in the morning though; he drank too much of the punch and was an absolute mess the next day!"

We enjoyed our laughter as we drove up the Kings Acre Road and on past dad's bungalow and up towards my village. Butch seemed to know just where we were because as we drove into the village, he sat up and took notice, panting and excited. Once through the village we were soon up my lane and outside my house. Dad helped me to carry all my bags into the house.

"So, are you going to come to the Bonfire Night that's lined up for tomorrow night?" Dad asked as he deposited my bags on the kitchen floor.

"Hmm, I don't know. I've already seen a firework display at the weekend…"

"Sheila and I will come for you at seven," dad said, firmly. I waved him off and then went to sort out my shopping.

****

When I took my delivery down to Madge the next day, there were already at least two huge fair vehicles on the field. On my way back, there were quite a few more. I stopped my car up the lane away from the wide gated entrance and watched them for a while. It was amazing how they built up those rides, laid cables and all sorts. Later, when folks started coming in, everything would be set up and look as though they had always been there. I didn't care for fair rides but there was no doubt they would brighten up the whole scene.

The bonfire was to be lit at seven and the fireworks would be let off at half past. The gates would be open for people to come in for the fair as from twelve-thirty. My other field opposite was to be used for car-parking again. I really liked being the owner of land used by the community. It made me feel even more that I was an integral part of the village.

Just before seven I wrapped myself up in coat, scarf, woolly hat, gloves and wellington boots with thick socks. I popped a small torch in my pocket. When the knock came at my door, I was all ready. The three of us walked arm in arm down the lane, dad in the middle.

"A thorn between two roses," he said happily and we all grinned at each other.

I could already hear the music when I stepped out of my house and, after we'd walked around the slight bend in the lane, I could see the lights too. Coming up close to the field, I could see it was teaming with people, all wrapped up in hats and coats. The fair was ablaze with lights and reminded me of the sea-side and holidays when I was little. We paid our entrance fees and went into the field.

The whole place had a 'holiday' feel to it; the music of the fair, the throbbing of their generators, the candy-floss, the big sweetie lollies that the children had, the smell of hot dogs and donuts in the air.

The bonfire crackled as the flames grew, gradually gathering strength as it licked at the dry wood on the pile. Already we started to feel the heat as it came off the fire. We greeted people as they came into our line of vision and we recognised them under their woolly hats and scarves. We stood around conversing with friends or made a fuss of the children as they proudly showed us prizes they had won at the fair.

Time passed quickly; we didn't have long to wait before loud music started echoing through the loudspeakers situated around the field. As 'The Dambusters' filled the night, the fireworks began, dancing and fizzing to the music which changed according to the display. It was impressive; it was just as if the fireworks had practised to the music. There were many 'ooos' and 'aaahhhs' from the onlookers and even the fairground music had dimmed, it seemed, while the display was happening. It went on easily a full twenty minutes, then all was dark again, except for the fire, still licking the skies and spitting as it burned. The guy on the top looked blackened and forlorn. For some reason, it made me shudder and I turned away.

"Come with us love, you look frozen." Sheila took my hand and, with dad on her other side, she marched me up to a van. Before I knew it, she had thrust a large cup-carton of hot chocolate into my hands. It was so hot, the heat seeped through my gloves quickly, which was lovely. I wished I had another couple of them, one for each foot!

"I haven't seen Ken at all," I said, "Isn't he here?"

"Oh, he's about somewhere," Sheila replied vaguely "But of course he has been in charge of the display so that's why we haven't seen him. He may well turn up now – oh, there he is!"

I turned to see him heading in our direction.

"Hello mum, Tom. Hello, Lucy, back from your travels? What did you think of the display?"

"I thought it was very good, impressive," I replied warmly.

"It improves every year, you do us proud, son," said Sheila. "Don't you think it was good, Tom?"

"It was excellent. Just as good as any I've seen of large, organised events – in fact better than some I've seen."

"Thank you, I'm learning all the time."

"I've seen loads of people I don't know," said Sheila, "I think news of our event is travelling."

"Bound to, I'd say," dad said and clapped his hand on Ken's shoulder. "In fact, all the events I've been to here have been impressive and mostly due to you and your mother here."

"I –" began Ken, to be interrupted.

"Oh Kenneth, there you are! I've been looking all over for you!" We turned around and there was the girl who had been at the party with him.

"Glynis, you know I've been seeing to the firework display."

"Oh yeah, but that's all done now. I wanna go on the fair. Come on."

"You know I don't like fair rides."

"Whatever – just come. We're goin' on the bumper cars, it's no fun on yer own."

"Sorry, mum, Tom, Lucy. I suppose I'll have to go."

"Have fun!" Sheila shouted after him and he turned round and gave her a wry grin then hastened his steps to catch up with Glynis.

"I don't know why he's still seeing her, I'm sure," remarked Sheila. "They are like chalk and cheese."

"Opposites attract." Tom put in.

"'Suppose," Sheila shrugged. "Oh well, each to his own, I suppose."

In that moment I felt utterly tired and very cold.

"Dad, Sheila, I think I'm going home. I suddenly feel extremely tired. My days in London catching up with me, I suppose. I long for my bed."

"Actually, we've had enough too," said Sheila and looked at dad. He nodded. "We'll walk up the lane with you then go on to my house."

So, the three of us walked back up the lane together. The sounds of the fair got fainter as we drew away from it until it was just a throbbing beat thumping through the ground. Dad and Sheila left me at my door, I kissed them both and went thankfully into my warm kitchen. When I looked at the clock, I was surprised to see it was gone nine. I closed my curtains, made myself a Horlicks and took myself to bed early with a book, thankful for my electric blanket to bring the life back into my frozen feet.

Chapter 30
Clarry

The run up to Christmas was very busy. I was grateful for my London shopping trip, for I'd pretty much bought all my gifts – that, at least, I didn't have to be concerned about.

Now that the fruit season was more or less over, I was making pickles. Thankfully, I'd had the forethought to make a large amount of mincemeat in the summer (although how I found the time I don't really know) and it wasn't long before mince pies were the order of the day – in fact, pretty much every day. Madge was selling them like hot cakes, and it seemed that almost everyone who came to the nursery café wanted them too. Every day, the thing that went into my ovens after the bread, were the mince pies. Strangely, I wasn't that keen on them myself but if others wanted them, who was I to object? They were bringing a good income to me. Madge was thrilled.

"Your mince pies are every bit as good as your aunt's," she said to me enthusiastically. "My customers love them. Will you take orders for Christmas week? Folks are bound to want them for the actual Christmas period."

"Of course. I'd like the orders the week before, if possible, so that I can make sure I fill all of them properly."

"No problem, that's what we used to do for Bea."

The weather was getting colder, the nights were dark early. Jim wasn't able to come so often because he said his works were very busy in the run-up to Christmas. As I always had a great deal to do, I was actually quite glad. When he did come, it was often too cold to go out anywhere, although we did used to eat lunch out sometimes, preferring to stay in the warm house in the evenings and eat at home.

I found that Jim got quite perturbed when he heard the Footsteps, which came fairly regularly. I'd got used to them and took no notice, but it made him edgy. We didn't hear any doors slamming again; that other time must have been a draught. Jim would pace the room, after going upstairs to look, poker in hand, to find nothing.

"I just can't figure out what it is," he would say. "I don't like it, Lucy, I don't like it at all."

"It doesn't bother me, Jim. I know it's nothing."

"You shouldn't be here on your own."

"It's okay, believe me. I'm fine. It doesn't frighten me at all."

"Well, I don't like it."

We agreed that we would spend Christmas with our prospective families this year as we were likely to be a married couple by the following Christmas. Jim said he would come and see me a couple of weeks before and then come after it in January and we would have our own Christmas together, just us. I was quite happy about this; I'd been invited to Sheila's for Christmas Day as obviously she invited dad. I looked forward to having a simple Christmas with my family. The past two I had spent with Jim and now I felt guilty about that, especially now Aunt Bea was gone. How she would have loved one more with the three of us together. I suppose there was no point in moping about it, but still, I was happy about this year's arrangements.

When Jim arrived two weeks before Christmas as promised, he was being very mysterious.

"I know we said we would have a time for our own celebrations after Christmas, but I have a special something that I have to give you now."

"Oh, won't it keep until later?" I asked, intrigued.

"Not at all. Go into the lounge and, when I say so, hold out your arms and close your eyes."

Even more puzzled, I did as I was bid. A few minutes later, I heard Jim say from the other side of the door, "Now, close your eyes and hold out your arms. Don't peek now."

I stood in the middle of the room, arms out, eyes closed, wondering what was going on. When I felt something small, warm and furry being put into my arms, my eyes flew open.

"Oh! Oh! Isn't he sweet? What is he?" I held the little white bundle that was squirming in my arms, a small nose and tiny pink tongue reached out for me excitedly.

"*She's* a Schnoodle – a cross between a Schnauzer and a poodle, which means she won't get big and she's non-allergic, which you need in an animal as you're making food. I looked into it all very carefully and decided this breed would be best for you."

"She's lovely, but really, why do I need a dog?"

"She will keep you company and maybe help you sort out those footsteps. Dogs sense when something is wrong. As I can't be here all the time, I'll be happy knowing you have her with you."

"Well, that's a very kind thought, darling," I said, although I wasn't too happy really, having a dog wasn't something I'd had planned on doing.

"I have everything you need; basket, blanket, food bowls and food, a harness and lead. She's still a puppy at the moment so you have the chance to train her. She's had all her injections too, so you don't need to worry about that."

'*Oh goody,*' I thought, '*A puppy to train, just what I need right now.*'

I had to admit though, that it didn't take me long to fall in love with my wee dog. I called her Clarrissa, 'Clarry' for short.

"Stupid name for a dog," remarked Jim but I noticed that he made a fuss of her whenever he got the chance. Just as well he liked her, for she would be with us when we were married.

When Jim had returned home on the Sunday evening, I called dad to tell him about my new 'baby'.

"We'll come round and meet her," he told me.

When Sheila saw Clarry, she was immediately in love.

"What a darling," she said as she held Clarry in her arms and the dog was trying to lick her face. "I'll help you to train her, I used to teach a dog training class, a few years ago. When I lost my dog, I hadn't heart to get another one."

"Well, now you have Butch and Clarry to share," I remarked. Was there anything this woman couldn't do?

"Yes, I love Butch of course. I think they should meet as soon as possible. We want them to be friends, don't we?"

"Oh yes indeed. I wonder what they will think of each other?"

"We will bring Butch over tomorrow evening."

"I must say that Jim has gone up in my estimation," said dad. "He must care about you and worry about you being here alone to give you a dog because I don't think he's that keen on dogs, is he?"

"Not usually, but he does have a sneaky liking for Clarry. I have to admit that I didn't really want a dog because I'm handling food all the time and have trays of freshly-cooked cakes and things sitting on worktops and tables when I'm busy. There will be times when she will have to be shut in the den, perhaps, but I admit I do rather like her – and I like that Jim cared enough to bring her for me. Like you, dad, there have been some times when I have not been sure that he really cares for me but I think this shows that he does."

The others nodded in agreement.

"I will be very grateful for any help and advice you can give me, Sheila. I've never had a puppy before."

"No problem at all, my love. I'm happy to help."

****

I was glad that it was near Christmas and, apart from what I supplied to Madge and the nursery café, I cut my work right down in order to be with and train Clarry. I had to admit, although a little challenging at times, I did enjoy having her. I was thankful that, because she was so small she didn't require long walks. Not that I minded walking, it was just that I knew that in my busy periods I just wouldn't have time to go on long rambles for the sake of my dog. She soon learned to do her business outside and in fact she was quite picky where she did it. Clarry was great company; she loved to sit on my lap and I enjoyed the cosiness and the closeness of her little warm body. She and Butch became friends instantly; I'm sure Butch thought he was her mother as he would fuss around her. As she grew though, it was obvious who was boss in that doggy duo!

Whenever Jim called me, he always asked how she was getting on and I would proudly report each achievement and he would be suitably impressed. Fortunately, she took to the den and was happy to stay in there in her basket when I was doing my baking. I had no wish to be in trouble with Food and Hygiene inspectors. It helped that she was non-allergic, being of poodle extraction she did not shed her hair, but would have to be trimmed from time to time.

The first time she heard the Footsteps, she growled at the door, then looked at me and whined. I took her on my lap and soothed her because she was shivering in fright. I'm not sure that it comforted me, having her quivering in fright on my lap! I hadn't been frightened of the Footsteps before and now I was more concerned with trying to make Clarry feel better. I hoped she would grow to be able to cope with the noises.

She slept in my bedroom at night. I used to take her basket up every night but she shunned it in favour of curling up on a blanket by the side of my bed and if she could she would sneak up to sleep on my feet. In the end, she just always slept there and I gave up and let her – after all, there was only the two of us. I didn't concern myself with any thoughts on how Jim would take it when we were married. Clarry seemed completely at ease when upstairs with me which was a relief to me; it showed me that there really was nothing there.

Chapter 31
Christmas in Sutton-on-Wye

Christmas Eve came at last and it was late in the day when I finally could allow myself to relax. I had fulfilled and delivered all my orders.

"Come on, Clarry, let's go for walkies," I called my wee dog, who capered around my feet excitedly. I just managed to catch her to clip her lead on and she then ran round the kitchen, the lead following her like a devoted snake while I put on my scarf, coat and gloves. Shortly afterwards we set off.

Clarry was getting quite good walking on the lead, although she did pull a bit. However, she was such a tiny thing that her tugging made little impact upon me. I decided to take her through the walled garden and into the grounds of Sutton Court. I knew Neil and Cessy wouldn't mind, especially if we kept on the path that ran along the periphery fence on the river side of their garden.

It was a lovely day, cold and crisp but bright. My breath puffed out like miniature ghosts before my face. We walked briskly and soon I felt quite warm. Clarry enjoyed discovering places she'd not been to before, sniffing and snuffling in the bushes.

"Hello there, Lucy, Happy Christmas to you!"

I heard a voice sing out and turned to see Cessy.

"Hello, thank you. Happy Christmas to you. Good to see you, we haven't met for a while."

"Well, we are both busy people." Cessy laughed as she caught up with me, a little breathless from hurrying. "I heard you had a little dog now. Isn't she sweet?"

She bobbed down on her haunches to pet Clarry, who greeted her enthusiastically, body wriggling so much you could hardly tell her front from her back. She licked at my friend's face, who held her off so her tongue couldn't quite reach. I waited while they became aquainted.

"So, how are things?"

"Oh, Lucy, don't you just love Christmas? Penny has come home for the holidays and so we are all together. She has been doing well at University but it's been so hard to have her away. It's the first time the family has been apart and we have missed her but we are really proud of her."

"I'm so glad."

"Will you be going to the torchlight service tonight?"

"What's that?"

"Oh, it's lovely. It begins at eleven o'clock and ends just after midnight because this is the night that Jesus Christ was born – or so they say – so we all light our torches to symbolise that the Light of the World has come. It's a joyful service and usually everyone in the village, even people who don't usually go to church, attend. For at least one night, the whole village is united."

"It sounds wonderful. I'll ask my dad if he is going with Sheila."

"I've no doubt he will. He seems to have become part of that family." Cessy looked at me, eyes twinkling and I laughed back at her.

"Yes, he has indeed. I've never seen him look so content and happy."

"Sheila looks happy too. She had a terribly sad time when her husband was ill and then died. She's such a lovely person, I am glad that she has found someone else to love. So, what about you, Lucy, any wedding bells coming up for you at any point? Your Jim has been visiting very regularly, I've heard."

"Can't keep a secret here," I grinned. "We are talking about possibly the summer, after I've been here for a year."

"You won't leave us, will you?" Cessy looked so alarmed that I was amused.

"To be honest, I really don't think I could bring myself to leave here. Jim will have to commute or something. We haven't worked out the mechanics yet but we've plenty of time."

"Oh yes, of course you have. I think we should move, I don't know about you but I'm pretty cold standing here."

"Yes indeed, it seems not at all bad but when you stop you realise you can't feel your feet after a few minutes! I will see you tonight at church then. Come on Clarry, I think we've had enough for this afternoon. Cheerio, Cessy."

"Cheerio, Lucy."

She hurried off across the lawn towards the big house and I hastened back along towards the walled garden with Clarry trotting at my feet.

****

At half past ten that night, I joined dad, Sheila, Joseph and Kenny and we all got into Sheila's car ('It's easier to park than the Land Rover') and drove down to the village. I had been invited to spend the night at the Nursery House and so Clarry and I had gone there earlier with the things we needed for a short stay. I was going to spend the day with them anyway so it made sense for us to stay – after all, there was plenty of room for us there. Dad was going to drive home and come back in the morning so I could use the spare room. I had protested that I could do that, after all, I only lived a stone's throw away and dad lived in Hereford but they all insisted so I gave in. I think I didn't really want to be on my own in the house at Christmas anyway; there's something sad about being alone at this time.

I spared a thought for all lonely or homeless people; somehow things like that seem worse at Christmas time and I knew I was so blessed to have a family to be with, even if they were not really my family (except dad of course) but they felt like family. Joseph was like a granddad to me and Ken was like a brother – well, almost like a brother but not quite. There was something about him that I couldn't quite fathom; I couldn't fault his behaviour, he helped me with my garden, with my deliveries and was always friendly but, ever since the day he came to me by the river, he's been a little distant, as if he'd stepped back a bit.

The village looked lovely with a large Christmas tree on the green, shining bright with many coloured lights and every street lamp (of which there were only about six) had a snowflake or a candle or a shooting star in lights and in between were strung loads of multi-coloured lights. There were also strings of lights along the path up to the church door and tiny lights were wound round some of the trees in the churchyard, transforming the place from a sombre graveyard to a fairyland.

The service was indeed, something quite special. The little old church was decorated with battery-operated candles (real candles deemed too much of a fire risk in these modern days) and Christmas Roses and greenery were on each one of the window ledges and at the ends of each pew. At the front of the church was an illuminated crib scene, also made attractive by more greenery. Cessy was right; it seemed the whole village had turned out for this service, children and all, it was a packed house.

This was not the usual sort of Parish church service; there were readings of scriptures or poetry or inspired pieces from – somewhere or other – and we sang lots of carols. There's something pretty special about carols sung to a church organ and the villagers gave it their all, singing their hearts out in joy, the children no doubt looking forward to lots of presents the next day and their parents hoping that the late night out would keep the kids in bed in the morning until a decent hour!

I noted that Joseph, sitting next to me and Kenny on the other side of him both had fine voices. Obviously runs in the family, I thought, but is there anything that Kenny can't do? The other thing that sort of surprised me was that, when the vicar, the Reverend Tony Trevithick, gave a very short sermon near the end, Joseph took my hand and held onto it on his lap. His felt a little rough and slightly papery, very 'old man-ish' but warm and I found it strangely comforting and was content to let my hand rest in his. When he let me go in order to pick up the hymnbook, he smiled at me and I smiled back, feeling a little teary but happy at the same time. Before I looked away from him, I noticed Ken also looking. He must have noticed his grandfather holding my hand. Our eyes met for a moment and I understood his expression was a mixture of approval and thanks. I smiled at him too and gave a slight nod to him to let him know I understood.

As we all filed out of the church, having our hands shaken by the vicar, it seemed that people were reluctant to go to their homes. They moved around, greeting each other with 'Happy Christmas' or 'Merry Christmas'. I received many hugs and greetings. It was lovely; I enjoyed it so much.

What happened next really surprised me. When every last person was out of the church, we moved as one body almost, down the churchyard path, out onto the road and along only a couple of minutes' walk to the village green and surrounded the big Christmas Tree.

When we were all there, we joined hands with our neighbours and sang 'O Come, All Ye Faithful' together. Obviously everyone knew the words because every verse was sung, ending with 'Ye, Lord we greet thee, Born this happy morning...' When we were done, the Reverend Trevithick, now with his coat on, put his hands in the air and said, 'Thank you, Father, for the Gift of Your Son.' Everyone said 'Amen' and then he said, 'Merry Christmas, everyone, and may you have a blessed day.' Everyone clapped and then gradually, the crowd dispersed. I watched them go in different directions, some smaller children, very tired now, being carried by their parents.

Dad put his arm around me.

"I've never seen anything like this before, dad," I said to him.

"Nor have I, Lulu. It's lovely, isn't it? I really like this village."

"Me too. It would be very hard to leave it now."

"What will you do when you get married? You'd have to live where Jim would want or need to live."

"Yes. Bit of a problem really." We stood in silence for a moment, then, "Well, I'm not going to worry about that now. Happy Christmas, Dad." I kissed his cheek and he held me close for a moment before offering his arm to Sheila. I watched them fondly and fell into step behind them with Joseph, who smiled at me and tucked my hand into his arm. Of Kenny there was no sign, I hadn't noticed him disappear.

"Oh, I expect he's gone off with that girl of his and her family. He'll be waiting for us at the car," was Joseph's explanation when I'd remarked on it. "Can't think what he sees in her, she's a madam. Especially with such a lovely next-door neighbour – he should be making a play for you, my dear – I know I would be if I was his age!"

"Why, thank you, kind sir!" I laughed. "But Kenny's not interested in me and besides, I'm engaged."

"Oh, since when did that matter? When I met my wife, God rest her soul, she was engaged to another chap."

"Was she? What happened then?"

"Well, as soon as I met her, I knew she had to be mine, so I made sure I was always there when she needed something doing or help in any way. I told her I loved her and it turned out she loved me! So she broke off her engagement and married me instead. We both knew it was right, you see."

I was to recall those wise words a few months later.

****

After that late night, I overslept but it didn't matter, for we were all late up, except for Sheila who was already bustling around the kitchen by the time I got downstairs. When I tried to apologise she waved me away.

"Oh don't you worry, dear. I just had to make sure I got the turkey into the oven on time. We don't like to eat a big meal too late in the evening, even Christmas Dinner. We will have dinner about five. In the meantime, I will lay out a light buffet so we can eat whenever we feel peckish. Now, what would you like for breakfast?"

"Oh, anything. A piece of toast will be fine. I don't want to put you to any trouble, Sheila, I'm just grateful to be here."

I put Clarry, who I'd been carrying, on the floor.

"I think I'd better just take this young lady outside. She must be bursting by now but she's been very good."

"You do that and I'll do your breakfast while you're out."

I took my coat from the hook by the door where I'd left it the previous night and this girl and her dog stepped outside into the chilly air.

When we came back (we weren't out long, it was too cold), the wonderful smell of bacon met my nostrils and made my mouth water. In spite of my protests that a piece of toast was enough, I was soon tucking into a plateful of bacon, eggs, beans, and hash browns – heaven! Sheila's two menfolk joined me soon after and were presented with their English Breakfasts too. The four of us sat in companionable silence while we ate. Sheila even presented Clarry with her own bit of bacon, all chopped up, which she ate with relish and then sat hoping for more. She had no chance!

"That was wonderful, Sheila, thank you so much," I said. "Can I wash up for you?"

"Oh no, they will go in the dishwasher, don't worry," she replied. She looked at her watch. "I think your dad should be here soon."

"Come through into the lounge," invited Joseph, and so I followed him through, Clarry at my heels.

The lounge looked beautiful, decorated so tastefully and yet very festive, with garlands around the wooden support columns or stanchions and along the mantle and the wrought ironwork balustrade that edged the upstairs landing that stretched over one side of the room. There was a fine Christmas tree here too and the lights already sparkled and twinkled.

As I joined Joseph on one of the sofas, I heard dad arrive, greeted by Sheila. Butch rushed in ahead of him and galloped up to me, greeting me in his usual enthusiastic way, then to Joseph and finally gave his attention to Clarry who was dancing around his feet. Joseph and I were laughing at their antics when dad came into the room. I hastened up to put my arms around him and kiss him.

"Happy Christmas, dad."

"Happy Christmas, my Lulu."

He turned to Joseph and shook his hand.

"Happy Christmas, Joseph."

"The same to you, son. Now, come on in, don't stand on ceremony! Would you like a drink or anything?"

"A cup of tea would be nice. I'll come and help you, Sheila, my dear."

Joseph and I smiled at each other as we watched dad follow Sheila from the room.

"Come and sit here, my dear while we wait for our refreshments."

I sat down next to him and he took my hand in his again. Clarry made herself comfortable on my lap.

"So, what did you think of our midnight custom last night?" Joseph asked me, his eyes twinkling at me. I found myself thinking that he must have been a very attractive man in his time for he was still handsome in a faded sort of way – and I realised how like Kenny he was.

"Well, I have never experienced anything quite like that before," I replied. "I liked it though, it made the whole village feel like family."

"It does. We have been doing that for many years, a tradition that's been handed down since the time we started having a tree in the middle of the village. Not sure when it started but it seems that everyone likes it and so it happens every year without fail, whatever the weather."

Joseph and I were soon deep in conversation about all sorts that for quite a while we failed to notice the non-appearance of dad and Sheila. About an hour passed when they finally made an entrance into the lounge, each bearing a tray. I looked up and noticed that Sheila was looking rather flushed. I looked from her to dad and saw that he was looking quite smug. What had they been up to?

Kenny reappeared from upstairs; he'd obviously had a shower and freshly shaved, his hair wet but combed neatly. I couldn't help looking at him; I rarely saw him like this. His eyes caught mine for a moment and he smiled but then he looked away from me to his mum.

"Hello, you look like the cat that's got the cream, mum. Have I missed something?"

Dad and Sheila had put down their trays on the table and now he took her by the hand.

"I have just asked your mother if she will marry me and she said yes," dad said, and he kissed Sheila's hand.

Kenny was the first to give her a hug and shake dad's hand, followed by Joseph and lastly me and I hugged them both. Then I admired the lovely ring that dad had just given her.

"Well," Joseph declared, "Thank goodness you've got around to it at last. I'm glad someone around here has some sense!"

We all laughed but as I did so, I again caught Kenny's eye briefly and he held the look for a few brief seconds then he looked down. Something stirred inside me and I felt confused – did I see what I thought I saw?

"Shall we have some coffee or tea to celebrate? It's rather early for champagne, we'll have that later." Sheila turned towards the coffee pot and started pouring.

"We usually play a game now until lunch, unless the weather is nice enough for a walk but it isn't really, it's very cold. What shall we play?"

We decided to play Cluedo and soon we were all immersed trying to find out who did it and where.

Lunch was a light finger buffet and we all made a concerted effort not to eat too much, knowing we had our Christmas dinner coming later. At half-past one, Sheila said, "We need to get ready now, I think."

"What for?" I asked, eyebrows raised.

"We go to Sutton Court to sing carols to the residents there. Didn't anyone tell you? We do it every year and some others from the village come too. We usually have a great time and the residents love it."

"Oh! No, I didn't know. I'm not very good at singing," I said.

Joseph squeezed my hand. "You're fine. I was sitting next to you last night and I thought you had a very nice voice."

"I think you're just biased towards me, Joseph!" I laughed. "But it's a wonderful thing to do."

"I need a few minutes' nap," said Joseph, "I'll follow you later."

"Why don't you, Tom and Lucy go ahead, mum, and I will bring granddad when he's had his nap?"

"Well, I think I should just give Clarry a little walk. Do you want me to walk Butch as well, dad?"

"No, we'll take Butch with us, he likes visiting Sutton Court."

"He's been there before then?"

"Oh yes, we've taken him a few times, haven't we, my dear?"

"Yes," replied Sheila, "the residents love to see him and he's so good with them. When Clarry is a bit older, you should take her to visit them, Lucy."

"What a great idea, I'll do that. But I'd better take her for a run now so I can leave her here when we go."

"I'll come with you, shall I, Lucy?" That was from Ken. I was a bit startled but I tried not to show it.

"That would be lovely."

"Will you all please go away so this old man can have a rest?" Joseph grumbled good naturedly.

I kissed him and then went to fetch my coat.

Ken and I walked Clarry along the river path towards my house. We walked side by side in silence. He courteously opened gates for me. Clarry had to run to keep up with us and then I let her off the lead so she could sniff at the bushes and trees.

"So, Lucy, what do you think of living here?"

"I love it."

"What will you do when you get married? Will you have to move away?"

"I don't want to move away."

"What if he insists?"

"I don't know."

A silence followed and I walked with my head down. I didn't want to think about it, didn't want to face a time when I would leave this place. I loved my farmhouse and my work and I loved the village. I wanted to be here with dad and have a family of my own, which Sheila's family would be. I liked Jim's parents, especially his mother, but somehow I couldn't see myself ever being comfortably part of their family.

"So…what about you? Is there a future for you and Glynis?" I asked, wanting to steer the conversation away from my uncomfortable thoughts.

Ken, who also seemed deep in thought, started slightly.

"Good grief, no!"

"Really? I thought you were getting on well with her."

"She's ok but she is not the marrying type. She's too set on having a good time. She's had a tough life growing up on the farm and she's making the most of her freedom now. I certainly don't think she would settle for being the wife of a nurseryman."

"Do you love her?"

He stopped and looked at me for what seemed like a long time but was probably only a few moments.

"No, I don't love her. I think we should go back now or we'll miss the singing at Sutton Court."

Without another word, we both turned around and retraced our steps back to the Baxter house.

Chapter 32
Boxing Day Beauty

The afternoon at Sutton Court was a wonderful time. Madge and her husband, Dot and her family and quite a few others from the village were there to sing the carols with us. Sheila was great as usual, encouraging the residents to join in with the singing. The vicar was there too, to offer a prayer and to join his lovely baritone with us. Butch was a star and was petted, patted and stroked by so many people and everyone looked happy.

After the singing we visited with the residents and their visiting families, if they had any, paying particular attention to those who had no visitors. Ken took Sheila home earlier than us so she could get on with the dinner; she refused my offer to go back with her and help, insisting that we should all stay and talk with the residents. Ken came back for Joseph, dad, Butch and me and we were back at the Baxter home by about four-thirty.

When we got back, the table had been set already; it looked beautiful with a festive cloth, mats and napkins with crackers at each place and four candles down the middle in between mats where the serving dishes would be laid. We all helped to bring the food dishes through, the delicious smells making our mouths water.

It was a wonderful meal; the food and the conversation flowed easily. The white wine that was served was light and of good quality – not that I was very knowledgeable about wine. We mostly drank water though; it was easy to see that this family were not big alcohol drinkers; the wine was a token gesture because it was a celebration. The meal was so good and filling that we were all grateful to have a light dessert of crème Brule that Sheila had made herself.

When we had finished the meal it was time for presents at last and I went upstairs to fetch my gifts for everyone. There followed a grand time of giving and receiving. I had found it quite hard to buy gifts for Joseph and Ken as I didn't know them so well but the beautiful soft Scottish woven scarves I gave them were well received. For Sheila I gave her a gorgeous leather handbag which I had fallen in love with and thought it perfect for her and she loved it, I could tell. Joseph immediately cuddled into his scarf and refused to be parted from it, even in the warm room! Ken smiled and said it would look very nice with his best suit.

Sheila gave me a scrumptious cashmere jumper and dad gave me a silver bracelet. Ken presented me with a book about wild flowers and herbs and Joseph gave me a tiny bottle of perfume. I felt very lucky indeed.

After the gifts, Ken brought in a bottle of champagne, popped the cork and when we had all filled our glasses, he stood up and proposed a toast to his mum and my dad, in celebration of their engagement. I hadn't often had champagne and I wrinkled my nose as the bubbles jumped up it. As I drank, I thought it quite overrated really but perhaps I could get used to it. However, with five people a bottle didn't go far. When I stood up, I thought it was probably just as well, for there was little doubt that and the wine mixed was taking effect. This concerned me because I was supposed to be going home that night, or so I thought, but there was no way they were going to let me go. For this I was thankful; not only was I not safe to be alone but I didn't want to be alone, not on Christmas night, so I didn't argue too much.

That night, in spite of the alcohol, I did not rest terribly well. My dreams seemed disturbing somehow, although I couldn't really say why, although it seemed shot through with Kenny's face and I kept hearing his voice *'no, I don't love her.'*

When I woke in the morning and could get up, I was thankful. I decided that I would have breakfast and go home as soon as I decently could. Engaged as I was, and, much as I loved being with this family, I felt that the less time I spent in Kenny's company the better.

However, Sheila and Joseph insisted that I stay because we were all going on a trip that afternoon. I was intrigued and felt that I couldn't go home without appearing churlish and I didn't want to upset dad at this special time of his.

Lunch was left-overs from Christmas dinner and was every bit as tasty as it had been the day before, only there wasn't so much of it. So today, Christmas Pudding was presented, with a choice of cream or custard. I only had a little, feeling that I'd eaten far too much over the past couple of days already.

Joseph decided that he would stay at home after all. "My old bones don't like the cold".

The dogs were coming with us this time and both were excited to get into the back of the Freelander. Clarry had to be lifted up but Butch was able to jump in. Dad and Sheila both got in the back, so that left me to sit in the front passenger seat next to Kenny. His face was impassive as he drove. I stole a glance at his side profile as he concentrated on the road. He wasn't bad looking, I thought, or perhaps I was just getting used to him now that I'd known him for a while? I recalled my dreams of last night and reflected that it was like a constant confirmation that Kenny wasn't in love with Glynis, but really, what was that to do with me? Although somehow I couldn't help feeling glad that he wasn't.

This was the furthest I'd been with him driving; before it had been short rides down to the village or nearby to deliver my jams. He was an expert driver, dealing with the winding Herefordshire roads with ease.

I looked in the mirror inset into the sun visor on my side and noticed that dad and Sheila were sitting as close as their seat belts would allow, his arm around her and she had her head resting upon his shoulder. I smiled to myself but also felt a pang that I wasn't experiencing something similar. Jim was fairly gentlemanly when we were in a public place but he wasn't very demonstrative. He rarely cuddled me and certainly never held my hand in the car or anything like that. Having said that, if Kenny wanted to hold my hand it would be nearly impossible in the Freelander; it wasn't built for togetherness.

I realised where we were going when we'd been on the road for about fifteen minutes; we were going up Hay Bluff, I thought. I was right. Kenny parked in a small car park and we got out and went for a walk. It was beautiful up there; even in the summer it was stark but now, in winter, it was much more so. The wind was cutting; our noses were soon reddened as were our cheeks. We were all glad we were well wrapped up. However, it was exhilarating. Dad and Sheila walked arm in arm, Butch at dad's heels. I followed with Clarry excitedly skipping around me, getting me twisted up in the lead and threatening to trip me up until Kenny came to my rescue and helped me to get untangled, laughing together. He was attractive when he laughed, I mused. I called Clarry to heel and made her calm down, which she did and we resumed our walk. Without being asked, Kenny took my hand and tucked it into the crook of his arm to make sure I didn't stumble on the uneven ground and I found that I felt content to let it stay there.

The view from up here was simply stunning; we could see for miles all around us. As we walked, the sun started to go down and the skies were painted with brilliant pinks and oranges. I stopped and drew in my breath. I turned towards my companion.

"Oh, isn't it wonderful? What a gorgeous sunset and it's even better from up here. Don't you think it's amazing, Kenny?"

He looked down at me, smiling. "It is. It's what we come up here for, especially on Boxing Day if it's a clear day. It reminds us that we live in a wonderful world and helps us to be thankful."

"You come up here every Boxing Day?"

"Yes, if the weather is okay and it's safe to come up here. It's not always possible of course."

"Thank you for bringing me up here with you today."

"Wouldn't have dreamed of coming without you, especially now."

"With dad becoming part of your family you mean?"

He drew breath to answer but at that moment, dad and Sheila joined us.

"Right, we've had enough now, we're cold, let's go," said Sheila.

We climbed into the Freelander and whatever Kenny was going to say was never said. I did wonder what he would have said but decided he was probably going to agree that it was because my dad was almost part of them so I was too.

On the way back down we came to a country pub and went in to have a drink and a ploughman's. We didn't have alcohol though, we opted for tea. Kenny wouldn't have drunk anyway; he was conscientious about drinking and driving and in any case, he needed all his wits about him to drive back along those twisty roads in the dark.

I stayed again for another night but then I said that I should go home. I kissed Sheila and Joseph and thanked them for letting me stay.

"It's the best Christmas I've had for a while," I said. "It's special to have the people you love around you at this time. I now feel bad that last Christmas I missed out on spending with it dad and Aunt Bea. I stayed in London because I had so little time off and Jim wanted me to spend it with him."

"Your aunt understood and so did I," dad assured me. "We kept each other company and we did talk with you."

I had indeed called them on Christmas Day. At that remembrance, I suddenly realised that I'd heard nothing from Jim at all over Christmas and I hadn't even noticed.

Chapter 33
A New Year

When I opened the door of River View, the house phone started to ring. I dumped my bag on the kitchen table and went to pick the phone off its cradle on the kitchen wall.

"Lucille, where have you been? I've been calling and calling your mobile but couldn't get an answer and I've been calling this number over and over." Before I'd even said 'hello', Jim's voice came at me, accusingly. I went over to my handbag and fished around for my phone. It was dead, run out of battery and I'd never even noticed.

"Oh Jim, I'm sorry, my phone must have run out of charge and I never realised," I said.

"But where have you been? I tried to call you last night and again today."

Suddenly, I was angry, although I couldn't give myself a good reason.

"Where do you think I was? Did you think I was going to sit alone in my house on Christmas Day, hoping you might call me? You decided not to spend Christmas with me, although I abandoned my family last year to be with you. Why should I be alone when I have family to be with?"

There was a silence the other end, then,

"But I tried to call you on your mobile, remember? It wouldn't have mattered where you were then. But it seems you didn't care enough to make sure it was charged so I could call you."

I was wracked with guilt then; the fault was mine, I hadn't checked and I was a little bit drunk last evening because of the champagne so no wonder I didn't think of it.

"I'm sorry, I think the champagne must have driven all coherent thoughts from my head."

"Champagne? Why were you drinking Champagne?" He was suspicious now, I could hear it in his voice.

"Dad and Sheila got engaged and we were toasting them."

"You were at *that man's* house for Christmas? I thought you would be at your father's."

"Well, I was with my father and as he was at Sheila's, I was too. They weren't going to let me be on my own at Christmas. "And 'that man', as you call him, did absolutely nothing wrong." (*'Darn it,' a little voice in my head said and I tried to push it away.*)

"He'd better not," Jim's voice took on a threatening edge. "How would you like to come to my parents' to see the New Year in? They'd love to have you."

"That would be nice," I said brightly.

"Fine. I'll come over on Thursday, stay the night and we'll drive down on Friday. See you then." The phone his end cut off and I was left staring at the phone my end as it buzzed in my hand. As I put it back on the wall, I had to admit to myself that I really didn't want to go.

****

Thursday came and Jim didn't arrive until early evening. About half an hour before he arrived a strange thing happened. I thought a car drove past the house – you know how it is, a light goes across the ceiling as the headlights show through the crack in the curtains, although I didn't hear anything. Clarry pricked up her ears and then lay down again. I thought it must have been someone who drove up the lane by mistake because there was nothing beyond my house, only the river. The lane came to a dead end just past my garden.

About five or ten minutes later, Clarry's ears pricked up again and she listened intently, head tilting from side to side and at one point, she growled. She scrabbled at the lounge door and when I let her out, she scurried up the stairs, barking. I followed, my heart in my mouth. She went to the end bedroom where Jim usually slept and faced the far wall, growling.

"What is it, Clarry? There's nothing there, it's just a wall."

She sniffed around the wall as if looking for something and turned to me and whined a little.

"Silly girl, Clarry! It's probably only a rat or something in the barn. Come on downstairs. Come on girl!"

I waited by the door for her to come to me, which she did, with a last listen at the wall. Her claws made a clicketty sound on the wooden floor. I picked her up and carried her down the stairs and we went back to the comfort of my armchair.

When Jim knocked on the door, I jumped. I had not heard his car come down the drive. Clarry greeted him in her usual effusive way and it wasn't long before he was sat down with her on his lap.

****

The weekend was fine; Jim's parents, especially his mother, seemed pleased to see me. The party went off with Caroline's usual flair, ending just after midnight with an even more spectacular display of fireworks. I couldn't help wondering why we felt it so necessary to celebrate the New Year with fireworks. I made sure that Clarry, who had come with us, was safely shut in my bedroom so that she wouldn't be afraid. Sunday was a quiet day; no doubt most of the population were resting in bed after a night of indulgence.

I couldn't wait to be home again; this weekend had shown me that I just wasn't cut out for this kind of life and I didn't want to live with Jim in this mansion, although it was beautiful, after his parents had left it. Jim seemed to assume that one day it would be his and would spend time with his father, looking at papers and discussing matter of estate business. I didn't know how I was going to tell him that I didn't want the life he had.

****

The night we got back from Jim's parents, the Footsteps came again. Clarry growled and Jim looked at me, scowling.

"There's that sound again. I hate thinking of you here when that happens. I worry about you, Lucy."

"You've no need. I know it's nothing. Whatever is making it, does nothing more than make the noise. It's strange, because I haven't heard it for some time, several weeks, I think."

"Maybe it decided to take time off for Christmas," he joked. Then, more seriously, "what if it becomes more than footsteps, what will you do?"

"How can it become more? It's only ever been just that. Admittedly, sometimes it comes at random times. I've heard it in the mornings. Apparently, Ken heard it when he discovered Aunt Bea's body and that was during a morning. It's strange but I suppose time has no significance in the afterlife."

"Hmm."

By the time we'd had this conversation, the Footsteps had stopped and Clarry was again snoozing on Jim's lap.

I saw Jim off in the morning, rather thankful to be left alone again, except for my little dog. I took her out for a walk, deciding to call in at Sheila's to wish them all a happy new year. The nursery was open again; Sheila and Ken were busy but they stopped for a moment to wish my greetings back to me.

"Go and see dad," Sheila said, "he's in the house today; his arthritis is playing him up but he'll be glad to see you, I'm sure. Tell him you've come to make him a cup of tea."

So, I made my way over to the house, Clarry trotting along at my heels. Joseph was pleased to see me and I gave him a hug and a kiss. As I hugged him, I felt how frail he seemed.

"No need to make me a drink, I've just brewed a pot. I hope you'll share it with me?"

I needed no second bidding and minutes later I was sitting cosily beside him on the sofa, my hands cupped around my mug and listening to one of his stories. I never noticed how the time went and was surprised when Sheila and Kenny came in to get some lunch. I was immediately invited to join them and I sat with them at the kitchen table, omelette and chips in front of me and listening to the warm chatter around me.

"This is where I want to be," I thought to myself. *"I want to be part of a family like this, where I am only expected to be me and loved for who I am, not trying to be something I'm not."*

At the end of the quick meal, Ken brought a bottle of Schleor to the table and opened it. He filled four glasses and then held his out.

"As this is the first time we have Lucy here to wish her a happy new year, let's do it now – sorry this is non-alcoholic, but we are working, as you know, Lucy. Here's to a very happy New Year to you, Lucy, and may all your dreams come true."

We all held up our glasses 'To the New Year' and drank. I smiled at them all.

"Thank you so much, such a nice thought. I wish I had been with you for New Year."

Sheila patted me on the shoulder.

"You were where you had to be," she said.

"Right, ma, I have to get back to work," said Ken, putting down his glass.

"I should go, it was only supposed to be a calling in," I said. "Can I help you clear up, Sheila?"

"No, I'll pop everything into the dishwasher."

"Thank you."

I kissed her and then Joseph, who held my hand and implored me to come and see him again soon. I promised that I would and then Clarry and I made our way home. As we walked along the river path, the sky looked full; the strange grey light a promise of snow. I shivered and walked faster.

Chapter 34
Snowed Up!

The snow did, indeed, come. I hadn't been home long when it started to fall. Big flakes drifted silently to settle on the lawn, the grass becoming covered easily while the patio and other stony areas were still only wet. I was thankful of the warmth of my home and the food in the freezer; it looked as though we might become snowed in.

The night was very quiet; I was glad of the television to lighten my evening and also the presence of my little dog. My phone rang and it was my dad, checking that I was alright. I assured him I was fine and told him not to drive out here in this weather. He told me that he was in fact already in Sutton-on-Wye and would be staying until the roads were clear. I was glad about that; I think I worried about dad as much as he worried about me. I was again glad of the comforting warmth of Clarry's little body as she lay in the crook of my legs on my bed that night. I actually put a blanket over her, being aware that she was only tiny and was afraid of her being cold. She looked so sweet with her face just poking out from underneath.

When I looked out of my window at the garden in the morning, it was to see an expanse of white, unspoiled by anything, no footprints on the lawn, no tyre marks on the drive or forecourt. Looking out of the other side of the house's windows, I saw that the field that usually held Farmer Price's cows was empty; he must have brought his animals in when he saw the sky. My heart softened slightly towards the man; he cared about his herd. They would be cosy in his cowshed, being fed with hay, or whatever cows eat when they haven't got grass.

Clarry wasn't at all impressed when she realised that I expected her to go out and do her business. She was so small that the snow came right up to her belly. She stopped a few inches away from the door and looked at me imploringly. I relented and brought her in. I donned wellingtons and my coat and carried her across the garden, loving the way the snow felt under my feet, it reminded me of icing sugar somehow. I found a place in the corner of the garden where the snow hadn't reached because of bushes and put Clarry down on the exposed soil. I hoped she would cooperate. She did; it seemed she was as anxious as I was not to linger in this strange white world. I was soon carrying her back to the house, thankful that I had a sensible pup. The two of us went in and shut out the world, gratefully.

I was surprised when a knock came at the kitchen door later. It was Ken.

"I just thought I'd pop over and make sure you're ok," he said. I invited him in and made him some tea.

"I'm just fine, there's no need to worry about me."

"Just being neighbourly," he grunted. "I'll pop by every day and if you need anything, just call."

I reflected that he had hardly 'popped by'; popping isn't something one can do in this weather. Walking was laborious to say the least.

"Looks like we could have more soon," was the gloomy prediction. "Are you sure you won't come and stay with us? Ma doesn't like to think of you here on your own."

"That's very nice of her but I'm fine and I'm not alone, I have Clarry."

Clarry thumped the floor with her tail at the sound of her name.

"I know, but it's not the same as human company. And have you heard any more strange noises lately?"

"Well, we heard the Footsteps again last night. I haven't heard them in a while. I think it's strange how random they are. Still, they don't worry me anymore."

"Random?" Ken frowned.

"Yes, they come at different times; quite a lot in the evening but I've heard them in the morning too – and you heard them yourself the morning you found Aunt Bea."

"That's right, I did. As you say, it's strange. One would have thought that a ghost would keep to the same time every night really."

"Yes. It is odd."

We lapsed into silence as we drank our tea. Eventually, Kenny got up, his chair making a scraping noise on the tiles.

"Well, I must be off. Thanks for the tea but don't forget to call me if you need me."

"I will, thank you."

When he had gone, the house seemed suddenly empty, as it never did when Jim left. Deep down, I wanted to call Kenny and ask him to come back... I gave myself a stern talking-to and went to put The Beatles on my radio-gram; anything to dispel the sudden loneliness I felt that I'd never felt before.

****

Very soon, the phone lines were down, the railways came to a halt, planes stopped and buses struggled to get through. The mobile phone reception became dodgy at times and Jim sent me a message to say he was sorry he couldn't come up just now. I text back to say I didn't expect him to and he was to stay at home and not take any risks trying to come here.

I filled my days baking, fortunately, I had plenty of flour and other supplies in and I would put on my wellingtons and plod down to the village shop carrying a basket of whatever I had made.

Madge was very grateful for anything that I could supply her with as other things were not getting through. When I had taken down some things she would put a large notice in her window saying 'fresh baking available now' and it wasn't long before everything would go. She always insisted that I sat down in her back room and had a warm drink before I made the trek back to the house.

I decided to try making a patchwork quilt because Aunt Bea had left loads of material off cuts and so I spent quite a bit of time in the den using her machine, with Clarry lying cosily at my feet in her little basket. I used the radio in this room and became quite hooked on Radio 4.

Every day, Kenny trudged over to check up on me. He never stayed very long, just enough time to sit at the table and drink a mug of tea or coffee or sometimes chocolate. If anything needed doing, which wasn't often, he would do it. He told me that the nursery wasn't open at this time although the plants still needed attending to.

"It's giving mum time to spend at home with granddad. He's not very good just now, the cold plays havoc with his arthritis."

"Poor Joseph. I should come over and visit with him."

"You don't need to, he knows what the conditions are like out."

"Well, I manage to get down to the village shop just about every day to make a small delivery so I could get over to your house."

"But if you had an accident on the river path, it could be so dangerous."

I could see his point; at least on my lane there was no danger from traffic or the river. However, if I had an accident in the lane, there still wouldn't be anyone to help...

The three weeks or so when we were snowed up had a surreal quality to them. I found that I was content to be shut up in the house for most of the time except for my daily slow trek to the village shop and the short visits to the garden with Clarry. It was restful, somehow, just cooking a bit, sewing and reading or watching television; rejuvenating, somehow, after the pre-Christmas rushing about. Although I wouldn't admit it to myself, the highlight of each day was the visit from Kenny. I found myself looking at the clock and wondering when he would come. He always came around a similar time but if he was a little late I found myself growing anxious until he put in an appearance. I didn't let him know that, of course.

Considering that Jim was my fiancé and was supposed to care about me, he didn't show it. In the whole time he only called me once. I sent him messages but he often didn't reply until the next day. I found that my mind was more focussed upon Kenny rather than Jim. At that time I didn't stop to examine why that might be, I just went with it.

A thaw started near the end of January and it looked like we were over the worst of it. The main road in the village was clear now. Once the villagers were sure the snow had stopped, all the men got out their spades and shovels and helped each other clear their drives and the main street. We still were not able to get out of the village but at least we could move in our small area.

The children had still been able to get to school because it was in the village, although one of the teachers could not get in; the others actually lived in Sutton. The children from the nearby villages who also went to the school were not able to get there so it didn't matter that they were a teacher down. I understand that a mother in the village who had been a teacher went in to help and between them they managed.

There was evidence everywhere that the children had enjoyed the snow; just about every garden had a snowman and the village green had a big one, surrounded by other shapes made of snow. Now that the thaw had set in, these once-proud models were looking a bit droopy and the faces were becoming lop-sided. However, it was good to be able to walk about easier. My lane was still snow-locked but one day I realised that Kenny and the men from the village had decided to rescue me too and they cleared the lane enough for me to get my little car down it. On that day, I provided a meal for them all; some delicious meat pies which they ate with relish halfway through their labour and I often brought out hot drinks to them to keep them going. I was so grateful, especially as my lane was not a short distance; I knew it was a big task. This meant that I could do a larger bake for the shop; I was not limited to what I could carry. I set to work the very next day and was able to provide bread and scones for the shop, although no cakes because I had run out of eggs. Still, it was bread people really wanted so that was okay.

Kenny made sure that my lane was well sand and salted, which I was grateful for because a few days after the thaw had begun, it froze again. This made everywhere very slippery and was actually more hazardous than the snow. Apart from my trips down to the shop, which I drove to very carefully, again, I went out very little, always being aware that I was somewhat isolated should I take a tumble.

I think we were all glad when the winter finally started drawing to a close towards the middle of February. In all this time I'd hardly heard from Jim; I had no idea what he'd been doing. I assumed he was busy in London, working. But I was too busy getting sorted here to be concerned over what he was up to. I had no doubt I would hear from him at some point.

It was roundabout this time when other things started happening in the house.

Chapter 35
A Terrifying Experience

Clarry and I were getting into bed one night when I first heard the sound. Clarry pricked up her ears and whined, snuffling at the bottom of my bedroom door. I picked her up and said 'shh'.

It sounded like sobbing, quite faint, as though in one of the other rooms. I stood still, heart thumping. What could it be? It only lasted a few minutes and I was trying to decide whether to investigate. Somehow, I was reluctant. Before I could make a decision, it stopped and I heard what sounded like light footsteps, much lighter than the usual ones I heard before, running along the landing and down the stairs. Then silence. Clarry whined again and I put her down. She ran straight to the bed and wriggled under her blanket and there she stayed. She was obviously frightened, I thought, and that didn't help me to feel calm. It might seem illogical now, but I locked my bedroom door and joined my pet in my bed.

I lay awake for quite a long time; afraid to go to sleep and listening hard but the sounds never came again. Clarry crept close to me so that we were both actually in the bed, with me cuddling her. Eventually, I fell into an exhausted sleep.

The next day, I checked all the rooms upstairs and down but everything was in order. I got on with the business of the day.

That night, the same thing happened again, in fact, night after night now it was the same – the sobbing, followed by the light, running footsteps down the stairs.

Kenny came round one morning; he wasn't coming so often now that the snow and ice had gone and life had returned to normal. I wasn't expecting him but was absurdly pleased to see him. However, he looked at me and frowned.

"Lucy, what's the matter, are you ill?"

"No, why?"

"You look so pale and you have dark circles around your eyes. I've never seen you look like that before. Mother was worried about you and said I should come to see if you're alright. You're not, are you?"

I sank down onto one of my kitchen chairs and put my head in my hands.

"I haven't been sleeping much recently," I said, tiredly. He put his hand under one of my elbows to raise me up. I looked at him.

"Come into the other room and tell your Uncle Kenny about it,"

I allowed him to lead me into my sitting room and I sat on the sofa with him beside me, holding my hand. Somehow, with my hand in his I felt better already; it seemed to give me strength.

I told him about the new noises that had been coming night after night, how scared Clarry and I were and how I dared not investigate and how it kept me awake, worrying about what it might be.

"Is it always the same?"

"Yes, always."

"And you say the footsteps are much lighter and they run down the stairs?"

"Yes. Very different to the footsteps you have heard."

"Hmm, very strange."

I nodded and we sat there in silence for a few minutes.

"Lucy, won't you come and stay with us? I don't know what's going on here, I never heard Bea talking about running footsteps or sobbing. I don't like to think of you here alone and frightened."

"I can't, Kenny. Much as I'd like to come, I have to stay here. The conditions of the will say I have to live here for a year, I can't just up sticks and live elsewhere instead. In any case, I don't think these noises will hurt me, it's just that they make me feel nervous, a bit jittery, you know? And I keep wondering what it is and why it's started now."

He put his arm around me then and I put my head on his shoulder. It seemed the most natural thing in the world to do and it made me feel safe. I didn't question it, I just went with it.

We stayed like that for about five or ten minutes, I don't really know how long, I just wanted it to go on forever; I wanted to stay in Kenny's arms and feel that he was there to protect me. Sadly, it did come to an end. He took his arm away and I sat up reluctantly.

"Do you feel better now?"

I nodded; I couldn't say that I had while his arm was round me but I didn't now that it wasn't, could I?

"I'd better go," he said, standing up. I stood up too. I wanted to say 'do you have to?' but I didn't, although I looked at him in silent appeal. He obviously read my expression; he put his hands on my shoulders and made me look at him.

"You are to call me if you need me. At any time, day or night. Understand?"

I nodded dumbly and looked down. He shook me slightly and I looked up.

"I mean it, Lucy, day or night, promise me."

"Okay. Thank you."

He let me go and strode off towards the door. I stood at the kitchen door briefly as he walked away from the house and watched him go with reluctance in my heart. However, I wasn't sure if it was because Ken in particular was leaving me or whether I just wanted another human being around.

After the severity of January and February, March was gorgeous. Sunny but still cold, the garden was bursting into colour with my favourite spring flowers. Bunches of primroses and Primulas of different shades lined the edges of the beds and the daffodils were unfolding their sunshine heads, dancing in the breeze.

In spite of the nightly ghostly 'visits', my heart lightened with pleasure at the sight of my garden, now being tended again by Ken or one of his workers. He took me into the walled garden one day to show me how he pruned the roses and the fruit bushes in readiness for the fruiting later in the year. Everything outside was under control.

Jim actually came up and paid me a visit the second weekend in March, the first since before Christmas. It didn't go well; he arrived unannounced in the middle of a big baking session and was annoyed that I couldn't just drop everything to go out with him.

"Have you forgotten that I have a business to run?"

"But it's Saturday!"

"I know it's Saturday but people still have to eat! I still have to provide the shop with their orders and there's always more on a Saturday because people order for the weekend. Madge's shop doesn't open on Sundays."

"Stupid in this day and age," he grumbled.

"She needs at least one day off a week," I said, sharply. "And if she opened, I'd have to work too and I appreciate not having to provide bread on a Sunday."

"I suppose so. I'll go for a walk or something and come back later."

And without another word, he was gone. He didn't reappear until the middle of the afternoon. I was annoyed with him and so didn't ask him where he'd been. I assumed that he'd had a pub lunch somewhere (and he said later that's what he'd done) but I hadn't known whether to make lunch for him. In the end, I didn't. He took me into Hereford to have dinner that night and we went to the pictures.

Later, after we'd gone to bed, the noises began. I heard his bedroom door being thrown open. Clarry went mad barking so I opened my bedroom door.

"What's going on? What's all that noise?" Jim was white-faced, standing in his bare feet at my door. At that moment, the running footsteps began. He stepped inside my room quickly. I almost felt a draught as the 'presence' run past us, although of course we never saw anything. Clarry backed away, growling. The noise stopped as always, once the stairs had been descended. I turned to Jim.

"That's it. Over."

"What the hell is it?"

"No idea. All I know is that it happens every night at the same time and as soon as 'it' has gone downstairs there's no more noises for the night."

"Good grief, Lucy, how can you stand it? This is a Godforsaken place; goodness knows what on earth has gone on here."

He stomped back to his room, banged the door shut and I heard no more from him. So much for him protecting and comforting me! I shut my own door and snuggled down in bed with Clarry, her warm body giving me the comfort that my fiancé should have given me. I shut my eyes and all I could think about was the arms of my potential step-brother around me; I could no longer deny it, I wanted Ken. I knew I had a problem.

Jim went home the following afternoon and I was glad. I had the feeling he wouldn't be staying here again; he said he couldn't stand the house and he hoped I would leave it when we got married.

"I can't live here, there's too many things that I don't like about it. I'd never feel comfortable," he told me over lunch. "I'll start looking around in London for another home for us, although we could live in my flat."

I nodded but said nothing. I wasn't going to leave here. In spite of everything, I loved this house, it was my place, it was where I felt I belonged. I didn't understand the noises but it was my feeling that if Aunt Bea could live here so long, it couldn't be anything to worry about.

****

It happened four nights after Jim had left.

The sobbing came just as I'd got into the bedroom that night. I was a little later than usual because I'd been watching a programme on television. The running footsteps followed and Clarry started to growl. She had got to the stage where she was no longer taking any notice of the noises, apart from pricking her ears when it started. Now, she ran to the window that faced over the garden and barked and barked.

"What is it, girl?" I asked and looked out of the window. I thought I caught a movement out in the garden and snapped off the light so I could better see outside. There was definitely something there; a figure, moving stealthily across the grass. If I expected to see a ghost, the figure looked exactly as I would describe one – long, wild hair, white nightdress down to the feet.

Now, it was one thing to hear noises, quite another to actually see a ghost. Clarry was going mad and so I decided, as I was still dressed, to investigate. Perhaps I shouldn't have done and perhaps it was stupid thing to do but I did it anyway. It's easy to be wise after the event. As I put on my coat and shoes downstairs, Clarry was going berserk, scrabbling at the kitchen door. The minute I opened it, she was out, barking and scurrying across the lawn. I followed; she seemed to know where she was going. When I caught up with her, she was at the edge of the pond, barking and running along and back, along and back. I hadn't thought to bring a torch out with me. At that moment, a cloud moved and the moon shone out and I caught sight of something in the middle of the pond. Floating on the water, I saw a long white nightie, topped with wild hair, arms and legs spread out, lifeless.

I screamed and ran back to the house. Without thinking what I was doing, I grabbed my phone and pressed the fast call button for Kenny.

He answered sleepily.

All I could do was cry.

"Lucy? Lucy, what is it?"

I couldn't answer him. I heard him say. "I'm coming!"

I sank down at the kitchen table, shivering. I didn't have to wait long. I heard a vehicle coming up the lane at speed and came to a halt abruptly, scattering stones on the drive. A door slammed and I heard hurrying footsteps, the kitchen door flew open and there was Kenny, gathering me up in his arms. I clutched at him and cried and he cradled me, murmuring, 'there now, there now,' as if I was a child.

"The pond," I managed to say eventually. "There's someone drowned in the pond. Go look, go look." I gulped. He looked at me and without a word, he went running out. Not long after, he was back.

"There's nothing there, Lucy."

"What?" I looked at him, wide eyed in disbelief.

"There's nothing in the pond," he repeated.

"I don't believe it. I saw it and so did Clarry. She was barking, barking like mad."

"I'm going to make you some sweet tea," he said and clicked the kettle on. In a short time he was handing me a mug. I wrapped my frozen fingers around it. I couldn't stop shivering, whether from cold or shock, I couldn't tell.

Kenny led me into the lounge and put on the gas fire. He sat me down on the chair closest to the fire and perched on the sofa nearest to me so we could talk face to face.

"Tell me what happened."

So I related to him the events, ending with me calling him. He looked grim.

"I don't like it, Lucy. I don't like you being here on your own. I don't know what's going on but I'm not happy with it at all. I don't remember Bea talking about anything like this."

Now that I was calmer and I thought about what I'd seen, it began to ring a bell in my mind.

"It reminds me of something that I found in the den," I told him. "Come through and I'll show you."

It was chilly in the den but I knew exactly where I'd left the paper and was able to find it easily. I handed it to Ken, who took it and we went back to the warm lounge. I waited while he read the paper and watched his face as he did so. He frowned.

"What is the date today?"

"It's the fifteenth of March," I replied. "Oh!"

"Oh indeed," he said grimly. "It is the anniversary of the drowning of this girl in 1952."

Chapter 36
Dealing with Decisions

I was in such a state of shock that night that Kenny stayed with me. We both laid, fully dressed, in my bed, Clarry in her usual place in the crook of my knees. I eventually went to sleep, safe with Kenny's arm across me. How much he slept, I don't know but I do know that this was something I wanted, always. In the morning I lay awake, still in his arms, and struggled to come to terms with this knowledge. I didn't know what I was going to do but I did know that I was not going to marry Jim. How could I when I loved another man? Even if Kenny wasn't interested in me, I knew I would not be happy with Jim. His life wasn't for me. If I had to live the rest of my life just being Kenny's step-sister, then so be it but I knew I couldn't be with Jim. Somehow, I had to tell him.

I tried to be cool in the morning. I gave Kenny breakfast and thanked him for everything. I assured him I would be fine; I hoped that was true. Now, I was less concerned with ghostly presences than with the affairs of my heart. Amazing how some things can dissolve with the appearance of daylight.

After that date, I never heard the running footsteps any more but I did occasionally hear the sobbing and the heavier footsteps. Clarry never seemed to be bothered about these and she didn't bark at the bedroom window again. Obviously, there wasn't to be a replay of the drowning now that the fifteenth of March was over.

There were two things I knew I had to do. I sent a message to Jim to say that I was coming to London the weekend after the ghostly drowning. I told him I was going to take the train down on Friday and could we meet in the evening as I was going to come home again the following day.

He agreed and said he would take me out to dinner that evening. I let my dad know I was going and asked Sheila if she would take care of Clarry for me until I got back and she agreed.

I had made an appointment to see the agents who were renting out my flat for me and when I arrived in London, that was where I went first. They were also selling agents and so I gave them instructions that I wished to sell my flat in Chiswick. They suggested that the current tenants might be interested in buying because they loved living there. I said that was fine if they wanted to do that, otherwise they would have to vacate within six months.

After that I called in to say hello to Sue and the others at my old place of work. While I was there, I told the boss that I would not be coming back. Then I wondered around the shops for a while. As I intended to go home the next day I had booked into a B & B not far from the station.

I got ready for dinner with care; it was going to be a difficult evening. I wore a fine woollen dress and jacket and I Had confidence that I looked smart. Jim looked at me with approval when I took off my coat in the restaurant. He ordered drinks for us and then ordered our meal. He was familiar with my tastes so I knew that I would like my food but I found myself being slightly irritated that he didn't ask me what I wanted. However, I let it go because I didn't want to start the evening off badly. I was glad of the aperitif that he'd ordered and I downed it pretty quickly, much to both our surprise as I usually drank very little.

"I was thirsty," I said and he didn't comment. When the food came, he told me about some of the things he'd been doing and about his parents. He asked me about what was going on in Sutton-on-Wye and I found myself telling him about the ghostly drowning episode earlier that week. Upon hearing about this, his face grew serious.

"Lucy, I wish you would leave that Godforsaken place! Goodness only knows what's going to happen next. Your aunt died there, something must have happened and I don't want anything to happen to you. I've been looking at houses down this way; we don't have to live in London, there's some lovely places in Sussex and I could easily commute after we're married. As you know, at some point we will have to live in my parents' place when I inherit it, in fact my parents might decide to give it over to me sooner. Come to that, there are some nice places very close to there that we could live in for a while and perhaps swap with my parents if they decide they want a smaller place."

He talked for quite a while about his plans and I said very little, just worked my way slowly through the meal; not that there was much of it, it was one of those places where you had to pay an arm and a leg for a tiny piece of fish, a couple of mange tout and a potato with a drizzle of sauce followed by the smallest round of sponge pudding and cream. However, I wasn't really that hungry.

"Lucy, you're not saying much. What's the matter?"

I looked up at him solemnly.

"Jim, I'm not going to move back down here. I am going to stay in Sutton-on-Wye."

I took the great rock of a ring off my finger and put it on the table in front of him.

"I'm sorry, Jim, but I'm not going to marry you." I fished in my handbag and took out the box the ring belonged in and put that on the table next to the ring. Jim looked at me in shocked silence.

"You can't mean that? But we've been together for ages, engaged for almost two years!"

"At least a year too long. You waited too long, Jim. If you had set a date before, I would have married you but now I know that I can't marry you, we are not suited."

"It's that man, isn't it – that fellow that owns the nursery."

"No, it isn't that." ('Liar', my conscious said but I did my best to ignore it.) "I have realised that we want very different things in life and it won't be possible for us to be together and both have what we want. One of us would have to sacrifice and I know it would be me." I drew in a deep breath. "I have come to realise that I don't love you enough to make that sacrifice, Jim, I'm sorry."

"We could work it out somehow."

"No, we can't. I've thought it through so many times; I've lain awake at night trying to work it out and I just can't. The simple fact is that although I care about you I don't love you enough to want to spend the rest of my life with you."

He grew angry then, I could see it coming on. It always happened when he didn't get his own way. When he started to speak, I interrupted.

"No, don't get angry, don't argue. I've had enough of being at the wrong end of your temper. I'm going now. Goodbye, Jim and thank you for what we've had."

I left then, the maitre handing me my coat on the way out. I hailed a taxi and gave instructions just as Jim appeared in the doorway. As I sat in the taxi, I think I should have been sad but all I could feel was relief; I felt that a heavy burden had been lifted from my shoulders.

****

When I arrived back in Hereford I was thankful I'd left my car in the station 24-hour car park. For the moment I didn't want to see anyone. I was feeling distinctly ruffled and unsure.

But as I followed the slow-moving traffic through the city, gradually picking up more speed as I turned into the Whitecross Road, up past Sainsbury's and Bulmers, then round the Whitecross Roundabout and onto the Kings Acre Road, my anxieties gradually dissolved and, as I passed Kings Acre Halt and onto the country road to Sutton-on-Wye, I felt at one with this beautiful place; the greenness of the English countryside soothed my feathers which were still ruffled, the result of having to break off my engagement.

Upon reaching the village, I went straight to Baxter's Nurseries in order to collect Clarry. Sheila and Ken were nowhere in sight but I got cheery waves from Ron and Joe as I passed through the nursery. I knocked at the kitchen door of the house and it was opened immediately by Sheila and, moments after, given a rapturous welcome from Butch and Clarry. I picked my little dog up and hugged her squirming body, then set her down again in order to pat Butch. Clarry wove through his legs and mine; how we all never ended up sprawling I don't know. Sheila laughed.

"Silly dogs! Hello love, I'm glad to see you back. How was London?"

I screwed my face into a frown and as I did so, dad came to see what all the fuss was about.

"Oh, hello Lulu! I'm glad you're home, I was wondering what time you would get here. Are you going to tell us why you went to London? You were very secretive before you went."

"Shall we go through? We have some tea and sandwiches in there already. Dad will be glad to see you, Lucy."

We went through to the dining room, the dogs still trying to trip us up, where Joseph was waiting, eating a sandwich. Kenny was there too, also eating. I went across to Joseph and gave him a kiss. I sat in the chair next to him and he smiled and held my hand for a moment.

"Well, the first thing I did was go to my renting agent to tell them I wanted to sell my flat. There's no point in keeping it, I'll never go back to live there now."

"Right. That's good," dad replied, "If you're sure."

"I'm sure," I said, firmly. "Then I popped in to see Sue and the others and looked round the shops. I had dinner with Jim in the evening. Then I came home this morning, as you can see."

"And?" Sheila prompted gently.

"And, I've broken it off with Jim. I've told him I'm not going to marry him."

I sat in the silence. Joseph took hold of my hand again and squeezed it a little.

"Well, my love," dad said, "I am glad you've got around to it at last. I can't say I'm sorry, he wasn't right for you."

There was a general murmur of agreement from Sheila and Joseph. Kenny said nothing and I dared not look at him. After a few moments, he got up and put his hat back on. "Well, better get back to work." And he went.

"Don't mind him," whispered Joseph. "He'll get round to it in his own time."

I could feel my face get warm and hoped the others wouldn't notice. Sheila, ever the diplomat, said,

"Have some tea, Lucy, and some sandwiches. I need to get back to the shop too so I'll leave you to it."

Dad stopped her by putting a hand on her shoulder.

"Eat your food, my dear and we have some news for Lucy, don't we?"

"What's that?" I asked, glad for the subject change.

"We have set the date for our wedding, haven't we, my dear?"

She nodded and patted his hand.

"We have indeed. Lucy, we are going to get married on Easter Saturday, 15th April. My daughter and her family can be with us then so it seems like a good time."

"That sounds perfect," I beamed at them. "I'm so pleased that I'll meet Kenny's sister at last, after all, she and Kenny will become my brother and sister. Won't that be fun?"

Chapter 37
Intruders!

If I thought that Jim would bother me with phone calls or texts, I was completely wrong. I never heard anything from him at all after my visit to London. To me, it told me with a loud voice that he never really loved me – surely he wouldn't give up that easily if he'd been seriously in love with me?

What did surprise me was that I actually received a letter from his mother.

'James' father and I were extremely sorry to hear that your engagement to our son has ended. We were very fond of you and we felt that you had a calming influence on James as we know he can sometimes seem a little wild at times.

We do not know all the details except that your engagement is off but we have asked James to reconsider.

However, we wish you well and hope you will make good decisions in your life. I will miss the woman to woman chats we used to have. I had looked forward to having you in our family. I hope you will forgive James in time.

With all good wishes,
Caroline Netherfield'

Obviously, my dear ex had let his parents think that he was the one who had called off the engagement. I shrugged, I didn't care, let him. I did think it was sweet of his mother to write to me though. So I dropped a little note back to her, sending her my love and thanks.

If I thought that it would make a difference now that Kenny knew my engagement was off, I was mistaken. Don't get me wrong, he was as diligent a friend as he had been before but he didn't get any closer, he never asked me out or anything. I didn't get it and neither did Joseph when I talked with him about it. I was glad of Kenny's friendship though, especially when other things started to happen around the house.

It started a few days after I'd been to London. Clarry and I were watching the television and I was doing some hand sewing. It was quite late, around ten in the evening. Clarry suddenly lifted up her head and started to growl.

"What is it, Clarry?"

It was as if the sound of my voice had given her permission to move, for she bounced up and ran to the window that faced the road, growling and barking. I looked up, and for a split second, I thought I saw a dark shape on the outside. I jumped, and closed my curtains quickly. (I often didn't bother to close my curtains because the house stood alone with no near neighbours.) I was glad that the front door was locked and bolted; I never used that door. I quickly ran to check the doors in the den and the kitchen. I had locked them both. Clarry was still barking, moving around the walls of the house, which indicated to me that the 'someone' was making its way round the outside of my home. I reached for my phone and pressed speed dial for Kenny. He answered at once.

"Lucy?"

"Kenny, there's someone creeping around the outside of my house," I whispered.

"Have you called the police?"

"No. Kenny, I'm scared."

"I'll call the police and I'll come over. Don't worry, I will be with you very shortly."

He was here in a remarkably short time. He was out of breath because he'd run along the riverside path. The police took longer.

By the time Kenny got here, Clarry had stopped barking. Kenny had walked all round the outside of the house; it was obvious no one was there now.

The police took a statement from me and Kenny, had a perfunctory look around and left.

"Fat lot of good they are," was Kenny's comment. "I'm going to stay here the rest of the night. I'll sleep here on the sofa."

A niggle of disappointment washed over me; I'd so wanted to sleep in his arms again like I had after the 'drowning' incident. I told myself off sternly. I must say I was relieved to think that he was here in the house with me as I went off to bed. I felt much safer when he was around. I'd brought him a duvet and pillows and he declared he was quite comfortable and not to worry.

In the morning, after checking that I was okay, he left. Wouldn't even have a cup of coffee, he said he'd have breakfast at his home.

"But I'll check on you again later and if you need me, just call."

"I will. I can't thank you enough."

His eyes held mine for a moment and I thought he might say something else. Instead, he kissed my cheek briefly.

"Take care of yourself. I'll see you later."

Later that day, dad came over to see me. I wasn't surprised.

"I don't know what's going on, Lucy, but I don't want you to be here on your own. I'm mindful that my sister died in this house because something had frightened her. I don't want anything happening to you. I think I should come and stay with you."

"Oh no, I don't think there's any need for that. I'll keep everything locked, no one can get in."

"Well, the offer is there. I'm worried about you, Lulu. Just let me know if you change your mind."

One night, when I had just put my light out when I was in bed, Clarry suddenly leaped off the bed and ran to the window, barking. She tried desperately to jump up at the window but she was too small. I got out of bed to see what she was upset about. I hoped no one was trying to get in the house. I saw lights, mysteriously floating above the pond. They were yellow and appeared misty.

I quickly got my mobile and called the police. Again, they took ages to come and the lights had long since gone. The police constable and WPC that came looked around the garden but again, found nothing. Upon taking a statement from me, somehow, they made me feel guilty, as if I hoped there would be a man in my garden. When they left, I felt cross, which wasn't like me.

So, when a few nights later I saw the lights again, this time they were blue, I didn't bother to call them but again called Kenny. Dad came with Kenny and together searched the garden and found nothing. They were as puzzled as I was.

"I think I am going to come here every night and morning to check up on you and you must call me if you are scared or worried," said Kenny to me, his hands on my shoulders in a repeat of an earlier gesture. I promised; I admit I was beginning to get a little jumpy and nervous.

When I saw them out and locked the doors behind them, I went back to my bedroom. I could feel I had a headache coming on. I opened my bedside drawer to get my cool stick to put on my forehead.

There, just inside my drawer, was a small card. 'D.C.I. Dan Cooke' I read. I had no recollection of the card being there but it seemed that 'Someone' wanted me to see it. I resolved to call Detective Chief Inspector Cooke in the morning.

I was sure that, just before I shut my eyes, I saw Aunt Bea and she was smiling at me and nodding in a satisfactory way. I went to sleep feeling that my aunt was watching over me and she wanted me to get D.C.I. Cooke in on this puzzle.

****

"Well, Miss Dixon, I am glad to speak with you again. I am very concerned to hear that these things have been happening. It seems that someone is trying very hard to frighten you into leaving this place. I believe you have to be here for a year or it will be sold; you told me before, if I remember correctly?"

I nodded as I poured him some tea and one for his sergeant.

"Yes, that's right. But I intend to stay; I like it here, in spite of everything. It's been okay until these lights and someone walking around outside. Even the Footsteps didn't frighten me but they have always been here because Kenny heard them the morning he found Aunt Bea."

"Footsteps? Ah, yes, I remember about them now. You are still hearing them?"

"Yes but it's obviously a resident ghost so that's not an issue. I'm more frightened of someone trying to get in."

"That is a worry and I'm sorry the force took so long to respond to your call."

"Well, we are a way out here, I've no doubt it takes time to get from the city to Sutton. I was upset, though, the way I was treated when I called them out because of the lights. I felt that they thought I was a neurotic female who hoped there was some man out there trying to get in to have wild sex with me or something."

The D.C.I. tutted. "I'm very sorry, you should not have been made to feel like that. I know you are a sensible woman. I still can't help feeling that your aunt's death was not entirely natural; maybe the same tactics were being worked on her as are on you, to try to force her out so that she would sell this house."

He took a sip of his tea.

"I have tried to find out who the man was that offered to buy this property and those around you but he seems to have disappeared without trace. There were no clues as to his identity; he left no cards, no one saw a vehicle and nobody has seen him in this area since. Whoever he was seems to have given up the idea of buying land around here."

"That doesn't surprise me; all my neighbours are adamant that they are not selling so there's no point in him hanging around here anymore."

"No. Well, do feel free to contact me if you find out anything more. In the meantime I'm going to have my men go over your property outside with a fine tooth comb to see if they can find anything at all. That should have been done already by the uniformed section. Heads are going to roll when I get back to headquarters."

He was as good as his word. His call to his headquarters brought four men out to examine the area and they were very thorough. However, apart from a thread of a fleecy jacket stuck on one of my rose bushes in the front garden, they found nothing.

"I think that could be off my neighbour Ken Baxter's jacket; he has one like that and he did look all around the outside the first night I had a prowler. Mind you, as he works in my garden a lot, he's quite likely to leave evidence of him around."

"We will get it checked out," D.I. Cooke said. "In future, Miss Dixon, anything you report will be taken seriously, I promise you."

I smiled at him as he shook my hand goodbye. I liked this man and was thankful he was determined to help me if he could. It wasn't until after he and his constable had left that I realised that I hadn't told him about the ghostly drowning but then decided that he couldn't do anything about a haunting anyway. If that was something I'd have to live with once a year then so be it.

****

Ghostly visitors etc aside, plans were afoot for the coming wedding. Sheila insisted that it was going to be a quiet affair but the way she was talking I thought it wasn't going to be exactly small. The marriage ceremony would be in the village church and the reception in the village hall. Offers to have the reception at Sutton Court or the Wye View Restaurant were politely turned down; Sheila had roped me in to help her with the catering and so I was busy filling up my freezers with all kinds of delicacies that could be defrosted on the day. Stephanie was going to make the cake; it was her speciality, apparently, and I was more than happy that she was doing it.

The coming wedding meant that I had to take a trip into Hereford to try to find a suitable outfit for the occasion. I thought it might take a few trips to find the right thing but I was very lucky and found it almost straight away. The two-piece in pastel shades of pink, lilac and blue was very pretty; I loved the way the skirt flowed around my legs. I found a jacket that toned in beautifully (after all, April can still be quite chilly) and then I needed to find accessories to go with it. Having accomplished my shopping, I happily carried it all back to my car and set off thankfully for home.

Now that there were no visits from Jim, I had formed the habit of spending much of Sundays with the Baxter family. Sheila was concerned about Joseph, who had not been terribly well lately. She was worried about him being alright while she was away on honeymoon. Ken would be here of course and he was very good but he had to work as well.

"I'll come," I volunteered. "Kenny will be here at night and I'll be here during the day. Clarry and I will come and watch over Joseph, he will be fine."

Although Joseph protested he would be okay, I was still determined I would come over.

"But you have your work, my dear," he said.

"I only have my bread order to do for Madge," I said. "This is a quiet time for me just now, before the fruiting season starts again. I love being with you, Joseph, you know that. It's the least I can do when you've all been so good to me. We'll be family soon, and families look after each other."

Joseph backed down after that and Sheila had her peace of mind restored regarding her father-in-law.

It had been decided that dad and Butch would move into the Baxter home because Sheila needed to look after Joseph and be near her work. Dad was going to rent out his bungalow and if a time should come when Kenny gets married, they would have dad's house to go and live in. I hated to think of some other woman running this house and being with Kenny but I didn't say anything. Nor did I want to think of a time when Joseph wouldn't be here.

"Sounds like a plan," I murmured, not daring to look at either Kenny or Joseph.

Because of the wedding, I was also going to meet the rest of the Baxter family, Kenny's sister Angela, her husband and children. They had been over since Christmas but I hadn't seen them because Jim had been here. It was just as well that they only lived in Ross, it wasn't that far away so they wouldn't have to have anywhere to sleep.

I helped dad to move his things out of the bungalow. He was going to rent it out furnished, so he was only going to take his personal things and some small pieces that he didn't want to leave behind for others to use – and Butch's things of course, his bed and bowls, although he already often slept at the Baxter house without his bed. Certainly, the move wasn't going to be traumatic for the dog – and he was someone else I'd be looking after while dad was away.

"You haven't lived here all that long, dad," I remarked as we were sorting. "Won't you be sad to leave it?"

"Not really. The very fact I haven't been here long makes it easier. It has no memories of you or your mother or Bea; it was much harder to leave the house. And I will be going to somewhere that I already love, will have a family around me, you a stone's throw away and, most of all, a woman to love and who loves me. I never thought I would find that again after your mother, Lucy. I had to wait a long time but I don't mind that because Sheila is right for me."

I nodded and agreed. Sheila was exactly right; just as Kenny was right for me – so upsetting that he didn't seem to know it.

Chapter 38
The Wedding

It was just three days before the wedding. Clarry and I had just gone to bed so it was around half past ten. I had picked up my book, intending to read for a while when there was a sudden, ear-splitting shriek. I sat bolt upright and Clarry flew off the bed, barking. She ran to the door while I was still trying to get myself together. The noise came again, this time it seemed further away – the first one was so loud it could have been just outside my bedroom door. At the second sound, Clarry rushed to the window that looked out over the garden. I followed her and peeped through the curtains nervously. Was I going to see a host of ghouls out there? However, all I could see were more lights hovering over the pond area again; this time they were blue.

'I've had enough of this,' I muttered and reached for my mobile. I tried calling Kenny but there was no answer, which surprised me somewhat. I called dad instead and he said he'd be right over. I also left a message for D.I Cooke on his phone.

Dad arrived quite quickly, Kenny with him.

"I'm sorry, Lucy," said Kenny, "My phone was switched off and charging because I forgot to do it this morning."

"It's ok, don't worry."

Of course, by the time they came, there was nothing to see or hear. But when I told them what had happened, dad said.

"Right, that's it. I'm going to stay here until the wedding and then I would be happier if you were to stay at the Nursery House until we get back. It won't matter if you are not sleeping here for a few days, you can always come here every day to do your baking but you really shouldn't be here alone at night. If you stay here and have to call Kenny, he will have to leave Joseph alone in their house to come to you."

That persuaded me; I couldn't have Joseph at risk on my account. Secretly, I was glad; I really didn't want to be here alone any more. I was getting to the stage where I wasn't sure if I wanted to keep the house after all.

Dad took Kenny home and came back with a small case of essentials for overnight. He pointed out that it was good for him to be here because a bride and groom shouldn't see each other on the day of the wedding until they met at the alter.

"Can't take any chances of anything going wrong." He grinned at me. I smiled at him; we both knew that nothing would go wrong, there was no way Sheila was going to change her mind. But at least it helped me feel that I was doing dad a favour too; he couldn't be at his bungalow because it was already being rented out.

I stayed up just long enough to make sure he was settled. I wouldn't let him sleep in the big room at the opposite end of the landing. I was suspicious of that room. In any case, I wanted dad near me so he went into the smaller room first on the right at the top of the stairs, next to the bathroom.

D.I. Cooke and his sidekick came out to see me again the next day. When I told him what had happened, his face grew very serious.

"This just doesn't sound right. I'm no expert on the paranormal but this all sounds very fishy to me. I'm going to get to the bottom of it somehow. In the meantime, be very careful, Miss Dixon, and if you can, stay somewhere else for a while, at least at night time."

"As a matter of fact, I'm going to be staying at my neighbours' house for a few days after Saturday and until then dad is going to stay with me."

"I'm very glad to hear it. I'll be in touch if I find out anything. Goodbye for now, Miss Dixon."

Although dad didn't stay with me during the day, it didn't matter because he always made sure he was back before dark. In any case, it was only three nights. The evening before the wedding, I packed a case and had it ready to pick up after the wedding, ready to move into the Nursery House.

****

The morning of the wedding was rather overcast. I got up early in order to get everything out of the freezers. Then I had to walk Clarry and make sure she was settled so I could leave her. Dad used the bathroom while I was out so I was able to go straight in there and have a nice, scented bath before I got ready.

The original arrangement had been that Joseph was going to give Sheila away and Ken was going to be dad's best man. However, because Joseph wasn't all that well, although he was coming to the wedding, Ken was going to give his mum away and I was going to be 'best woman'. It hardly mattered that we were rearranging the traditional. Dad declared he would rather have me, after all, who knew him better than his own daughter? With the possible exception of Sheila, who seemed to know him better than he knew himself.

By the time we stepped out of the car at the church, the sun was trying hard to come through and when we came out, the sun had made it, just in time for the photos. I guess I shouldn't have been surprised to see that the church was packed; it seemed the whole village had turned out to see Sheila wed. So much for a quiet wedding!

The village hall was equally packed; I hoped the mountain of food I had prepared would go round.

Ken did brilliantly in his speech as the 'bride's father' and I received many compliments on my speech as 'best man'. It was a joyous occasion and dad and Sheila shone with happiness throughout. Joseph, too, was moved by it all. He sat next to me at the bride's table and I held his hand and we smiled at each other. I knew he was thankful that Sheila had found someone else to love – and that it wouldn't mean things would change for him, I knew he had been worried about that. I knew that my dad wouldn't take her away from her other menfolk; he got on extremely well with them both and fitted in as if he'd always been there, as did Butch.

I saw Cessie, Neil and Sylvie, Madge and her husband Len, Paul Gamble, Alex and Stephanie, Joe, Eddie, Roger, Patch, Gerry Mike, Ron, Mavis and Janice. The nursery had been closed for the day because of the wedding ('because we just have to have everyone there,' Sheila had declared) and the restaurant would not open until the evening. Their families were there too, of course and I must say, the children did very well on the whole, they were pretty good. Sylvie came rushing up to me at one point, and I greeted her cheerfully.

"Hello there Sylvie, how are you? I could have done with your help with all this baking I had to do!"

"Yeah, sorry, Lucy, I got invited to stay with a friend the first week of the holiday and I only got home yesterday – couldn't miss this wedding!"

"Where's Penny, isn't she home for Easter?"

"Oh no, she's gone somewhere with some friends she's hooked up with at Uni. They're going walking, I think she said. Rather her than me!" Sylvie giggled.

"Well, I suppose it's hard, learning nursing. I expect she felt she needed to get away for a while and get some exercise and fresh air. I don't suppose the air is always very fresh in a hospital."

"No, I suppose it isn't. Oh, look, Kenny seems to be having a fight with his girlfriend!"

Startled, I looked where Sylvie nodded and saw Kenny and Glynis not far from the door. She looked like she was having a good go at him, her face screwed up in annoyance. Her whole body language conveyed anger, while he just stood, impassively letting her vent. She turned and flounced out of the hall, slamming the door loudly behind her. It stopped the conversation momentarily but it soon resumed.

I realised it was time to cut the cake and so I banged on the table for attention. Everyone watched while the couple put the first cut in the wonderful, three-tiered creation that Steph had made. It had flowers of all colours all over it, a tribute to the nursery no doubt, with a big heart on the top. Cameras flashed as they posed. Sheila looked wonderful in a blue suit and matching hat; it set off her brown hair to perfection and somehow I was reminded of the Queen, I was sure that I'd seen Her Majesty wearing an outfit like that.

I took the cake into the back room and deftly cut it up into slices and put them on napkins on trays for the waiters to give out. The waiters from the restaurant had volunteered their services, which I thought was good of them.

When everyone had had their piece of cake, dad and Sheila decided it was time to leave and so I announced that they were going and everyone filed out of the hall to wave them away in dad's car.

When they had gone, we went back in to finish off the food still there and to clear up. Kenny soon had his men organised to stack chairs and tables and sweep the floor. As I watched the piles of food being swept, I had a moment's lapse in thinking about the twelve baskets of food that was left after the 'feeding of the five thousand' story in the Bible. Thank goodness there weren't twelve baskets of left-overs here!

There were some things still in the kitchen, rolls, parts of quiches or flans or gateaux which I gave to the helpers' wives to take home, or to the waiters if they wanted them. I really didn't want to be taking any of it home with me, or maybe just a few bits for Kenny, Joseph and me to enjoy tomorrow.

Dad and I had come down in his car so that he and Sheila could leave in it. That meant I was without a car and I looked at my high-heels ruefully, thinking the walk back to River View was not going to be easy.

"Don't worry, I'll take you," a familiar voice said at my side. 'How did he know what I was thinking?' I wondered, as I looked at Kenny gratefully. "Well, you didn't think I was going to let you walk home after all the work you've done? It's your hard work that made this wedding, you know. You must be exhausted."

Come to think of it, I was. Now that I had finished, I knew I was worn out. I dared not sit down in case I couldn't get up again.

"Come on, love," said Kenny, offering me his arm. "Granddad's already in the car."

'Love? Did he call me 'love'?' Somewhere in the tired fog that was now my brain, I registered that he produced an endearment for me that he'd never used before.

****

The week that I spent at the Nursery House was like a breath of fresh air after all the frights I'd had lately at the farmhouse. I loved walking the two dogs, which I did twice a day. I went to church with Kenny and Joseph so I could help keep an eye on Joseph but I found I liked being there and started to find some peace within me which had been missing for some while.

I found that both the Baxter men were quite capable around the house but having me there to produce lunch and dinner saved Ken having a lot of time away from work. Joseph couldn't do much because he was still recovering from the severe flu that he'd had which had left him weak and he soon ran out of energy and slept quite a bit during the day. However, he made a mean pot of tea to go with the scones I made.

I concentrated on making meals to help rebuild Joseph's strength and he did appear to be better towards the end of the week. He had more colour in his cheeks and was sleeping a bit less. I hoped Sheila would be pleased with me.

Every day I went back to my own house, taking Clarry with me, to do the baking to provide Madge's shop and the nursery café with the orders, delivered them and then drove back to the Nursery House afterwards. Kenny and Joseph were great company; both men seemed to know just when to be companionable or when to give space. Not that I needed space; I was very happy to have their company, especially in the evenings and also to have the knowledge that I wouldn't be dogged with paranormal activity or prowlers to disturb me.

One thing that did happen though was on the Sunday afternoon, Kenny decided to come walking with me and the dogs. His granddad insisted he would be fine, he was going to have a nap. We walked along the river path, watching the river as it rushed along towards the city, where it would get wider and slow down a bit to wind through Bishop's Meadow and on towards Ross-on-Wye and beyond to the beautiful Wye Valley.

It was pleasant walking; the dogs were ecstatic and spent lots of time sniffing around the undergrowth. We passed the place where the weeping willow with the seat was and I felt a pang of memory as I looked towards it.

Kenny must have felt my hesitation as he reached out and took my hand and we smiled at each other.

Not a word passed between us but a little bubble of happiness rose up inside me. After we'd walked only a short way, Clarry started to bark. We looked around us but couldn't see what she might be barking at. She ran towards us, her little feet almost leaving the ground as she tried to get our attention.

"What's the matter, girl?" I asked. She ran away from me and up to a spindly Silver Birch, putting her forefeet onto the trunk of the tree and continued to bark, look at me and back up the tree.

"Look!" Kenny pointed towards the top of the tree. There, hanging off a twig and almost hidden by the newly unfurled leaves, was something blue.

"What is it?" I asked, squinting to try to see better.

"It looks like a balloon," was the reply.

"Oh, is that all?" I held out my hand to Clarry, who was still jumping up the tree. I'm sure she would have climbed it if she'd been able. "Why are you fussing about an old balloon, Clarry? Come on girl, let's go."

I got hold of her collar and pulled her away. She came, reluctantly and followed us but she kept turning round, barking a little and showing she was not willing to come really. As she did so, something shifted in my brain. I stopped.

"What's up?" asked Kenny. I turned, went back to the tree and peered up at the balloon. Yes, that's what I thought...

"I must call D.I. Cooke," I informed Kenny. "I think we might have a clue to what's been happening. That balloon is the exact shade of blue that the last lot of mysterious lights were in my garden the other night."

Chapter 39
Disturbing Evidence

Detective Inspector Cooke had police swarming all over the banks of the river, both sides. They got the balloon down from the tree, and, stuck in the mud not far from the tree, was a tiny halogen light. On the other side of the river, the remains of a pink balloon were found.

D.I. Cooke held up the plastic bags with the blue and pink balloons and the little light so I could see them.

"I think the mystery of your floating lights is solved, Miss Dixon," he said gravely.

We were in the lounge of the Nursery House then, with Kenny and Joseph there. Joseph pointed at them with a shaky finger.

"They look like the balloons that we sell in the garden centre," he said. "They are shiny ones. We sell those, I'm sure we do."

D.I. Cooke raised an eyebrow.

"Could I see them please?"

"Certainly," said Kenny. "I'll just get the keys."

He went off and was back a few moments later. "I'll take you over there."

I went with them and saw that the packets of balloons, sold in single colours, did indeed look the same. Not only did they have pink and blue but yellow and white too. It seemed that the mysterious 'lights' could have come from this very place.

"Hmm, yes, I see. Could I have a packet of them, Mr Baxter?"

"Help yourself."

The detective took a packet of blue ones.

"Thank you, sir."

"No problem."

"All these things will be sent to Forensics for testing. We will see what they come up with. At least you don't have to worry that you're being haunted, Miss Dixon. However, it seems someone wants to frighten you."

"Why would someone want to frighten me?" I was genuinely puzzled. Kenny put a protective arm around me and pulled me close to him.

"Don't worry, Detective Inspector, I'll look after her."

"I am very glad to hear that, Mr Baxter." He hesitated as if he was going to say something else then decided not to. "Well, we will be off now then. I will be in touch if we find out anything. In the meantime, if you find anything else, please let me know."

"You can be sure that I will."

"Good."

We made our way back out of the garden centre buildings and saw the police off the premises. We returned to the house where Joseph was waiting for us. I made light of the discoveries because I didn't want the elderly man to be too troubled. However, when I went to bed that night, I stayed awake quite a while, trying to figure out who wanted to frighten me and why.

****

Another thing I did while Sheila was away was to serve in the garden centre, which I did in the afternoons. This gave Joe and Mavis the time they needed to fill the shelves and also give advice to people, which they were both good at and I found that I really enjoyed it. Customers were pleasant and happy to spend a few minutes chatting. Some of them I knew lived in the village and they stopped by to tell me how much they'd enjoyed the wedding and my food.

I was pleasantly surprised how busy the garden centre seemed to be most of the time. Of course, some pensioners would come in to wander around and then have a coffee and cake in the café, managed by Janice. I made the cakes for the café in the kitchen here, rather than at home. That way, I was able to keep an eye on what was being used and make sure that everything was as fresh as it could be.

I thought I saw Glynis a couple of times; perhaps she was trying to make things up with Kenny, I thought. Other than Sunday afternoon when he'd held my hand a few minutes and put his arm around me when the D.I. was with us, Kenny had not taken things any further. He could be so annoying! Maybe he didn't want to make things a little awkward while I was staying there; after all, it would be tempting to kiss and cuddle and we couldn't do that in front of Joseph. But maybe Glynis had managed to make it up with him.

Apart from that, everything was fine. That is, until Friday afternoon. It was after the garden centre had closed and I was going to take the dogs out before we had our meal. I'd put a casserole on at lunch-time before I went to help at the garden centre. The dogs were excited to be going out. I knew Kenny wouldn't be coming with me, he always had things to do after the shop closed. As soon as I opened the kitchen door, Clarry shot out of the house, barking.

"She's been barking a lot this afternoon," grumbled Joseph. "I don't know what's got into her."

"Sorry," I kissed him. "Try and have a rest now while we are gone."

Butch came to heel when I called him but Clarry rushed out into the yard. She headed straight for one of the outbuildings where Kenny kept his gardening vehicles and other things. I hastened after her, calling her but she took no notice. She scrabbled at the door of the building.

"What's up, girl?" She looked at me, tongue hanging out, for all the world as if she was smiling at me, then scrabbled at the door again. I suddenly remembered how she found the balloon on Sunday. Could it be that there was something else in this building? I opened the door and she shot inside. Butch and I followed her. At first, I couldn't see her but then I spotted her in a corner where there were bags of peat, fertilizer and potting compost stacked up. She was jumping up and down like a Jack-in-a-box. I wondered what she could be after. Then I spotted a bag, just an ordinary plastic carrier bag, half hidden amongst the bags of stuff. I had to put my foot on the pile in order to reach it and I only just managed.

When I had it in my hands, Clarry stood waiting, tail wagging slightly. Butch came up and pushed his nose on the bag. With shaking fingers, I untied the knot in the top. When I saw what was inside, I gave a little scream and dropped the bag. Butch was on it in a trice and he pulled out what looked like a scalp of blond hair. I realised it was a wig. What was a wig doing in a carrier bag in this shed? There was something else in the bag too, something quite substantial. I drew it out and held it up. It was an old-fashioned nightdress, made of thick white cotton with lace around the high neck. All at once, I knew what these were – they were the 'floating body' in my pond. I stuffed the things back in the bag and pulled out my mobile with shaking hands. I made my call, then sank down on the pile of compost bags and waited for the police to come.

****

Give D.I. Cooke his due, they weren't long. The D.I. was a bit cross with me because I hadn't told him about the 'drowning' incident. The blue lights and sirens must have given Kenny and Joseph a clue that something was going on because Kenny appeared in the doorway of the shed moments after the police arrived. He stared at the bag in the Inspector's hands.

"What's going on? What's that?"

"Miss Dixon just found this in your shed amongst your bags of compost, sir. Do you have any explanation?"

"What for? What is it?" Kenny was wide-eyed, I'd never seen him look so flustered.

The D.I. lifted the wig out of the bag with a gloved hand. Kenny looked puzzled. Just as the detective took the nightdress out of the carrier, Joseph came into the shed, leaning heavily on a stick.

"What's all this? Why do you have my wife's nightdress in your hands, D.I. Cooke?" he asked in a quavering voice.

"This is your wife's garment, Mr Baxter?"

"My late wife's yes. I haven't seen it for many years but I'm sure it was hers."

"What about this wig?"

"Never seen that before."

"We will have to take this to Forensics." He turned to me. "When is your father back, Miss?"

"Tomorrow."

"May I suggest that you take great care." He then looked at Kenny. "I assume you are not planning on going away anywhere, sir?"

"Are you accusing me of something?" Kenny looked directly into the detective's eyes.

"Not at the moment but I advise you to stay in the village, sir."

"I can't believe it! You can't think my grandson would do anything to Lucy? He loves the girl, any fool can see that! Someone has planted those things to try to make him look guilty."

Kenny put his arm around the old man. "Come on now, granddad, let's go back to the house. You mustn't get upset and you're right, I haven't done anything. I'm sure the police will sort it all out."

The D.I. asked me to tell him exactly what had happened the night that I thought I'd seen a body floating in my pond and he wanted to know why I hadn't called the police. When I explained that when Kenny came there was nothing in the pond, he nodded.

"Right. Well, we will see what this lot can tell us and I'll be back if I think of anything else I want to ask you. Don't hesitate to call me if you think of anything you think I need to know."

The police left and I followed the Baxter men back to the house, the dogs trailing after me, having been cheated of their walk.

Dinner that night was a quiet affair, each of us taken up in our own thoughts. Eventually, Kenny broke the silence.

"You don't think I am responsible for what has been happening, do you, Lucy? What possible reason would I have?"

"I don't know. I don't know what to think any more. This whole thing has been so confusing and frightening. Perhaps I've made a terrible mistake in coming to live in the farmhouse. Maybe I should go back to London after all."

"No! Don't go back to London. Don't leave here, Lucy," Joseph held onto my hand and I looked at him lovingly. "We all love you, you belong here."

I got up from the table.

"I thought I did but now I'm not sure."

I took the crocks through and put them in the dishwasher. When I came out, Kenny and Joseph were sitting in front of the television. I could tell that they weren't really paying much attention to it. Kenny looked like he wanted to say something but I didn't give him the chance, I just wanted to get away.

I went straight up to my room. Clarry came with me and I locked my door and settled down in the armchair and picked up a book. However, I found it very hard to read and I kept thinking of the things that had gone on and thinking about Kenny. Did I really believe he could or would have done those things? What possible motive could he have had? All those times he stayed with me to 'look after' me, was he laughing up his sleeve at me because he was the perpetrator? Again, to what purpose? He'd never taken advantage of me, so that couldn't be the motive. Had I fallen in love with a man who was a psycho on the quiet? Had I given up the prospect of a comfortable life with a rich man for someone who was prone to doing strange things? I had to admit that I was not happy and even more than that, I was extremely confused.

Dad and Sheila were due back tomorrow. It was not going to be a good welcome home.

****

In the end, I decided that the best thing to do was to go home before they got back. I left an hour before I knew they would be here. I kissed Joseph and whispered that I loved him and not to say anything to them today about what's happened. They would find out soon enough and now that I knew that it was a person, not ghosts haunting me, I knew I would be okay back at the farmhouse. *'Let them do their worst,'* I thought, although I had no idea who 'they' were.

Deep inside of me, I couldn't believe it was Kenny, even though the evidence was damming. He, of course, was busy at the garden centre because it was open all day Saturday until about seven in the evening.

I was glad to be back in my own home again (well, it was nearly mine, still had a couple of months to go before I'd fulfilled the conditions of the will), not least because I didn't have to talk with anyone about what was going on and my fears and feelings about what I might do. I'd stayed in the house for ten months; was I really going to give up now? Even if I didn't stay here, I felt that after all I'd been through I deserved to have the money that the sale of the house would bring. I just didn't know what to do. I had burned my boats with London in every way – my job was gone, my fiancé was no longer my fiancé and my lovely flat was in the process of being sold. I knew there was still time to back out but I felt that I really didn't want to go back there, it wouldn't be the same as it had been. Perhaps I should stay here, sell up after it was mine and start again somewhere else; after all, this place and all the ground would fetch a tidy sum which could set me up in business and get me a decent house. I didn't need one as big as this, it was a large house for one person, and it should be a family home.

Anyway, I couldn't do anything for another couple of months; perhaps things will have changed by then.

Dad came round to see me on his own the next day. He looked very serious. He'd come to ask me what was going on because neither Kenny nor Joseph would tell them anything but it was obvious there was an atmosphere.

"Has there been a row over something? I thought you would be at the house waiting for us when we got back."

I decided there was no point in stalling; I'd always told my dad everything anyway. I made him a cup of tea and sat down with him to tell him everything that had happened.

After I'd finished my narration, he was very quiet. After a while, he said,

"I really can't believe that Kenny has got anything to do with all this. He's such a genuine man and I'm sure he wouldn't try to hurt you in any way. In any case, there's no reason that I can think of for him doing such things. Sheila will be very upset about all this."

"And you think I'm not?" I got up and paced around. "I've been the victim here! I am the one who has been suffering because someone has decided to make my life a misery – to try to get me to believe my house is haunted! Why should anyone do that? I've not done anyone any harm, in fact, I've tried to help people, to be a good neighbour and a helpful member of the village! And all you can worry about is your new wife – what about me?"

He got up and caught me, put his arms around me and I sobbed on his shoulder and when I stopped I felt wrung out.

"Of course I care about you, my Lulu," he said gently, offering me his clean white handkerchief. "But I also care about Sheila, Kenny and Joseph. It will hurt my Sheila so much if she thinks that you think that Kenny is doing this to you and think how she will feel if he gets arrested over this."

I had thought about it and about Joseph and how it would affect him; it could make him ill all over again.

"Oh dad, what are we going to do?"

"Well, we can't do anything until the police have the results of the forensic tests; maybe that will shed some light on it all. In the meantime, I want our family to stay close and support each other. Kenny is innocent, I'm sure of it. I think someone planted those things in his shed. If that is not the case, how come none of the nursery workers had found the bag before? They are in and out of there all the time, getting stocks out."

That made sense.

"Actually, before I found the bag, John told me that Clarry had been barking a lot that afternoon. Normally, she doesn't bark and hadn't all week until then. I think Clarry knows who is doing this and she knew it was that person she heard in the yard that afternoon."

Dad stroked his chin thoughtfully.

"Hmm, I think you are right there. I think we need to tell the D.C.I. when we see him again."

Chapter 40
A Monumental Find

As it happened, I didn't have long to wait. D.C.I. Cooke was back at my house on the Monday morning. I had just put my loaves of bread to rise when he arrived with his usual sergeant and a woman P.C., who he introduced as WPC Ruth Jones. I nodded to her in acknowledgement.

"We have had the forensic report on the balloons; they are the same. We are not saying that they definitely came from the garden centre but it seems likely. The lights appear to have come from a small electrical shop in the market in Hereford; they come in packets of five. We have questioned the shopkeeper but he had no idea who bought them. We found part of a finger-print on the blue balloon but it doesn't match any of our records."

"So, we are none the wiser as to who did them then?"

"Not at this moment, no, but you never know what will turn up in an investigation like this. Now, what I want of you, Miss Dixon, is to tell me the whole story of everything that has gone on in this house since you arrived, even if it seems insignificant. I want to hear about every mysterious sound, every strange thing you've seen, every time your dog has barked for seemingly no reason – you know that dogs can hear things we can't. I want to know everything."

Phew! That was going to take a while.

"In that case, I think we need some tea or something to keep us going, " I said.

"My sergeant will make it, won't you Grant?"

"Yessir," was the stalwart reply and D.C.I. Cooke took me by the elbow and guided me into my lounge, followed by WPC Jones, who sat herself down unobtrusively on an upright chair in a corner and took out her notebook.

"Now, Miss Dixon, tell me everything you can remember."

It did indeed take quite a while to tell him all that had happened, beginning with the Footstep noises. The constable came through with four mugs of tea after about ten minutes and I took mine gratefully, wrapping my frozen fingers around it, appreciating the warmth. Briefly, I wondered why my hands were so cold, it wasn't that cold out. Perhaps it was because I was still suffering from shock.

When I reached the part about the ghost and the pond, D.C.I. Cooke stopped me.

"Um, you seemed unsurprised that you should see a ghost in your pond, why was that?"

"That was because of the date – March fifteenth," I explained. "It was the date of a real drowning there back in the early nineteen-fifties."

"How do you know that?"

"Because I found a paper in my aunt's files about it."

"Do you have it still? Can I see it?"

"Of course."

I took him to the den, the other P.C.s trailing after us. I found the paper where I'd left it and handed it to D.C.I. Cooke, who looked at it carefully.

"Hmm, can I keep this?"

"Yes, no problem."

"When did you find this paper?"

I realised then that I had forgotten about the day I'd found it, so I told him about it. "I was surprised to find it because I'd gone through all my aunt's papers and thought I'd seen everything. However, I must have missed it somehow."

"Unless it wasn't there before," mused the detective. I looked at him sharply.

"What do you mean? How could it have just appeared there?"

"I'll give it some thought. Let's go back to the lounge and finish our tea."

So we returned and I finished my narration. When I got to the bit where Clarry had barked at the wall in the bedroom, he looked up again.

"Can we see the bedroom?"

So then I found myself guiding them up the stairs and along the landing to the long bedroom.

"You say it was here that the dog was scrabbling and barking?"

"Yes."

"Hmm, doesn't seem to be anything here. Very strange. What's on the other side of this wall?"

"The hayloft. You get to it through the upper barn."

"I think we need to do a search, if you don't mind, Miss Dixon?"

I replied that it was fine, to go ahead. He barked some instructions into his phone and we went downstairs.

I continued with the things I remembered. He'd heard about the mysterious lights but was interested again in the screaming. Where did I think it had come from? I had no idea; it sounded like it was very close.

Eventually, his questions ceased. I looked at my watch, it had taken at least an hour. I remembered the bread and hastened through to check on it. The loaves were well risen so I put them all in the ovens and set my timer; I couldn't afford to waste so much produce. I was watched interestedly by my companions.

"We will search the house and the grounds, with your permission, Miss Dixon? I feel we really need to get to the bottom of all this."

"I am happy for you to do anything you feel you need to. Would it be alright if I make my deliveries to the shop while it's going on?"

"Of course you may, you're not a suspect you know! I must say that bread smells very good."

The search squad arrived just as I was taking the loaves from the ovens. They did indeed smell good. I turned them out of their tins and put clean cloths over them so they could cool.

"This is Sergeant Chambers, Miss Dixon. He will be in charge of the search team. I'm going over to the Nursery House; I need a few words with them."

"Please bear in mind that Joseph Baxter is an old man and doesn't need to be upset," I said.

"Don't worry, Miss Dixon, I'll be gentle. Come, Grant and Jones, you're with me. And Sergeant, don't hesitate to call me if you find anything."

"Would you mind not searching my kitchen until after I've taken the bread away? This is supposed to be a kitchen that's hygienic because I sell my bread. It won't be with your team all over it."

"Don't worry, miss, we can wait. We'll do the rest of the house first, if that's okay? I'm not expecting to find much, although I think we need to concentrate on the den and the large bedroom."

I was left to get on with my work and, truth be told, I was glad to drive away from there with my car full of the bread order for Madge.

"I'm sorry that I've no cakes for you today," I told her as I unloaded. "I have police all over my place, not possible to bake I'm afraid."

"Come and sit down, you look like you need it, lamb." She wasn't far off. I found myself telling her something of what had been happening and she was all sympathy. All ears as well, I knew and I also realised it wouldn't take long for it to go round the village. But now, I didn't care, I needed a woman to talk to and although I might have talked to Sheila, I felt I couldn't now that her son seemed like a possible suspect. I didn't mention that to Madge though.

"What a terrible thing! Someone wants you out of that house but what a way to do it. Do you think you will stay now? I'm not sure if I would if all those things happened to me."

"To be honest, I don't know. Perhaps I will sell up and move away. Dad doesn't need me, he's happy with Sheila and I don't want to go back to London now that my engagement is off."

"You poor lass. If there's anything I can do to help you, just call me. Me and Len are right behind you, we don't want you to leave and I'm sure that most of the village would want you to stay."

'Except at least one person,' I thought to myself.

As I drove back, I was trying to think of just who in the village might want to see me gone. They all seemed very friendly, with the exception of Elwyn Price. However, I knew that it wasn't personal with him, that's just how he was with everyone.

When I got back home, the place was crawling with police searching everywhere. I'd been home about half an hour when a shout came. 'In here!'

The man who had made the find stood at the top of the stone steps leading up to the barn. I had been here nearly a year and I'd never been in it, had no idea what was up there. I followed the inspector up the steps and into the barn. It was big, with small windows along the walls either side. The floor was made of the same painted wooden planks that were along the landing in the house. There were various mysterious shapes, hard to see in the dim light but I guessed they were the sort of junk people usually kept in their attics.

At the far end there was another door and the man led us through that. This was the hay loft; it had the wooden door in the wall and a metal contraption that was a chain and pulley for getting the bales of hay up and down.

There was no hay in here, just a few old sacks and some old chairs. They were stacked in one corner and were now being moved by a couple of constables. I felt it was odd that they were here when all the other junk was in the main barn. Then I saw why; they had been put here to hide something.

Attached to the wall was something like a very small computer, even smaller than the notebooks that children used in school; it was, in fact, not much bigger than a mobile phone. Attached to it by electrical wire was a bulky piece of black plastic casing and, when one of the men turned it around in his gloved hand, we could see that it was in fact a large battery pack.

I looked at the Sergeant with questioning eyes.

"I think we may have found your 'ghost', Miss Dixon," he said gently. "I'll contact the D.C.I." He nodded to the entrance and I took the hint and went back through the doorway into the barn and out down the steps.

It didn't take long before the D.C.I.'s car was crunching to a halt on my driveway. Without any preamble, he went straight to the barn, up the steps and disappeared inside. It wasn't long before he was out again and this time he came into the house to find me. I was in the lounge again, totally unable to do anything.

"So, we are making progress, Miss Dixon! We will get our experts over here; this will be our biggest lead. Somewhere, someone is controlling it. We should be able to crack that, find out who is behind all this.

"Oh, by the way, Mrs Dixon insists she gave that nightdress away, along with other things just before Christmas. Says she took it down to the Hospice shop herself. Couldn't have been the old man's wife's nightie but we will look into it, of course."

He stood up.

"Right, I'm out of here! I feel there's no point in searching the grounds anymore and it's obvious there's nothing in the house. We have taken some finger-prints in various places; I would be glad if you would pop into the police station in Hereford at some point to give us your finger-prints so we can eliminate your prints from the clues."

"Of course I will," I replied. "Thank you for all you have done and are doing."

He looked at me and smiled. I realised he was quite an attractive man, especially when he smiled.

"We are making some real progress at last. I always felt there was something not quite right with your aunt's death and if she had some of this going on, I am not surprised she eventually had a heart attack; it got too much for her, poor woman."

"I hope you manage to find out the scum who has been doing this. I wouldn't normally use such expressions but I feel that's just what they are, whoever they are."

"You're right there, miss."

I saw him to the door and watched him and his two sidekicks get into his car and they set off with a crunching of stones on the drive.

Half an hour later, the search squad had all gone too and Clarry and I were left alone. I felt wiped out but restless; the quietness of the place fairly shouted at me. I felt I just wanted to sleep and sleep forever; I wanted to shut out the thought that someone in this village hated me so much that they were willing to do almost anything to get rid of me.

Chapter 41
The Mystery Begins to Unravel

My peace didn't last long; soon, another car drove up. This was just a plain black saloon and two men got out. They looked barely more than teenagers; however, they were professional in their approach. They were the computer experts who had come to crack the device in the hay loft.

I showed them where to go and they examined some chairs up there. Having found two that were serviceable, they dusted them off, positioned them in front of the device and proceeded to unpack the cases they had brought with them. I left them to it; I hadn't a clue what they were going to do or how they would do it but they looked like they were confident.

Although I'd been thinking of going for a walk, I decided against it, feeling that I couldn't really leave my property while these men were in my hayloft.

I decided to do some baking and so I made some Victoria sponges and some scones. I took two scones, fresh from the oven, up to the men in the hayloft. As I got up there, the one with the spectacles, who reminded me a bit of Harry Potter with his dark hair and a very Potter-like half grin, took his headphones off.

"Well, we have got what we came for, I think. We are going to leave this device here working for now so that the other end doesn't become suspicious. Please ignore any noises you hear. When we have found the source, we will come and take this away. It has been fingerprinted by the other team, so we now have all the evidence we need from it."

When they had gone, I decided that I needed to get out. I called Clarry and she skipped up to me joyfully and we set off together. I didn't bother with the lead, my little dog was very obedient and we were in the country anyway. I did make sure I locked everywhere up; I didn't want my invisible enemy to gain entrance to get up to any new tricks.

I decided that I needed to go over and see dad and Sheila; I felt bad that I hadn't stayed on to welcome them home on Saturday. I was somewhat worried about how Sheila would react to me but I needn't have been concerned for she was as sweet as she always had been.

"Come and see Joseph, he's been worrying about you," she said. I followed her through and went straight to the elderly man in the chair. He held his arms out to me and I went to him, putting my arms around him and kissing his cheek.

"Oh Lucy, love, it's so good to see you," he said, his voice quavering a little. "I thought you didn't like us anymore."

"I love you, you know that. I've just been having a bad time, that's all."

"Tell us what's been going on today. The police came over and I told him that I had given that nightdress to the St. Michael's Hospice shop along with quite a few other things. I took them down there myself," said Sheila.

"I know, he told me. It couldn't have been the one from here. I hope they find out some things from it. They have had a search squad over at my place and they found something interesting."

I told them about the little computer and the experts who had been this afternoon.

"I have no idea how it works but it seems it is a mini computer, connected to my wifi in the house but controlled by another computer elsewhere. It acts as a receiver and speaker, putting out the sounds that I hear in the house as if it is ghosts."

"And you say it's in the hayloft?" mused dad. "Very clever; no wonder Clarry went mad in there. She knew where it was coming from – from behind the bedroom wall!"

"Yes, she's a clever little girl."

"I can't help wondering what this is all about though," Sheila said, thoughtfully. "Just who would want to do this to Bea and to Lucy – and why?"

"Well, that's what I can't work out."

"Let's hope the police can find out for us," said dad. "That Detective Inspector seems like a clever man; he's always been suspicious about Bea's death. My goodness, I hope no-one is trying to kill our Lucy!"

"Oh no," Sheila was quick to reassure, "I'm sure they wouldn't be after killing her. I think they just want her to leave the house."

"So, who gets the house if she leaves it?" asked Joseph.

"Various charities," I answered. "The house gets sold and the proceeds go to charities of Aunt Bea's choice."

"Hmm, perhaps we should get in touch with Paul Gamble to see if he knows what charities they are," said dad thoughtfully.

"I'll call him, invite him round for tea," said Sheila. I put a hand out to stop her.

"No, don't do that. I have to go into Hereford tomorrow, they want my fingerprints. I will call in on Paul's office while I'm there, if he's not busy."

At that, we dropped the subject and I asked about where they had gone on their honeymoon. The time passed very

When Kenny came home from work, he smiled at me. My heart jumped and I knew that I would never believe it was him trying to frighten me.

I helped to clear up after the meal and I declared it was time I went home. I bade them all goodnight and collected my coat and called to Clarry. I had just reached the river path when Kenny caught up with me. I stopped and looked at him, he wore a troubled expression. I wanted to put my arms around him like I had with Joseph but my arms stayed by my side.

"Lucy – I – sorry, I had to speak with you."

"That's alright."

"You don't believe it is me that's done those things to you, do you, Lucy?"

I gazed at him searchingly. I could not see anything in his face, only open honesty.

"No," I said at last, "I don't believe it's you, Kenny."

"Thank you. That means a lot to me. I would never do anything to hurt you."

"I know."

"But the police don't know. I could still yet be in trouble for this. The balloons came from my shop, although anyone can buy them. And those things were found in my shed, although if I'd done it, I would hardly keep them on my own premises, would I?"

I touched his arm.

"Don't worry, the Chief is a good man. He'll figure it all out."

He nodded and then turned around and walked back to his house. I watched him go and a feeling of great sadness filled my whole being.

****

It was only a couple of days later that I had another visit from D.I. Cooke and Sergeant Grant. It was afternoon and I'd done my deliveries to Madge's and to the nursery café. I was having a quiet rest after my morning's work.

"Won't keep you long, Miss Dixon. I've just come to give you an update. The computer control was traced back to a flat over an empty shop in Credenhill. We found the computer in question; it had been disabled. Our experts are looking at it as we speak."

"I don't know anyone in Credenhill."

"You don't have to. It's my guess it was just a convenient place; they didn't want the control too far away from the receiver in case there were any problems; it is a short-range receiver. You may also be interested to know that we have also talked to the staff of the St. Michael's Hospice Shop in Hereford. We found that the manager, a pleasant woman name of Mrs. Brown, was very helpful. When we showed her the garment, she remembered it – not only that, she remembered when it was sold. She said she recalled it easily because it was regarded as a vintage item, of which they didn't get that many. She remembers a young woman buying it; apparently the woman told Mrs Brown that she wanted it for a play that she and her acting group were putting on later this year. She said it was just what she was looking for."

"Well, she has performed her play alright," I remarked. He nodded and continued,

"So it seems that, in a roundabout way, it was Mrs Baxter's nightdress after all, although it obviously didn't come straight from the house. Now, Mrs Brown is an extremely helpful lady; she came down to the station this morning and helped us to compile an identikit picture of the young woman." He nodded to P.C. Grant, who produced a paper from a folder he was carrying.

"Does this face ring any bells, Miss Dixon?"

I took the picture, looked and gasped.

"You recognise her?"

I did indeed; although it wasn't exactly right, the identikit was a very good likeness of Kenny's girlfriend, Glynis Price.

****

After the policemen had gone, my mind was in turmoil. Having been convinced of Kenny's innocence, I had to admit that it didn't look good for him again. I didn't want to think of him wanting to frighten me; he'd always done such a good job of coming to me and helping to soothe my fears, making me feel safe. How could he possibly be in on this? I wouldn't believe it.

"Clarry! Come on, girl, we have to go out." Clarry, ever willing for a walk, was up in a trice, waiting at the door, wagging her tail. I fetched my anorak, locked the door and set off for the river path. I reasoned that I had some time if they were going to take Glynis in for questioning; I wanted to warn my family, it was the least I could do. In particular Kenny, I wanted to warn the man I loved

\.

****

Two days later, Kenny was brought in for questioning. I learned later that Glynis had held out for that length of time, refusing to talk. In the end she said 'he told me what to do and how to do it.' However, she wouldn't say who 'he' was. So, D.I.Cooke took it upon himself to bring Kenny in. I happened to be at their house when they came because I had formed the habit of calling in every day. The detective didn't come himself, he simply sent Sergeant Grant and another policeman to fetch Kenny.

"Just tell the truth, son, if you tell the truth you have nothing to fear," Sheila said as she hugged him. I wanted to hug him too but I couldn't. Our eyes met for a moment; I hoped he saw what I wanted to say in my eyes. I desperately wanted him to be innocent and pushed down the little niggling doubt that threatened. I just couldn't understand why Glynis would do things like that and inside me I knew she would have had to be motivated by someone else.

Twenty-four hours later, they let Kenny go; they had nothing definite to pin on him, apart from the wig and nightdress being found on his premises and the balloons having come from the garden centre shop. It was obvious that he'd had nothing to do with the computer business in Credenhill; he was always in and around the garden centre. In any case, he didn't have that much computer expertise.

Although the nightdress had been Mrs Baxter's, where the wig had come from was not yet established.

Kenny was released from the station; he hadn't been arrested but had been told to stay in the area. He looked terrible when he came home; his clothes were crumpled and he was unshaven and unkempt with dark circles under his eyes. My heart went out to him. It was obvious that he didn't know what to to do first, eat, shower or sleep. Sheila of course made him eat, convinced that they hadn't fed him properly at the station, although I suspected that they would have fed him and probably gave him disgusting coffee. Then he went off to shower.

I went home; I felt responsible somehow and wanted to be out of the way. At least I knew there would be no more creepy noises at my house. I should have been able to relax but somehow I couldn't. There was more to all this than met the eye and I was desperate to know what it was.

Chapter 42
A Terrible Shock

After the dramatic identification of Glynis, and Kenny's interrogation, everything went quiet. I could do nothing only get on with my work supplying Madge's shop and the café. Business at both places was building up again, for we were well into May now. People were coming out to enjoy the weather, stocking up their gardens and stopping in the café for a drink and a cake. At the village shop, people were after cakes and pastries that they could eat on the move.

I also threw myself into the gardening; there was always so much to do out there. Kenny came to help but there was little interaction between us; I felt to blame, although I hadn't done anything. Much of the time he sent someone else to work in my garden and I understood that; there was a definite atmosphere between us. In any case, he needed to be at the nursery most of the time, he was the boss after all, although I knew the nursery people well enough now to know they were perfectly able to function without him there all the time.

The days drifted on without hearing anything. Every day when I got up I hoped that this was the day that I would hear something from D.I. Cooke and every night as I went to bed, I sighed because there'd been nothing.

It was some two weeks later that I finally got a call from the detective.

"Miss Dixon, could you meet me at the Nursery House in about half an hour? We have some results and I think you should be with your family when I share our findings with you."

"Have you made an arrest?"

"We have indeed, Miss Dixon but I will tell you about it when I see you."

I didn't get a chance to question further because the connection was abruptly cut off.

When the call came, I was about to take my order to Madge's and to the nursery. It fitted in well with my schedule; I was going there anyway. I loaded my car quickly, popped Clarry in a small dog carrier (she didn't like that but I couldn't have her all over the car while I had produce in it) and put it in the well in front of the passenger seat so she was beside me.

I didn't linger at Madge's; in any case she was busy serving, so I just carried the trays in and left them for her. Then, it was off to the nursery. I made my delivery to the café and then took my car around so it was near the house – in fact, not far from where I'd found the bag on that fateful day. I let Clarry out and she rushed to the door of the house, wagging her tail. Sheila was surprised to see me and immediately called dad, who was busy writing upstairs. He came down.

"Hello Lulu, this is a surprise." He kissed me.

"You haven't had a phone-call then?" I asked. It seemed they hadn't.

"I had a call from Detective Chief Inspector Cooke, asking me to come here and he's coming to see me, to see all of us. Apparently, they've arrested someone."

"Oh!" Sheila sank down on a kitchen chair. "That's such a relief. They don't suspect Kenny any longer then, obviously. Tom, would you mind fetching him over?"

"Of course I will. Won't be long." Dad hurried off in the direction of the garden centre. Sheila decided to make a pot of tea in readiness and told me to go in and say hello to Joseph.

I did as I was told and made a fuss of the old man. When I told him why I was there, he rubbed his hands together in glee.

"So, we get to find out at last! About time too."

D.C.I. Cooke arrived dead on time with the ever-faithful Detective Sergeant Grant. Dad and Kenny followed them in. We all went through to the lounge and Sheila dished out mugs of tea to everyone. D.C.I. Cooke stood and the rest of us were sitting.

As I looked around the room, I was suddenly reminded of all those Agatha Christie programmes on television where all the suspects are gathered together to hear Miss Marple's or Hercule Poirot's revealing of who the killer was and how they did it. I wanted to giggle for a moment and then a horrible thought struck me – what if they had come to reveal that someone in this room was guilty after all? That horrifying thought silenced any potential laughter.

"As you know, Glynis Price was behind your mysterious 'ghosts', Miss Dixon. She has admitted to us that she pretended to be a ghostly entity drowned in your pond and produced the floating lights by way of small halogen lights inside balloons. However, she refused to tell us who had got her to do it." He glanced towards Kenny, who gazed steadily back at the detective. I felt a sudden dip in my stomach – surely not, please…

D.C.I. Cooke continued,

"So, we turned our attention back to that wonderful little device we found in your hayloft. As you know, we traced the source back to a flat in Credenhill. Our experts were able to establish that it was, in fact, the device that had controlled your one. They were able to produce the footsteps, the sobbing and the screaming that you described, Miss Dixon."

"The footsteps too?" I asked, surprised. "But they were already there, my aunt had heard them because she wrote about them – and Kenny heard them the morning he found Aunt Bea."

The detective nodded.

"Indeed. We were able to establish that the device had been installed quite some time before the death of your aunt. However, the sobbing and the screaming were added much later – this year, in fact."

"We decided to turn our attention to the flat itself, had it been rented or had someone just managed to get in and occupy it? We found that the premises had been rented by a person called Bartholomew Westrupp. We felt that it shouldn't be too difficult to trace a man with a name like that but we found that he didn't seem to exist.

"However, although attempts had been made to eliminate all evidence, it seemed our man must have had a hasty departure because we managed to find part fingerprints and also DNA from the computer itself. It led us to one Brian White, he was on our records. We have a picture of him here."

P.C. Grant handed the picture out and it was passed around. It meant nothing to me; I knew I'd never seen it before. However,

"That's the bloke who came here wanting to buy this property!" exclaimed Kenny.

The detective nodded, unsurprised.

"Yes. We have shown it to others who have identified him as the man who was trying to persuade owners here to sell up. It will be the man your aunt wrote about, Miss Dixon."

"I can't get my head around this," I said.

"The day your aunt saw him was not the first time he had been to her property. He had discovered all about her – that she was an elderly lady, living alone and was the owner of most of the land. It seems she didn't just own the house and garden but she owned the fields surrounding the property.

"He had found out that she was unlikely to sell and his boss wanted that property so he planted the device in the hayloft; he had just come out of there when your aunt came back and saw him. So he pretended he was lost and asked her if she would consider selling. As you know, your aunt sent him away with a flea in his ear but it didn't matter because the device was now in place ready to start the 'frightening campaign.'

What they never bargained for was her great love of her home and her stalwartness in dealing with a sudden ghostly occupation which had not been there before. It didn't move her one bit. So, they decided to keep on with the plan in the hope that they would win her over; they would up the 'persuasion' as they did with you, miss. However, there's one drawback to that device; the battery pack has to be renewed about every three months and it seems that it was when she heard someone creeping around her house that she had her heart attack and died. It was, of course, Brian making his way to the hayloft in order to renew the batteries."

"Oh, poor Aunt Bea!" I shook my head.

"Yes indeed. Of course, now that the old woman was dead, they thought that the place would go up for sale; however, the conditions of the will meant that you had to live there if you wanted to inherit it, Miss Dixon."

"Yes. I can see how that would have disappointed him."

"It did indeed disappoint him dreadfully, even more than you can imagine. Brian's boss had already invested a lot of personal life in order to be in line for your property, Miss Dixon."

I frowned, puzzled. "So this Brian guy was working for someone else?"

"Miss Dixon this is going to come as a shock to you but I'm afraid his boss is your ex-fiancé, James Netherfield."

There was a stunned silence in the room. My thoughts were racing – Jim! No! Surely not! I didn't know what to say. If I hadn't been sitting already, I would have fallen. My knees suddenly felt like jelly and I found I was shivering.

"Shock," pronounced Sheila. Drink this, sweetheart." I took the mug of tea that she had picked up and spooned more sugar into. Dad tucked a soft, fleecy blanket over my knees and Kenny wrapped one around my shoulders. He left his hand on my shoulder and I covered it with my own shaky hand.

It was down to dad to ask the questions, 'How? Why?'

"I'm afraid that Mr Netherfield owns a big consortium. As you know, he is very rich and he has taken over his father's business. However, unlike his father who was honest and a good man to work for, James isn't. He has fingers in a few shady pies. Quite why he was so set on having your property, I'm not sure. And his methods do seem rather extreme.

"It seems that once he had his sights set on River View, he also set his sights on you. He found out all about your aunt, what family she had, who she was likely to leave it to if she died. He knew her only family were you, Mr Dixon and you, Miss Dixon. When he first met you, he didn't know who you were but of course he looked into your background and hey presto! You had fallen right into his hands, how amazing was that? He only had to make sure you were in his life, then it was hopefully only a matter of time.

"Of course, he hoped you would sell right away; he never bargained on you actually wanting to live here – that came as a shock to him.

Once you had made your decision to come here, he tried to make sure that you would stay with him; he got worried in case you would decide to stay here.

He got Brian to resume the 'footsteps' and played his own part in pretending to be scared of them and worried for you. He was convinced you would be afraid and decide to leave but you didn't. He gave you your dog as part of the act of 'being afraid for you' and even went so far as to suggest that you married once your year here was up, although he'd actually got no intention of marrying you once the place was sold.

When you broke off your engagement and was so firm about it, he realised that he had to go back to his original plan of trying to scare you into leaving. He gave instructions to Brian to up the haunting campaign; he'd already planted the paper in your den with the supposed drowning (that didn't actually happen, by the way, the people who lived here then weren't even called Jones), just in case, as he suspected already that you were going to need more persuading to leave the property."

My shock was leaving me; now I was feeling angry. I pushed off the blankets and sat forward.

"So, how did Glynis get involved in all this?"

"It seemed that Mr Netherfield had an eye for the ladies," he paused, looking at me apologetically.

'Didn't I know it?' I thought, ruefully, remembering how he'd lusted after Penny at her party.

"He said he met Miss Price on one time when he was over here and you were busy. He used to take himself out sometimes when you had too much on. He recognised her as Mr Baxter's girlfriend, having seen her with him and started talking to her. He told her she was attractive and would make a good model and he could help her. He, erm, seduced her, gave her money and told her he would get her a job with a model agency if she would help him with a couple of things first. There was no danger in it, just to play some jokes on you, Miss Dixon.

She went along with it and followed his instructions; she didn't like you, Miss, she thought that her boyfriend, Mr Baxter here, paid you too much attention. Brian provided the wig and the sound effects and she did the visuals. She had no concept of the seriousness of what she was doing, she just thought it was a lark and he flashed a lot of money around her.

"Unfortunately, she realised that Mr Baxter's attentions were, um, wondering, shall we say, especially after you broke the engagement off, Miss Dixon. She had a big row with him and wanted to get back at him so she planted the nightdress and wig on this property; she knew we were looking into the ghost business and she wanted to get him into trouble. Of course, she had no idea what was really behind it all.

Mr Netherfield was desperate to get you to leave your house before the end of the year; he knew you wouldn't leave after that, it was the only chance he had to get hold of it. He was willing to pay for it, it wasn't that he wanted to get it for free, although it's likely he would try to knock down the price considerably, but he knew that if you fell in love with the place that you would never sell."

"I just can't understand why he had to have this property; there are loads of places all over the country that he could have had."

"Oh, believe me, he knows that – he has procured all kinds of properties through various means, some of them shady. But this is a prime location, this is Herefordshire and business people from London want to retire here or have a holiday place here. It's particularly beautiful and the pace of life is much slower; it's a popular area for the rich. He would make a fortune building here."

I thought about this area covered in expensive houses for the elite; the fields gone, Mr. Price's cows gone, River View Farmhouse, gone. Or would it have been left and done up for some rich Londoner to swan about in, to boast that he lived in a four hundred year old black and white farmhouse?

I shuddered at these terrible thoughts. I picked up Clarry and cuddled her.

"We will never let that happen, will we, Clarry?" She wagged her tail and tried to lick me.

"The ironic thing is," said the Detective Inspector, "that if Mr Netherfield hadn't given you your dog to keep up his charade, the balloon in the tree might never have been found, nor the wig and nightdress, and therefore we might never have found out the answers to all of our questions. Clarry is a heroine."

Chapter 43
A Magical Evening

May quickly turned into June and very soon I had completed my year at River view. Paul Gamble did all the necessary legal stuff and now the farmhouse and all the land belonged to me.

"What will you do now that it's all yours? Will you sell?" he asked.

"Of course not! I would never do that after all that's gone on."

"Shocking business. But now you are free of it all, free to get on with your life."

Indeed I was free to get on with my life. However, the next few months were so busy it hardly felt like freedom at all. Once again the race against time was on to pick all the fruit and get the jams made; I barely had any spare time and sometimes it was so hot in my kitchen I wondered why I was doing it.

Sylvie came as often as she could, being off school now for the holidays. She only had one year to do at sixth form then she would be going to the Catering College in Hereford. She had already learned much with me; she would be an expert in Food Health and Safety and had learned various techniques for icing and making sauces. She was also becoming a dab-hand at jam-making. She remembered everything from last year and was extremely helpful.

Kenny was very busy too but he came to make my deliveries for me, knowing that the trays of jams were heavy for me.

Sylvie chattered away to me; it was delightful to have her company. I acknowledged to myself that I was lonely at times. One day, after Kenny had taken another batch of jams for me, she said thoughtfully,

"I just don't know why he doesn't ask you out, Lucy. It's obvious he adores you. Can't you see the way he looks at you? And you like him, don't you? I can see it in your face."

I was startled; was it that obvious? I could feel the heat coming into my face and it wasn't being caused by the cooking. Sylvie chattered on,

"Kenny is lovely. He is so much nicer than your Jim was. I remember what Penny said after her party about Jim. She said that he couldn't take his eyes off her cleavage and when he looked at her from across the room, he reminded her of a weasel just taking stock of its prey."

A weasel! Penny said that James reminded her of a weasel. I recalled the lone sentence that my aunt had written 'he reminded me of a weasel'. Could she have been writing about Jim? Suddenly, I understood everything. Aunt Bea had met Jim that time in London and, although she never said anything to me, she hadn't liked him. So, she went home and changed her will in the hope that I would decide to come here instead of being with him. I smiled; wasn't that just like Aunt Bea? *'Well, it worked, Aunty,'* I said to her in my head. *'I can't thank you enough.'*

The summer fete was just as successful as last year; I was into it now. Thankfully, I was able to enjoy it without Jim appearing and ruining the day. How things had changed since last year. I recalled the lovely moments that I'd spent under the Weeping Willow with Kenny, however, there wasn't going to be a repeat of that experience, sadly.

Summer passed in a flurry of jam-making and other baking. The plums, apples and pears followed the soft fruits and still I was very busy. Sylvie had gone back to school of course but she often appeared on a Saturday to help me. Sometimes, she would simply take Clarry for a walk for me if I was in the middle of something I couldn't leave. The time was flying by almost unnoticed and I was often working into the evening and then collapsing in front of the television.

Every Sunday I went to church unless I was too tired to get up early enough and afterwards to the Nursery House for a meal. Sheila was lovely; it was just like having a mother. Dad was obviously very happy and content and Joseph was looking much better. Kenny? Well, Kenny was just as he always was. Sometimes I wanted to slap him about and ask him why he wasn't asking me out.

September slipped into October and work was easier now. The fruiting was over and I was back into just making bread and cakes for the shop and the café. I often thought I should make an effort to find other places I could supply but somehow I didn't. I found I could live on what I earned and that satisfied me. Why should I slog myself to death for money I didn't really need?

As life was a bit quieter at this time, I had my bathroom 'done up'. It was tiled completely and a lovely walk-in shower installed. I kept the beautiful roll-top bath; there was loads of room and I loved the luxury of relaxing in scented bubbles. However, it was a joy to have a shower and so useful when I had to be in a hurry. I realised the bathroom now wasn't really in keeping with the rest of the house but I loved a 'posh' bathroom so decided it didn't matter. I would be doing other things to the house but they would be done eventually.

Now that we were into October, I was making toffee apples in readiness for Halloween. It was strange to think that I'd done all this before. This year I wouldn't be going to a posh ball in a rich mansion; this year I was going to the village Halloween party.

I wondered what I was going to wear; there would be no Regency ball gown for me. Then, I remembered that I'd seen something in a cupboard in the small bedroom. There was a long black dress and a large black woven shawl. There was even a long grey wig and a pointy hat.

The dress and shawl were a bit grubby, so I took them downstairs and carefully washed, spun and hung them up to dry. They should be okay by tomorrow, I reasoned.

Then, a thought struck me. I called Madge.

"Hello Madge; do you think the organisers of the party would like some toffee apples and maybe some apples for bob-apple or something?"

"I'm sure some of your wonderful toffee apples would be very welcome, my dear but the apples for the games and so on are already provided."

"Ah, okay. How many toffee apples do you think I should make?"

"Can you manage fifty, do you think?"

Fifty! I needed to get onto it without delay.

"That's fine, fifty it is."

That night, I went to bed totally exhausted but I had fifty toffee apples, each wrapped in cellophane, ready for the party the following evening. They looked lovely all laid out on my trays and I was quite proud of myself. I slept well that night!

The next afternoon, I was having second thoughts about going to the party. For the first time I realised I would be going in alone and going to a fete alone was one thing, but entering a party on my own would be different. However, I decided to put on the costume and see what it looked like on me. It was a little too big in places but with the shawl wrapped around and held in place by a silver and black broach that was with it, it didn't look bad. I put on the wig and the hat and really liked it.

Wearing the costume brought me into the spirit of the thing and so I decided to put some make-up on my face to make me look more like a witch. It was a little early, so I took the clothes off and hung them up again. I would get dressed again about half past five, to give me time to get the make-up on and get down there.

I would wear my black ankle boots and black tights to help keep me warm under the dress.

Actually, the dress was made of quite heavy material, which was good.

I had an hour or so before I needed to get changed, so I loaded up my car with the toffee apples and drove down to the village hall with them. I found – guess who – Sheila, of course! She was directing proceedings and Patch, Ron and Mike were busy decorating the hall and getting things ready.

"Oh Lucy, that's marvellous! They look wonderful, you're a star! I didn't like to ask you to do any more, you already do so much for us."

"I wondered why I hadn't been asked! Is there anything else you need help with?"

"No, I think we're just about done now. I will be going home shortly to get changed and so will these lads. They will be bringing their families, won't you guys?"

"Oh yes," grinned Patch. "Will you be coming, Lucy?"

"Yes, I'm coming," I smiled back, glad that I'd decided I would. As they didn't need me, I got in my car, eager to go home and get ready.

Just over an hour later, I re-entered the village hall. It was aglow with eerie lighting, spotlighting the stage on which a witch sat, stirring her cauldron. She had long, flowing white hair and a hooked nose. Her clothes were similar to my own. I had absolutely no idea who she was.

I looked around the room which was crowded with ghosts, witches and wizards, more than one Harry Potter lookalike (of course, wizards are so 'in' these days!) skeletons, ghouls, devils and all sorts and of various sizes from very small to quite large adult. I barely recognised anyone but I found my hand being grabbed and I was pulled into the room by a silver-haired witch, who I realised was Sylvie.

"You look amazing, Lucy!" said Sylvie. "It took me a few minutes to realise it was you! Doesn't Sheila look great? She always does that and I'm always gobsmacked about how different she looks."

My eyes widened.

"That's Sheila up there?"

Sylvie giggled. "Yep. And look over there – that's Ken!"

I followed her point and I saw a wizard in a tall, pointed hat and a long, dark blue cloak covered in moons and stars. He wore a wig of long, brown hair and to me he was the most stunningly wonderful sight in the room. If he took off the hat, it would seem like he'd just walked off a film set about swashbuckling heroes. As I looked at him, his eyes met mine. He kept his eyes on me and walked from the other side of the room straight to me.

"Is this a new witch for the coven, Witch Sylvie?"

She giggled.

"Yes, Oh Master! This is Witch Lucy."

"Oh yes? May I introduce myself, Mistress Lucy? I am Kenneth, Grand High Wizard of the Sutton-on-Wye Coven and these" – he swept his hand over the room – "are all my minions."

I stooped low before him in a bow of respect, although I had to hang onto my hat.

"I am honoured, Oh Grand Wizard of Sutton-on-Wye."

"Come." He took my hand and held it up high as if we were a grand lord and lady. I had trouble keeping my face straight. What a sight we must have looked! But as everyone else looked ghoulish too, it was fitting. We went around the room and people bowed to us and stood back as if we were royalty so we could watch the games being played in different areas. There was much fun going on with Bob Apple, Donuts on a string, Whack the Rat, and others that I couldn't put a name to.

I learned afterwards that Ken, as Grand High Wizard of Sutton always choose a 'queen witch' to escort for the evening and I had obviously been chosen for that particular night. However, at that point I had no idea of that and just enjoyed being with him and the silly pageantry of it all. Everyone was having a good time.

Eventually, we sat down on two seats especially for us and we were served hot dogs (called hot toads laced with human blood – ugh) by two people dressed as vampires and I enjoyed mine, in spite of their gross name, mainly because my partner wouldn't let go of my hand as we sat there, although he held it low down behind the folds of our clothes. It was almost impossible to converse because of the noise but every now and then he squeezed my hand a little and smiled into my eyes. There was so much electricity flowing between us I was sure we must have lightening around us and that the whole room must see it. However, no one stopped to stare and so I relaxed.

We had been there about an hour when the lights flashed off and on, off and on. I wondered what was happening. Obviously the others were unperturbed about this but they all stopped what they were doing and focussed their attention upon the stage. Now, not only was Sheila up there, stirring her cauldron again but there were also a number of 'imps' on the stage with her.

Some strange music began and they began to dance around the stage as she sat calmly stirring. Then, the music changed and Sheila stood up and started to sing, 'Come, little children, I'll take you away' from a certain film about witches. My word, she was good! I saw my step-mother in a whole new light as I watched her sing and dance. When she finished the song, she returned to her pot, the 'imps' gathered around her as then as she stirred she chanted:

'Hair of dog and eye of cat,
Toe of frog, or something like that.
What shall I add to my special brew?
Maybe a little child or two?

At that line, the imps jumped off the stage and pretended to run after some children, who screamed delightedly and ran before them. A couple of children were 'caught' and brought to the front of the stage. Sheila pointed to them and chanted:

"Will it be you, or maybe you?
I think there's enough in my witches brew
Who would like a cup or two?"

The two 'caught' children were the first ones to come up on the stage to collect their drinks. One by one, the children lined up to go onto the stage and Sheila ladled the drink into each cup. The 'imps' helped them down the steps the other side. When the children all had a cup of brew the adults were able to go and get theirs. The serving vampires brought some to Ken and me. I eyed the blue-green liquid in the cup and tentatively took a sip. It was lovely, fruity and quite refreshing. I looked at Ken and he laughed.

"I have no idea what it is! Alex and Stephanie concoct something different every year, I don't know how they do it. It's a well-kept secret. Do you like it?"

"It's delicious. How clever of them to make it look so gruesome and have it taste so lovely!"

"I am constantly amazed by the wealth of talent we have in this small village of ours."

"Oh my goodness, you are right! Your mother is something else – is there nothing she can't do?"

He laughed heartily; I loved the sound.

"Do you know, I can't think of anything, although I don't think she can play the Bassoon!"

I nudged him.

"You are silly!"

He laughed again and I became aware that he'd actually put his arm around me. I could hardly breathe and I was convinced he would be able to hear my heart hammering away nineteen to the dozen. We sat in contented companionship as we watched the iron cauldron being man-handled off the stage by Ron and Patch – at least, I think it was them – and brought down to a place at the back of the hall where it was easier for people to help themselves. Sheila came over to speak with us. Ken's arm came from around me, which I was disappointed about, but I couldn't really ask him to put it back.

"Hello, you two, you look wonderful."

"So do you – and you performed up there so well, you are amazing. Pity dad couldn't see you doing that!"

"Thank you, my dear, it's my yearly pleasure! And your dad did see it." She pointed to where two males sat, one dressed as a scarecrow and the other as Herman Munster and I realised that it was in fact Joseph and my dad!

"Oh, I had no idea they were here! I must go and speak with them," I said, turning to Ken. "Do I have permission to leave the Grand Wizard's side for a few minutes?"

"Absolutely not! I will come with you."

The three of us went over to the scarecrow and Herman.

"Dad! Joseph! I didn't know it was you!" I hugged and kissed them each in turn. "Are you enjoying the evening?"

"We are indeed lass," the scarecrow that was Joseph answered me. "This is one of the best Halloween parties we've had. You have made a wonderful Queen Witch, my dear."

I gave him a very un-witchly grin. "Thank you very much. What fun this is, I don't think I've ever been to anything quite like this, have you, dad?"

"Well, of course I was here last year but this year is even batter. My lady is wonderful, isn't she?" He reached out and took Sheila's hand and there was no mistaking the obvious affection in their eyes for each other. I felt a lump in my throat. I turned a little and spotted a tall and gangling 'skeleton' seated near the two men and suddenly realised it was Paul Gamble, the solicitor.

"Paul, it's good to see you too! I hadn't realised you were here."

"It's hard to recognise people in their costumes, my dear, although I admit that I wear this every year!

"You look, erm, hungry." I grinned. "I think you should come up and sample some of my apple pies."

"Apple pies eh? How can I resist? I'll be up as soon as I can."

I was quite sorry when the evening came to an end. It had to end early because of the children. I noticed that some families with very young toddlers had already left.

"Can I see you home? It's the Grand Wizard's last duty to see his queen safely back to her lair."

"Erm, well, I have my car parked at the end of my lane. I knew I would be alright in the village with everyone around but I didn't relish having to walk up my lane in the dark. I didn't know I would have a Grand Wizard to escort me home," I said regretfully.

"Well, perhaps I can see you to where your broomstick awaits?"

I agreed to this and we bade all our friends goodnight and off we went. The village outside the hall and around the green was abound with imps, fairies, witches and ghouls of all kinds as they walked home in groups. Ken took my hand and together we wandered, quite slowly, up the main street of the village and out towards the lane. We didn't talk; I think we were each of us struggling inside.

When we got to my car, he watched me as I fished around in the pockets of my skirt to find the keys. I put the key in the lock and opened the door of the car.

"Thank you for a wonderful evening," I began, "and thank you for choosing me to be the queen witch, it was so much fun."

"Who else would I choose?"

I looked up because his voice sounded funny, a bit horse really, not like him. He was so close but he stepped closer and put his arm around me.

"I am going to invent a new tradition for the Grand Wizard and his queen," he said, huskily and before I knew what he was doing, he put his hand around the back of my head and kissed me, full on the lips. Oh, my goodness! It was the sweetest kiss I'd ever had! My heart was racing again and I wanted the moment to last forever. Sadly, it didn't.

"Goodnight, my queen."

"Goodnight, Grand Wizard."

We stood there, inside my car door, looking at each other, searching with our eyes. A few moments later, he said.

"Go on then, you'll be getting cold."

I got in the car, although I didn't want to, and he shut the door and stepped back. I had no choice but to start up the car, put it in gear and drive off. As I drove, I could see him in my rear view mirror, still standing in the road where I'd left him, looking after me – that is, until he was enveloped in the darkness as I drove further away.

When I'd finally managed to get all the muck off my face and fell into bed, I drifted asleep on Cloud Nine.

Chapter 44
Happy Ever After

The next day was Sunday, which was the real Halloween day. The party had been last night because there was no way that Sheila would put on a party on a Sunday. I was going there for dinner again.

I went to church and sat between dad and Kenny. I was very aware of him so close to me. Joseph wasn't with us this morning because he was still tired after last night. My happiness knew no bounds when Ken took my hand in his during the sermon. I was hard put to concentrate on what the vicar was saying. When we came out, he again took my hand and walked with me back to the Nursery House. Dad and Sheila went in the car because Sheila wanted to get the dinner on and check that Joseph was alright.

We didn't talk, we just walked, content to be with each other.

When the meal finished, Kenny pushed back his chair and said,

"Lucy, would you like to come out for a ride with me?"

Would I?? "I'll get my coat," I said, trying to quell my jumping heart.

"Have a good time, you two," grinned Sheila and Joseph winked at me. I smiled back at him and followed Ken out to his mother's car. The Freelander stood ignored; I was happy we were going in the car. The Ford Mondeo was a smooth ride, much better than the Freelander, which was built for rough country.

He headed through the village and out onto the main road. He took my hand in his and that's how he drove. I liked it. He didn't even let go when he changed gear; I let my hand go with his, no problem.

I looked at him sideways, loving the profile of his face. He must have felt me looking, for he gave me a self-conscious grin.

"What?"

"Oh, nothing," I said.

Once again we went to Hay Bluff and he parked the car in pretty much the same place as he had before.

"I brought you up here to see something special," he said, "but also to talk with you. I know I should have done it before."

"Perhaps," I said. I wasn't going to help him out. Not yet anyway.

"It's been a difficult time," he began. "It's been a long time since I have been in the position when I haven't known what to do. And I'm the kind of person who has to be sure."

I nodded, I had realised that.

"Anyway, for now, just sit and watch. We will talk again later."

Talk again? We hadn't talked yet! But I did as I was bid and he stretched out his arm and put it around me and pulled me close to him. I couldn't help shivering.

"You're cold." He switched on the engine so that the heater came on and then pulled me close again. I put my head on his shoulder and wished that we could stay like that forever. As we sat there, the sky gradually turned to fire as the sun went down. Before me was an expanse of sky that was all pinks and golds, turning more gold as the central fiery orb sank lower behind the Black Mountains. I felt that this was a show that Nature was putting on just for us; it reflected the emotions going on inside of me.

"Gorgeous," I murmured. Ken's arm tightened around me and I knew he was feeling the same as me. We watched until the sun was no more than a slither of gold atop the mountain and then it was gone. The glowing sky remained for a while and started to darken.

Ken took his arm from around me and I sat up reluctantly. He took hold of my hand again.

"Lucy," he said. "I have to tell you that I love you. I have loved you since the first day I met you and it has been torture to me for see you with someone else. I tried hard not to feel like this because I felt guilty loving another man's woman but I couldn't help it. I had a problem with Glynis too; she just wouldn't let me go, she threatened all sorts. Then, when you broke off your engagement I thought I might have a chance but I wanted to wait a little while to be sure you weren't on the rebound. Then you seemed to believe that I was behind all those things going on. I was devastated to think you believed that I was guilty, that I could do something like that to anyone, let alone you. I would give my life trying to protect you and I was so upset with myself that I couldn't keep you safe. I was frantic with worry that something might harm you but I was also frantic that I might lose it and take advantage of you during the times I stayed with you. You have no idea how much I wanted to just take you in my arms and love you but you belonged to another man."

He stopped when I took my hand from his and put my finger to his lips.

"Sshh, don't talk. Just kiss me. Please."

At that, he wrapped his arms around me and kissed me, gently at first, then more hard and demanding. I put everything into it, to hopefully show him how much I loved him. When we came up for air, he said, "Does this mean?"

"Yes," I said, gently stroking his cheek. "I love you. I have loved you for months. That's why I broke my engagement, there was no way I could marry someone else when I loved you, even if you didn't want me. Everyone kept telling me it was obvious you loved me.

"They could see it but the time just kept going by without you telling me. I was getting desperate, especially as last year was leap year and I just don't think I could have waited another three years.

I don't think Joseph could wait that long either, he was getting worked up and cross about it all. He knew a long time ago how we both felt about each other. He even told me how his wife was engaged when he met her but he made her change her mind."

"He told me that too! Dear old granddad, he's soppy about you himself you know."

"I love him to bits too. But not how I love you, of course."

We sank into another kiss and I was in heaven. I could hardly believe this was happening to me at last.

"You have no idea how much I wanted you to kiss me that time when we were under the willow," I said. He laughed.

"You have no idea how much I wanted to!"

"I wish you had; I would have broken off my engagement much sooner."

"Now she tells me!" he groaned and he drew me to him tightly and kissed me again. Then, he let me go and started the car. Again, he wouldn't let my hand go and I watched the dark road before us in a haze of happiness.

I'm sure that our glowing faces when we got home was noticed by everyone but only Joseph quietly growled 'and about time too.'

The week passed by in a whirl. Every evening Ken came and spent with me and we talked and talked about just about everything. I just adored sitting with him on my sofa with his arms around me, talking and kissing. Clarry always made a fuss of Kenny and he of her and she would sit on his feet if she couldn't sit on my lap.

The following Sunday was a beautiful day, sunny and unseasonably warm for early November. When we'd had dinner and after we'd helped clear the dishes, Ken asked me if I'd like to go for a walk. I agreed and we said we would take the dogs.

We set off, the dogs happily running around us, tongues hanging out. Kenny guided us towards the river path as if going back to my house. We came to the steps leading down to the willow tree. I could see they had been cleared of the grass and other undergrowth and realised he'd made sure they were safe. The tree was not looking quite as green and lush as it had the last time we'd sat there because it was autumn and it had lost a lot of the green but it was still lovely to me. Ken drew me down on the seat and kissed me.

"Lucy, I know this might seem quick because we've only been together for a week. Lucy, I love you and want you to be with me forever. Will you marry me, please?"

I threw my arms around his neck. "Yes! Yes, yes, yes, yes!"

"One yes would have been enough," he grinned at me. I just loved his grin, it turned my heart over. He took a little box out of his pocket. "I chose this because I thought it was the sort of thing you would like. If you don't like it, we can change it."

I looked at the ring; it was a cluster of tiny diamonds around a sapphire.

"Oh, it's beautiful, I love it."

He took it out of the box and slipped it onto my finger. It fit perfectly. I held my hand out to admire it as it glinted in the sunlight.

"I love it, and I love you," I said, as I put out my hand to stroke his face looking at me anxiously. He stood me up then and we kissed long and tender, then he took my hand and we climbed back up the steps and continued our walk.

There was much rejoicing when we got back to tell our family. We decided that we didn't want to wait a long time to get married; there was no need to wait really, we were sure – we had both been sure for a long time. We had so much in common and we enjoyed and understood each other's work and shared a love for the countryside and for growing things.

Not to mention that Kenny said if he had to wait to make love to me much longer he would burst! (But we're not mentioning that).

We set the date for the 4th March; it would be a good time to go away as it was a quiet time for my business and Kenny knew that he could rely on his workers to see that things were right in the nursery.

Christmas came and went, as did the New Year. I was going to have Sylvie and Angela's little girl Louisa as my bridesmaids. Sheila was amazing; she made my dress and the bridesmaid's dresses. We decided they had to have warm jackets to wear because it could still be quite cold in March. So I bought furry jackets for all three of us.

It was dad's turn to give me away and he whispered that he was so proud of me and how my mum and Aunt Bea would be proud of me too. We walked down the aisle together towards my beloved Ken. His eyes widened in admiration when he saw me 'looking like a princess' as folks say that brides look on their wedding day.

The reception, held at the WyeView Restaurant was wonderful. Steph and Alex did a gorgeous sit-down meal for us and our guests. Many people from the village came to attend the church ceremony but the reception was for invited guests only. We had to do that because of it being a hot meal.

We got through the speeches, the cutting of the cake and then we were away on our honeymoon in Greece, which was wonderful – and I'm not telling you about that!

River View Farmhouse was going to be our home; this was the best arrangement so that dad, Sheila and Joseph could stay in the Nursery House.

****

When the case finally came to court, James and Brian were found guilty of harassment with intent to harm. They were also found guilty of other similar crimes not connected to me. Brian turned out to be a computer genius but he was working under the orders of James so it was James that got the heavier sentence; he got six years. Brian got three years. They were also accused of manslaughter with regard to my aunt but the judge said there was not enough evidence for that so they were found not guilty. However, he did say that, if it were not for the lack of evidence, he would happily have sentenced them for it because he believed they were indirectly responsible for causing my aunt's death. I was happy with that really.

As for Glynis, the judge told her she was 'a silly girl, influenced by money and empty promises and also driven by jealousy.' He accepted that she was ignorant of the serious motive behind what she had been asked to do but he also said that, as she professed to be an adult, she should have realised that trying to frighten a woman living alone was not something that anyone should be doing. He put her on six months' probation and told her to 'grow up and do something useful with her life.'

So that was that. I did spare a thought for James' mum and dad, who I had liked very much. I was sorry that they had a son who was a waste of space but was also glad I'd had a lucky escape.

****

Aunt Bea always said this was a house for a family and our children would grow up here, swimming and boating on the pond and playing in the garden and in the barn. We had four children, two boys and two girls, John, Archie, Rosemary and Beatrice and we were a happy family. We loved having the grandparents so close and the children never tired of hearing how their dad and I got together.

The children all adored Joseph, who thrived at all the attention he got from his great-grandchildren. Every Sunday we spent at the Nursery House and often Angela came over with her children too. Sometimes, when I wasn't too busy with babies, I cooked dinner for everyone at River View and it was a joy to hear the children's laughter as they played together out in the garden; Angela's children, being older, were deemed capable of keeping an eye on the younger ones and we were all glad the cousins were close friends.

Every year we had two anniversaries, the first being that of our wedding, the other was the village Halloween party, whichever night it was on, because that was the night that Kenny finally showed me how he felt. For the first few years we carried on the tradition of being the Grand High Wizard and his Queen Witch but once we had a brood of children to keep an eye on, the tradition had to be changed and so Kenny would choose which young man (and in some cases, an older man) would be Grand Wizard for the night. We saw a few romances begin that way over the years – I reflected that true love obviously didn't depend entirely on beauty! But the party remained our own special night.

The nursery went from strength to strength, especially when they decided to specialise in organic growing because organics were becoming popular with gardeners.

Penny eventually became a 'Sister' in the Nottingham hospital where she had been a student nurse. Sylvie fulfilled her dream and trained as a chef and got herself a top job in Birmingham. I missed her cheerful face around my kitchen.

Cessy took pity on Glynis and offered her a job at Sutton Court. Surprisingly, Glynis proved to be very good at it and so she eventually did her qualifications to be a carer.

The biggest surprise was Mary, Glynis' mother, who turned up one day soon after the trial to my house. She told me how sorry she was that her daughter had treated me so badly and offered to help me in some way. She and I became friends and I became a regular visitor to West Bank Farm.

As for Elwyn, well, he became positively friendly – for him – and if I saw him he would actually manage to grunt a grudging greeting rather than glowering at me, quite something for him. 'He likes you,' Mary told me and although it was hard to see it, knowing him as I did, I understood.

****

When I had my first baby, John, and I was home from hospital with him, we had a visitor. It was Paul Gamble and he had brought me a letter. When I saw the writing on the envelope, I felt a lump rise in my throat; it was from Aunt Bea. I handed the baby to Ken and opened it with shaking hands.

'My Darling Lucy,

If you are reading this, it's because you have fulfilled the conditions I gave to my dear friend Paul.

You will, by now, have worked out why I made the conditions of my will the way I did. I did not like your James; to me there was something not quite trustworthy about him. I hoped that if you were even a little unsure about him that you would decide to come and live in my house and in so doing you would eventually meet my Kenny. I have felt for a long time that he was right for you but didn't know how I could get you to meet. I am sorry this was rather a drastic way of doing it but as you have this letter I know that I have achieved my aim. So, I hope you will forgive me for the wiles of an old woman. But I am an old woman who loves you as if I were your mother, and mothers always want what is best for her children. This you will know now too because Paul was not to give you this letter until you and Kenny had your first baby.

I wish I was still here to be grandmother to your baby but you know that I will always watch over you from heaven if I am blessed enough to go there and if I am allowed.

Your ever loving
Aunt Bea'

Wordlessly, I handed the letter over to Ken, who juggled the baby so he could take it from me to read. A few minutes later, he handed the baby to Paul, and he took me in his arms and rocked me as I cried.

"The old schemer!" Kenny laughed. "We were being set up; we should have known!"

"No," I said as I wiped my eyes, "She loved me like she was my mother and she loved you too. I understand now; my Aunt Bea's real legacy to me was how to find true love."

When I put my baby in his cradle in our bedroom, which had been Aunt Bea's 'quiet room', I thought I saw a figure wearing a straw hat standing the other side of his bed. She looked at baby John and then at me and smiled.

"Thank you for everything, Aunt Bea. I love you."

She blew me a kiss and in moments she was gone.

If you have enjoyed this story (or if you didn't!) please leave a few lines of review on Amazon for me. That helps to sell my books. Please tell your friends! Thank you. J.T.F.

Look out for the next '**River View Mystery**', due to be published later in 2017:

By The Gate When Farmer Elwyn Price digs up a skeleton in the meadow belonging to Lucy Baxter, it launches D.C.I. Cooke's investigations into a seventy year old murder.

Other books by Jeanette Taylor Ford
Rosa, a psychological thriller
Bell of Warning, a ghostly novella
The Sixpenny Tiger, a story about a boy that will touch your heart

The Castell Glas Trilogy:
The Hiraeth
Bronwen's Revenge
Yr Aberth (The Sacrifice)

Mostly About Bears, a small book of short stories and poems about children and childhood. For adults, but some of the contents are suitable for children. (Paperback only)

For Children:
Robin's Ring a fantasy adventure. (Paperback only)

About the Author.

Jeanette Taylor Ford is a retired Teaching Assistant. She grew up in Cromer, Norfolk and moved to Hereford with her parents when she was seventeen. Her love of writing began when she was a child of only nine or ten. When young her ambition was to be a journalist but life took her in another direction and her life's work has been with children – firstly as a nursery assistant in a children's home, and later in education. In between she raised her own six children and she now has seven grandchildren and a beautiful great-granddaughter.

Jeanette took up writing again in 2010; she reasoned that she would need something to do with retirement looming, although as a member of the Church of Jesus Christ of Latter Day Saints she is kept busy. She lives with her husband Tony, a retired teacher and headmaster, in Derbyshire, England.

22244119R00171

Printed in Great Britain
by Amazon